ESCAPE!

The beam hit Chandler full in the face. From below, he heard a confusion of shouts and barking dogs. Anne-Marie was already backing away from the light.

"The window," Chandler said urgently. "Jump."

He saw her scramble up onto the sill. As she jumped, a rifle shot cracked by his head and sang away into the darkness. Seconds later he hurled himself through the windowless opening and landed, rolling, in the bushes outside.

He reached out for Anne-Marie in the wet grass beside him. "Run!" he said. "Get into the water. Run, for God's sake!"

Three of the Germans were now firing into the darkness. The fourth, still in the lane below, struggled against the dogs' wild excitement to unleash them. As the catch loosened they leaped forward, still joined together by a yard-long chain . . .

James Barwick

THE DEVIL AT THE CROSS- ROADS

BERKLEY BOOKS, NEW YORK

THE DEVIL AT THE CROSSROADS

A Berkley Book / published by arrangement with
G. P. Putnam's Sons

PRINTING HISTORY
G. P. Putnam's Sons edition / March 1986
Berkley edition / July 1988

ISBN: 0-425-10950-X

A BERKLEY BOOK ® TM 757, 375
Berkley Books are published by The Berkley Publishing Group,
200 Madison Avenue, New York, New York 10016.
The name "BERKLEY" and the "B" logo
are trademarks belonging to Berkley Publishing Corporation.

PRINTED IN THE UNITED STATES OF AMERICA

10 9 8 7 6 5 4 3 2 1

THE DEVIL AT THE CROSSROADS WILL
ALWAYS TAKE THE HINDERMOST.

Old English proverb now shortened to:
The devil take the hindmost.

THE DEVIL AT THE CROSSROADS

Prologue

IT HAD ALWAYS seemed to the Reichsführer-SS Heinrich Himmler that the banners which draped the inner courtyard of Wewelsburg Castle had restored the authentic medieval Germanic flavor to his SS headquarters near the Westphalian town of Paderborn.

Originally a free gift to the SS from the local community, the castle had, by 1940, cost thirteen million marks to restore to what Himmler believed was its original condition.

Now the vast triangular fortress housed the SS central library, a unique collection of old German weapons, and a dining hall nearly one hundred and fifty feet long. But most of all it was to Himmler the clan center of his new Aryan Order of Teutonic Knights.

From the imposing stone castle set in tree-covered hills directives went out that shaped the clan. The pagan midsummer festival was to replace Christmas. The SS marriage service, conducted by an officer of the order, was invented; large families were encouraged with SS gifts made in SS-owned factories; the Lebensborn breeding homes were established, and as the war began the first kidnappings of fair-haired, "racially valuable" children from Polish families were practiced.

High priest of the order was Himmler himself, part schoolmaster, part crank, fighting, as he saw it, to protect the racial purity of the German people. Under him a group of senior SS officers gathered from time to time at Wewelsburg. In one of the great stone rooms of the castle the Reichsführer had created a chamber inspired by a ragbag of myth and pagan history. Twelve banners hung behind twelve pigskin chairs reserved for his SS leaders at an Arthurian Round Table.

Intellectual SS generals like Heydrich concealed their contempt for this fairyland Himmler had created. Ex-street fighters and bullyboys like SS General Josef "Sepp" Dietrich squirmed uneasily in their ornate chairs as each year the "Knights" gathered to pledge themselves anew to defend German womanhood and Teutonic culture against the menace of the Jew. But the deadly, school-masterly seriousness with which the Reichsführer himself took these annual ceremonies precluded levity. Indeed, levity was a note seldom struck in the purlieus of Schloss Wewelsburg whether Himmler was in residence or not. There were too many talebearers among the staff who might report a smirk at the Teutonic hunting horns that summoned SS officers to dinner, or an indiscreet joke during the salt pledge at an SS wedding.

The two visitors who were checked through the castle's main gate this morning offered the sort of contrast not uncommon among SS officers. They were both Gestapo functionaries, both were attached to the Ahnenerbe, the SS Ancestral Heritage Bureau, where ancestries were checked to ensure that every SS family was quite free of racial contamination. Both were dressed in civilian clothes, but the elder of the two, Colonel Reichenau, his hair graying at the temples, his suit an expensive product of a Berlin tailor, clearly came from a different back-ground than his companion. Gestapo Inspector Krebs was in his thirties, ten years younger than Reichenau, a moon-faced Hessian country boy whose winged collar bit at his powerful neck and whose bowler hat looked out of place in his huge hands.

As they left the main gate the visitors were conducted across the flagdecked courtyard by a uniformed SS-Standartenführer, Dr. Otto Grollich, a recruit from the once great universities of Germany. Walking beside the visitors in the brilliant sunshine, Grollich was, this morning, absorbed with the subject of piano wire.

"I have been working on a not uninteresting academic problem," he announced, pacing the courtyard between Reichenau and Krebs. "In Austria, Czechoslovakia and now Poland we have assumed responsibility for some sixty million additional individuals, some of whom may not be totally resigned to the New Order. Punishments for infringement of our decrees is my special field of study. The Reichsführer himself gave me the commission only last week. Of course we have our *Kz Lager,* our concentration camps, but there remain several categories of crime, for example treachery and treacherous activities toward the New Order, for which the mere death sentence sometimes seems inadequate."

Krebs nodded as if in agreement with this obvious intellectual. Head down, Dr. Grollich concentrated on the polished toes of his knee-high boots as he stepped out across the graveled courtyard. "Consider the case of a treacherous attack on a senior SS officer. An attempt perhaps on the life of the Reichsführer himself. Could anyone suggest that death by shooting, a soldier's death, is an adequate, appropriate sentence for the miscreant? This was the problem that the Reichsführer put to me."

He paused, expecting and receiving Krebs's look of awe.

"This question of how the convicted individual is rendered lifeless by the community is, of course, one that has involved societies from the earliest times. I was forced to reject the hemlock of the Greeks on the simple grounds that Socrates, at least, exacted dignity from his death. The guillotine of the French Revolution intrigued me. But its association with the death of nobles was distressing. For a long time, gentlemen, I toyed with the idea of death by fire. Few men can restrain their panic when the flames leap about their legs. Yet again there was a subtle historical association, in the Wars of Religion particularly, with martyrdom. Having therefore considered objectively all the possibilities," he said slowly, "I concluded that hanging was the only satisfactory answer. But—" he paused dramatically, raising a finger in the air, "but not by the rope, gentlemen. I have advanced the view that every shred of human dignity will be stripped from the miscreant only if the noose he is confronted with is not of honest hemp but of sharp, unforgiving piano wire."

His hand dropped to his side. "Yes, gentlemen, for major crimes against the state, death by hanging will be the formal sentence. And it will be for the condemned prisoner to shudder in his lonely cell as he contemplates the thinness of the noose."

Krebs gaped open-mouthed. Reichenau gravely adjusted the brim of his pale gray homburg as if in silent salute to the doctor's research. "Grollich," he said, "I would enjoy discussing the problem on another occasion, but our appointment is for 11:30. It would be unthinkable to be late."

"Indeed," Grollich agreed with a start. "This way."

Bounding up the steps, Grollich passed through the guard at the main doors of the castle with Reichenau and Krebs a pace or two behind.

"Curb your enthusiasm for Grollich's noose," Reichenau hissed in Krebs's ear. "If this meeting goes badly, we could well be the first to sample it."

At precisely 11:30 Grollich knocked on the door of Ernst Kaltenbrunner's office and ushered in Colonel Reichenau and Inspector Krebs.

Kaltenbrunner, in his late thirties, long headed, his

face scarred from political street fighting in his native Vienna during the early days of the Nazi movement, lounged behind his desk. He would later take over as chief of the RSHA when Reinhard Heydrich was assassinated near Prague. At the war's end, he was to be hanged (by a conventional rope) in the prison gymnasium at Nuremberg.

"Leave us," Kaltenbrunner said to Grollich, who was hovering near the door. As soon as they were alone he indicated that Reichenau and Krebs should sit, then leaned forward in his chair, meshing his large fingers together in front of him.

For a few minutes they sat in silence, then a small door opened at the back of the room. Krebs and Reichenau leaped up, and uncurling his long legs, Kaltenbrunner, too, came to his feet. In black trousers, boots and brown uniform shirt, the small, clerkish figure of Heinrich Himmler stood blinking in a shaft of sunlight.

Politely returning the Hitler salutes of Reichenau and Krebs, Himmler turned mildly to Kaltenbrunner. "I'll sit here, in the corner," he said. "Ignore me."

He took a seat by the window and gestured to the three men to resume their seats.

Kaltenbrunner slid down into his desk chair and fixed his eyes on Reichenau. "Begin," he said.

"The Reichsführer-SS is perhaps aware of the special responsibilities Inspector Krebs and myself have been given under the Ancestral Heritage Bureau?" Reichenau looked awkwardly from Kaltenbrunner to the earnest face of Himmler.

"The Reichsführer is aware I have appointed you both," Kaltenbrunner said briskly, "to the supremely delicate task of protecting the names of the leadership of the Reich against foreign slander. Your particular function has been to ensure that the obviously impeccable racial origins of Germany's leaders can never be represented as otherwise. So far we are totally satisfied with your work."

"I am gratified to hear you say so," said Reichenau.

"Your message spoke of a matter of the highest seriousness." Kaltenbrunner shifted in his seat.

"And delicacy," said Reichenau.

Kaltenbrunner restrained a smile of satisfaction. He was virtually certain from Reichenau's coded message that the subject of the meeting was his superior and rival, Reinhard Heydrich. There had been rumors circulating in Nazi circles for years about the uncertain origins of Heydrich's grandmother. Heydrich had even had her tombstone removed from the Berlin graveyard where she was buried. If Reichenau and Krebs had substantial evidence of Heydrich's Jewish ancestry, it would be the end of his spectacular rise to power in the SS.

"Before we go further," said Kaltenbrunner confidently, "we must know the identity of the particular Party or SS leader under discussion."

"Reichsführer . . ." Reichenau turned toward the corner seat.

Himmler's hands fluttered upward. "Please ignore me."

In the silence, Inspector Krebs's close-cropped head sank into his heavy shoulders.

"Continue," snapped Kaltenbrunner.

Reichenau ran his tongue along his upper lip, his mouth suddenly quite dry. "The subject of our investigation," he said softly, "has been no less a person than the Führer himself."

"Cheap British and American gutter slanders on Adolf Hitler's parentage have already been exposed as completely false," Kaltenbrunner said in a relaxed voice.

"Allow me to explain, gentlemen," Reichenau said desperately, "that this is an entirely different problem."

"Which nevertheless concerns the Führer?" Kaltenbrunner leaned forward in his chair.

"Yes."

Kaltenbrunner glanced quickly at Himmler, but the Reichsführer's face remained impassive. "Very well," he said, nodding for Reichenau to continue.

"As you know, gentlemen," Reichenau began, "for some time now the Foreign Intelligence Section SS has, under cover of a youth hiking scheme, been mapping areas of military importance in northern France. Ten days ago a report came into our hands from an agent who had stayed at a small French village near the Belgian border. The agent booked a room at the one café-hotel in the village, the Hôtel de la Paix, owned by a woman named Arlette Claudel. Her husband, it appears, served in the French Army from 1914 until the end of the war. He died some three years later."

"Is all this necessary, Reichenau?" asked Kalten-brunner.

"Indeed," said Reichenau. "The evening he stayed at the hotel our agent spent some time talking to Madame Claudel. During this evening it is reported that the woman spoke openly of her affection for the German infantry who occupied the area for much of the war."

Himmler leaned forward, his eyes blinking behind the rimless spectacles. "Her affection for the German infantry who occupied the area?"

"Yes, Reichsführer," said Reichenau, half rising from his chair.

"The Führer served in the infantry, the 9th Bavarian Regiment."

"Yes, Reichsführer. The 9th Bavarian occupied the area throughout 1918."

"Are you saying the lady in question claims to have been acquainted with the Führer?"

"That is what is reported, Reichsführer." Himmler sat back, turning to stare out of the window. "Ignore me. Ignore me. Continue."

"In November 1918, a few days before the end of the war," Reichenau said, "Madame Claudel gave birth to a child. A girl. It is impossible for it to have been her husband's child. He was, after all, in the French Army, on the other side of the front lines."

"Yes, yes. What exactly does this Frenchwoman say?" asked Kaltenbrunner harshly.

"She says . . . she claims that she knew the Führer during the early months of 1918." Reichenau's voice now became barely audible. "She claims that he is the father of her child. A girl."

Above his collar Krebs felt his bull neck running with sweat. Kaltenbrunner's face was as gray as chipped stone. Himmler was breathing in rapidly, his fingers nervously tapping at his mouth and chin. Reichenau was fully on his feet now, searching for a way to continue.

A premonition of what he was about to say suddenly gripped Kaltenbrunner. "This woman Claudel," he rasped, "is of pure French ancestry?"

"She was born outside France, in Algeria," whispered Reichenau. "Her maiden name was Zindel."

Kaltenbrunner felt the room swim before his eyes. "Zindel?"

"She is a mongrel," stammered Reichenau, "of a sort not uncommon among the French *colons* in North Africa. Part Greek, part French, part Jew."

Kaltenbrunner's elongated face seemed to drain of its last vestige of color. "Part Jew."

Himmler's voice floated from the corner of the room. "Who knows of this?"

"No one outside this room, Reichsführer," said Reichenau eagerly.

"You forget the agent hiker." Himmler stood up abruptly. "The woman's child," his hands fluttered about his face, "by now she will be more than twenty years old. Consider this," he was trembling, "if the woman Claudel is telling the truth our Führer, Adolf Hitler, has, somewhere in France, a fully grown Jew daughter."

Three days later a report from Birkenburg, a small German town near the French border, was dispatched to Gestapo HQ in Mannheim. It concerned the suicide of

Carl Heinz Ohlsen, Foreign Intelligence Section SS, who had recently returned from undercover operations in northern France. It appeared that Ohlsen, for no apparent reason, had hanged himself in a washroom with a length of piano wire.

Chapter
One

THEO CHANDLER WALKED jauntily down the Rue de Rivoli, hands deep in the pockets of his open black evening overcoat, cigarette in an amber holder jutting from the corner of his mouth. Paris, he decided, was the city for him. London was stuffy, overly formal; his hometown—New York—crude, pushy; Berlin was all politics and flags with hooked crosses. But Paris, even Paris at war, was freedom, the sort of freedom he'd been looking for all his adult life. He strolled on, half a head taller than most of the jostling crowd.

He was more than a little drunk. He had eaten langoustines and châteaubriand at his favorite restaurant, the Vendôme. He had talked to an old Frenchman about the progress of the war and drunk a half bottle of champagne and nearly a bottle of good Burgundy—plus a calvados or two while the old man explained why the German Army would never dare launch an attack on the impregnable defenses along the border. The arguments seemed compelling enough—the huge guns, the thickness of the concrete caissons, the vast stores of food and ammunition. Marshal Pétain had broken the German Army at Verdun in the last war. The Germans would not be stupid enough to hurl their youth at the might of the Maginot Line.

Perhaps the old man was right. Since the outbreak of war hardly a shot had been fired in anger on the Western Front.

Chandler sniffed the sharp scent of roasting chestnuts and admired a befurred, bejeweled and long-legged Parisienne stepping from a taxi. He was drunk and he was broke. He had not succeeded in selling more than a hundred francs' worth of paintings since he had lived here. In his bank account at the Société Générale on boulevard Haussmann he had just twenty-two francs. He had another fifty or so in his pocket and a few pawnable items like a gold watch and some expensive suits from his more affluent days, in the wardrobe in his studio apartment on the Île St-Louis. The strident voice of a new singer named Edith Piaf blasted from the entrance to a tiny café on the street corner. Chandler smiled to himself. Something would turn up. It always had so far. He might even sell a painting.

People streamed past him; Parisian families enjoying the crisp bite in the night air; soldiers in rough olive uniforms, their arms around the waists of girls; severe, straight-backed elderly ladies in pairs, their umbrellas rapping the pavements.

Above the boulevard a light fall of snow drifted down through the bare branches of the plane trees, sparkling below the dull canopy of wartime's restricted lighting. The métro station at Pont-Neuf still spilled people out onto the Right Bank, newspaper vendors tried to interest the crowd in news of another quiet day at the front, on every street corner stalls sold oysters in the pale yellow light of carbide lamps.

Chandler walked on past open-fronted restaurants, past street performers struggling to free themselves from padlocks and thick chains or belching fire from the corners of their mouths, and paused before the cinema on the corner. It was too early to go home. After the Vendôme he had no wish to stop at a café. He stepped into the cinema foyer. A balding man with a thin mustache leaned forward from the *guichet*. "Last performance," the man said. "You'll just catch the beginning."

The American gave him ten francs and collected his ticket and the change. He thought of asking what movie they were showing but decided against it. Any movie would do.

He crossed the foyer and, pushing open the swinging door, stepped into the blackness. On the screen a newsreel showed French troops training behind the Maginot Line. It all seemed relaxed and leisurely. Perhaps the newsreel commentator, and the old man in the restaurant, were right. Perhaps the Germans had no stomach for an attack on the Anglo-French positions. Perhaps the war would just fade away.

Standing in the flickering darkness, he saw the outline of the usherette approach. She used her flashlight to indicate the aisle.

"Where would you like to sit, monsieur?" she asked. She stood beside him, the warm scent of her body rising to his nostrils.

"I don't care where I sit," said Chandler.

"At the back, monsieur?"

"At the back, sure."

"This way, monsieur."

Again she lit her flashlight, leading him to the back row of the house. The newsreel was now reporting on the United States. Long, shuffling lines of workless men were shown in New York, Chicago and Philadelphia. Then back to France and film of men and girls working and laughing together as the huge shells rolled off the production line in a munitions factory. What was the propaganda message, Chandler wondered. That it was better to be at war? More work, more fun? Especially if the armies at the front weren't actually fighting. Yet.

The usherette had stopped, beam flashing along the back row.

Chandler sat down in the end seat and fumbled in his pocket for the customary few centimes to hand to the girl.

"If you'd like to move over," she whispered, "I could take the seat next to you."

Even in the half-light he could see she was a pretty girl, no more than twenty or so. He stood up again, his senses running warmly, and moved over a seat. She extinguished her flashlight and, with a quick glance toward the rear of the cinema, sat down next to him.

From the few heads amid the curling tobacco smoke between him and the screen, Chandler could see that it was not a busy evening. He moistened his lips, unsure how to proceed.

The girl showed no uncertainty. Undoing two or three buttons on her uniform blouse, she took his hand and slipped it inside.

He was exhilarated by the feel of smooth flesh and the soft dimpling of her hardening nipple. Leaning toward him, she kissed him full on the mouth, her tongue briefly forcing between his lips. Then, as he made to move his other arm around her, she sat back and deftly took his hand from inside her blouse.

"What's wrong?" he whispered.

She began to button her uniform.

"Wait a minute," he said. "You're not going?"

She smiled. "Why, would you like me to stay?"

"Of course I'd like you to stay."

"But I daren't," she said. "Perhaps the manager will come in."

"Okay. What time do you get through here?"

"If you wanted to meet me tomorrow," she whispered, "we could have lunch."

"I'd like that," Chandler said. The full heat of his excitement was ebbing only slowly. "Even better, why don't you come to my apartment for a drink when the movie's finished."

The girl shook her head vigorously. "No," she said. "That's impossible."

"Then come tomorrow, I can fix lunch at my apartment."

Again she shook her head.

He turned to face her, resting his elbow on the seat arm between them. In profile, he could see that she was indeed as pretty as he had first thought. But he was baffled by her quick, determined reactions to his suggestions.

"We'll have lunch," he said, "where you choose."

She relaxed immediately. "Hôtel Clemenceau," she said. "Do you know it?"

"On the Rue Albert?"

"That's the one," she turned toward him, smiling again.

Only faintly uneasy, Chandler thought to consolidate his apparent conquest. "After, we can go to my place," he said. "Or yours if you prefer."

Again the girl shook her head forcefully. "No need," she said. "We can take a room at the hotel."

"They won't make problems?"

"Of course not."

"All right, if you're sure."

"Naturally, the room will not be cheap."

He smiled. "Naturally." He understood now.

"You're a foreigner; you can afford it."

"I'm sure I can," he said. If only she knew.

"One o'clock tomorrow, then, Hôtel Clemenceau."

"One o'clock, Hôtel Clemenceau."

"I must go," she said. "If the manager caught me sitting with a customer, I'd lose my job." She stood up, straightening her skirt, then leaned back close to him.

"You won't forget, or decide not to come because of your wife?" she whispered.

"I don't have a wife, at least not in Paris," Chandler said. "And I won't forget."

"Until tomorrow," her hand lightly brushed across his crotch as she turned to go.

"What's your name?"

She turned back. "Jacqueline. Jacqueline Claudel."

Colonel Reichenau sat writing at a small table. He had dragged it into the center of the room to make the best use of the single, dim light bulb that hung on a frayed wire from the center of the ceiling.

Outside in the darkness, a steady rain, driven by a rising wind, splattered against the unshuttered window of the small hotel café outside Wewelsburg.

Krebs sat, hunched forward, on the end of a creaking, double bed, his elbows on his bulging thighs, toying with a length of piano wire he had acquired shortly after his encounter with Dr. Grollich. The room was large but sparsely furnished. Apart from the bed, table and chair, the only other item was a huge, ornately carved wooden wardrobe that seemed to tilt at a strange angle.

The air was chill, damp. Reichenau laid down his fountain pen and blew into his hands, consoling himself with the thought that a hotel room such as this could never be considered an extravagance. It was a well-known fact to Gestapo agents that Reichsführer-SS Himmler himself would occasionally take it into his head to wander into SS Central Accounts and select at random a fistful of expense sheets from the agents in the field. He would then sit at his desk long into the night going through them, checking to the last penny. Extravagance was rooted out and the culprit reprimanded.

Krebs stood up from the bed, stretching his arms over his head, then walked to the window.

"It's still pissing down out there," he said, scratching himself.

Reichenau continued writing; he was almost finished.

Krebs turned back into the room. "I said—"

Reichenau interrupted his subordinate. "I heard what you said."

It was the thought of sharing the double bed with the uncouth Krebs that had convinced Reichenau, although it was almost midnight, to complete his latest report now.

Krebs would take it immediately to Kaltenbrunner in person. It was the one authorized method of communication on this most delicate assignment. The use of the mail was forbidden, and the telephone could only be used in an emergency. The importance of absolute security and total secrecy had been made abundantly clear.

The report was short and to the point. The investigation was proceeding well, if a little slowly. It had become much more difficult to operate in France, but one vital fact had been established. The target subject, the daughter of Madame Claudel, had left her home village for Paris several years ago. It was only a matter of time now before success was achieved. Reichenau folded the single sheet of the report, slipped it into an envelope and sealed the flap.

"You will leave immediately," Reichenau said, holding out the envelope to Krebs.

"Of course." Krebs carefully put the envelope in the breast pocket of his coat, then donned his bowler hat, making sure it was square on his close-cropped head.

Reichenau looked up. Krebs had made no move to leave the room.

"Something wrong?" asked Reichenau.

"No," said Krebs, then paused again. "How much do you think the Führer knows?"

"About what?"

"About the Jew daughter."

"How would I know?" said Reichenau. "However, if you would like my opinion, I would venture he knows nothing."

Krebs grunted; Reichenau took it as a sign of disapproval.

"I take it you think the Führer should be told," said Reichenau. "Perhaps, my dear Krebs, you would like the dubious privilege of informing him yourself. It would be interesting to see how our leader reacted to your news."

Krebs's eyes narrowed for a moment, then he turned on his heel and left the room.

Reichenau crossed to the window. It was raining harder

now. For a moment, in the street below, he saw the figure of Krebs hunched against the wind and rain; then it was gone, lost in the night.

It was early evening and the setting sun had dropped below the rooftops, silhouetting the crooked chimney pots across the Paris skyline. In the bedroom at the Hôtel Clemenceau, the retreating light was already softening the edges of the heavy furniture, leaving deep corners of darkness.

"What's the hurry?" Chandler asked.

Jacqueline Claudel threw back the sheet and rolled off the side of the bed. Standing naked, she said, "It's time to get up. There's a friend of mine who wants to see you."

He lifted himself onto one elbow. "A friend of yours."

"An art dealer." She began to dress. "There could be some money in it for you."

Chandler sat up on the side of the bed and searched for a cigarette. Lighting it, he watched her pale shape move back and forth across the window. It was their third meeting, and already he was beginning to feel that familiar loss of excitement.

"You told me you needed money," she said.

"I said I wasn't selling a lot of paintings. Who is this friend?"

"I told you," she said irritably, "an art dealer. A good friend of mine. He said he'd seen some of your work."

In spite of himself Chandler found his interest quickening. "He saw my exhibition at the gallery?"

Jacqueline shrugged on her dress. "Who knows. I don't follow these things. Last week I told him I was seeing an American painter, and he said he'd like to meet you."

Chandler pulled on the cigarette. "What's his name, for Christ's sake?"

She turned to face him, fully dressed, hands on hips. "Bilescu."

* * *

"Peter Bilescu," said the man opposite Chandler at the café table twenty minutes later. Chandler shook the offered hand, noticing the sparkle of the diamond ring on the little finger.

"Jacqueline, *chérie*," said Bilescu, smiling a flawless smile, "I want to speak to Monsieur Chandler alone. Run along now."

"I thought a glass of champagne at least," the girl said sullenly.

"Later," Bilescu dismissed her.

The two men watched her go, her high heels clicking angrily along the pavement.

"So, Monsieur Chandler," Bilescu ran his hand back through golden blond hair. "A glass of champagne."

Chandler watched him as he took the bottle from the ice bucket and filled two glasses. Bilescu appeared to be about forty but was probably older; the face was tanned and unlined, though the color of the hair could hardly be natural. The eyes were blue gray as far as Chandler could tell, and the mouth very straight, framed by thick, sensuous lips. His suit was soft gray flannel. His shirt cuffs, cream with a pale blue stripe, were fastened with heavy gold Second Empire cuff links.

"You saw my paintings?" Chandler asked.

Bilescu smiled. "I'm afraid so. Why don't you take up photography?"

Chandler accepted the glass of champagne, stony faced. "Jacqueline told me you liked my work."

"I thought it was simpler if she believed that." Bilescu smiled again. "She's got a good body, but her mind . . ." He raised an eyebrow in a gesture of despair.

"Why did you want to meet me?" Chandler cut him short.

"I might have some work for you. Well-paid work."

"If you don't like my painting, why the hell should you offer me work?"

"It's not a commission," Bilescu said, his smile fading. "And I am by no means sure you are the right man. But Jacqueline said you were broke."

Chandler nodded. "More or less."

"Paris is a marvelous city if you have money. I came here from Bucharest in 1934. I had just ten francs in my pocket. I found nothing marvelous about Paris for the first six months I was here. Now I have a house on the Avenue Foch, a fine motor car and an application for French citizenship, which will be processed shortly."

"So you made it."

"Indeed." Bilescu's smile was back.

"But not from buying and selling paintings?"

"As you've rightly guessed, Monsieur Chandler, I am engaged in a variety of pursuits."

"What do you want from me, Bilescu?"

Bilescu leaned forward. "Tell me, have you ever heard of the Jewish Resettlement Agency?"

"I guess so," said Chandler. "They help Jewish refugees in Paris. Apply for residence permits, that sort of thing."

Bilescu nodded. "Since the outbreak of war the flow of refugees has dried up. The Franco-German border is, of course, closed. Yet there are still some, many, who would like to leave the Teutonic paradise." His eyes narrowed as he looked at Chandler. "Are we beginning to understand each other?"

"No," Chandler said flatly, "we're not. The Jewish Resettlement Agency is not in the business of smuggling Jews out of Germany."

"What do you think of the champagne?" asked Bilescu.

"I like it," said Chandler. "Clean on the tongue. I'm just not so sure about the aftertaste."

Bilescu drummed his fingers on the table. "Very well," he said at last. "I have no connection with the Jewish Resettlement Agency, except that any Jews I bring out of Germany they are pleased to look after here in France. I bring them out, and for that I charge."

"So you're in the business of being a Scarlet Pimpernel," Chandler said. "Except you get paid."

Bilescu sat upright. "Those who get out, Chandler, are

grateful for the chance to pay. You know what's happening in Germany. I don't want any moral superiority from you. I want an answer. You are an American; you can travel into the Reich. You can travel back. I pay well, and you'll have the satisfaction of knowing you've done more for German Jews than any number of resettlement agencies in Paris.''

Chandler lit a cigarette and stared thoughtfully across the plume of smoke at Bilescu as he poured more champagne. How far could he trust this Rumanian with dyed hair?

Bilescu pushed the refilled glass across the table. ''Try it again,'' he said. ''You'll find it improves with the second glass.''

Through the sunlit pine trees, between the steep Alpine slopes, the ancient locomotive, puffing wood smoke, dragged the two-car black-and-gold passenger train along the single-line track. Apart from the swastika flags that draped the infrequent grade crossings, Leo and Magda Beckerman might easily have imagined that they were back in the Austria of their childhood, sixty years ago. Around them in the coach, farmers sat with their wives and children played along the central aisle between the slatted seats; chickens clucked in rough wicker cages; boxes piled with carrots and onions surrounded each family. As the market town of Beringen came into sight, the farm people rose, nodding politely to their two well-dressed traveling companions, and began to allocate baskets and boxes to each of the children to carry.

Leo Beckerman pressed the side of his face against the glass of the window. Between the rising hillsides he could see the spire of Beringen church and the gabled facades of the houses clustered around the market square. He leaned forward and touched the hand of his wife, whose eyes had closed again in the heat of the morning sunlight shining through the window.

''We're here, Magda. Beringen.''

She came fully awake, confused and fearful.

"It's all right, Magda," Beckerman said quietly. "Everything's as it should be."

"I was asleep," she said.

He nodded.

"What dreams," she sighed. "Will they ever end?"

He smiled, rising to hand down the suitcases. "Soon. Very soon."

Beckerman was a conspicuously tall man and his wife was a tall woman. Among the jostling crowd of stocky farmers and their families, they stood out on the narrow platform, physically, as well as because of their city clothes.

"We must not even think," Magda Beckerman said firmly, "of what will happen if he isn't here."

They began to follow the crowd. At the gate an official in a red-topped peaked cap took their tickets. The square before them was a replica of a thousand Austrian market squares, surrounded by tall timbered buildings with sharply pitched roofs, squeezed together like a crowd waiting for a parade. The shops were low, medieval; apothecaries and bootmakers, bakeries and corn chandlers. The *Gasthaus* stood opposite the station, beyond the already bustling market stalls. Outside the café stood a single-deck blue bus. Stenciled along its side, in English and German, was the legend: German-American Friendship Club. An American flag was painted on the engine cover.

"It's there, Leo," Magda Beckerman said excitedly. "It's there."

Lifting their suitcases, the Beckermans began to cross toward the bus, averting their eyes from the timbered balcony of the guildhall and the great swastika flag weaving lazily in the warm air currents above the square.

The blast of brass-band music struck them like gunfire, halting them in their tracks. From half a dozen loudspeakers set high on the old gables, drums thundered and cymbals clashed out the Horst Wessel song, the anthem of the Nazi Party. Then, as abruptly as it had begun, the music stopped.

The market was silent. The stall-holders paused, some halfway through a transaction, a cabbage or a string of sausages still proffered to the housewives before them. The voice of a radio announcer echoed in flat tones across the square.

"*Achtung. Achtung.* This is a special announcement. Today German troops crossed the borders into Belgium and Holland to safeguard their neutrality against Anglo-French aggression. At the same time the Wehrmacht High Command issued the following statement: 'This morning at dawn powerful German forces launched a series of attacks against the Anglo-French Armies in the west. Supported by continuous air strikes, German forces have broken through the enemy's defenses along the whole length of the front.'"

Again the Horst Wessel song blared out over the square, filling the silence as people stared at each other. Somehow, after months of inaction on the Western Front, they found it difficult to believe that the war against the French and British had begun in earnest.

Standing beside the blue bus, Chandler studied the bewildered couple in the middle of the square. He had watched them leave the station. Their height alone made it virtually certain they were the Beckermans from Vienna. Their age and appearance fitted the details given him by Bilescu. And the woman was wearing the green tweed skirt and jacket as arranged. He moved out into the square toward them.

The Beckermans hesitated. The man walking across the square was dressed in light, casual clothes most Europeans associated with America. But neither of them could resist a moment's dry-mouthed fear that he was in fact Gestapo.

"My name's Theo Chandler. I'm glad you made it," Chandler said, taking Magda Beckerman's suitcase.

"Hardly as glad as we are," said Leo Beckerman. "I think you can be sure of that."

Magda Beckerman looked up at the faces peering anxiously down from the bus windows. The announcement had obviously had a disturbing effect.

"Will the start of the fighting affect us, Herr Chandler?" Magda asked.

Chandler shook his head. "Within an hour we'll be in Italy," he said. "By this evening we'll be safe in France," he spoke with more confidence than he felt. If Italy entered the war today, there would be little chance of reaching France.

"You make crossing frontiers sound a very easy matter, Herr Chandler," said Leo Beckerman, handing up his suitcase.

Chandler helped Frau Beckerman onto the bus. "We'll find a way," he said.

The other occupants, the Mendels, were sitting at the back of the bus. Chandler made the introductions. "Herr Beckerman, Frau Beckerman, this is Professor Mendel, his wife, Golda, their son Felix and his wife, Sarah."

The two families exchanged polite nods of greeting.

Leo Beckerman settled his wife and their luggage and then sat down on the bench seat beside the professor. "It's a pleasure to meet you, Professor Mendel," he said.

"I'm delighted to meet you, Herr Beckerman," Mendel said. The voice was soft and cultured. He was a short, dapper man of fifty with iron-gray, curly hair and soft brown eyes. He was dressed immaculately in a three-piece pin-striped suit, a neat tie held in place with a pearl-headed pin.

"Do you think there will be trouble at the border?" Beckerman asked.

"Trouble?" said Professor Mendel. "For a busload of German Jews with false American passports. How could there possibly be trouble?"

"It's a small joke from a small man, Herr Beckerman," said Golda Mendel. "Better he was a comic in a music hall than a professor of literature."

It broke the tension; they all smiled.

Chandler stood by the driver's seat, looking back at the expectant faces of his passengers. "Just relax and enjoy the scenery," he said. "Behave like Americans. Point at things as we go through the villages. And wave at any policemen we pass.''

As Chandler slid behind the wheel, Professor Mendel leaned over to his wife. ''A woman of your age, Golda, waving at policemen.'' He shook his head in feigned disapproval.

As they drove through the mountains toward the Italian border south of Villach, the professor came forward and sat next to Chandler.

''What will the French military think of this attack in the west, Herr Chandler?'' said Mendel. ''Will they conclude that, at last, Adolf Hitler has overreached himself?''

''I'm no expert, Professor,'' said Chandler, ''but from what I hear in Paris, this is just what the British and French generals were waiting for. As the German Army comes forward, the Allies move in and destroy it.''

Chandler was watching the sharp curves in the road ahead, but even out of the corner of his eye he could see that Mendel was nodding dubiously.

Chapter
Two

IT WAS THE fifth night of the Great Exodus. During this one night nearly a million people from the northern towns and villages of France would trudge through the great boulevards, heading for the safety of the south. Tens of thousands more had already been overtaken by the speed of the German advance.

It had been a military breakthrough on a scale nobody could have anticipated. Not the French High Command, nor their allies in Churchill's newly formed government in London, not even the German generals themselves. Sweeping through the Ardennes, the Wehrmacht had brushed aside the French Armies and gone on to the British Expeditionary Force against the Channel at Dunkirk. A naval miracle had brought the bulk of the men safely back across the Channel, but almost every tank and gun the British Army possessed had been left in France. Thus, the Maginot Line, in which a whole generation of Frenchmen had been told to put their trust, had been bypassed, rendered obsolete by plan *Sichelsschnitt,* the sweep of a scythe. France was left wide open to the invader.

And then the Wehrmacht had turned toward Paris. Before their racing armored columns, grotesque rumors emptied the towns and cities, turning peasants and townsmen alike into frightened refugees. In a week 180,000 people fled Lille; only 20,000 inhabitants remained. Small villages were left without a single inhabitant as the *curé* and the *maire* led the exodus south.

Among the stumbling refugee columns, the extraordinary rumors spread, hastening their flight; rumors of German paratroops dressed as nuns; of poison powders in the water supply; and of "French" and "Belgian" officers speaking only German.

Above the crowded roads, the Luftwaffe flew unchallenged. The crookwinged Stuka dive-bombers, fitted with air sirens to terrorize their victims, screamed down on bridges and supply points. French reservists, struggling toward the front, were demoralized by horror stories long before they saw their first German tank. Desertion became commonplace.

By the second week of June the chaos of fleeing people—the greatest movement of refugees the Western world has ever seen—had spread into the Paris area and central France, overwhelming military supply columns and reinforcements that tried to reach the front. Eight million people were now wandering homeless in the countryside between Orléans and Poitiers, a locust army of unfortunates, seeking food and water from the bewildered rural population. Farmers who had given bread to the first refugees now defended their land with guns, or themselves joined the great mass straggling southward.

Near Tours, where the French government was now established in the ancient château on the Loire, dependent for communication with the rest of the country on a rural telephone system whose operators left work at six each evening, Premier Paul Reynaud struggled alone against the defeatism of his cabinet.

Generals proclaimed the war lost. The mistresses of ministers held boudoir meetings to promote an approach to the Germans. Marshal Pétain, the hero of the First World War defense at Verdun, was now an octogenarian figure, enigmatic and even sinister in his anxiety to sue for peace.

And meanwhile the panzer divisions raced forward. Dieppe and Rouen were already occupied. The Seine had been crossed that morning. On the road to Paris, Compiègne had fallen, and no reliable estimate of the speed of the advance was available to the French government.

Winston Churchill flew to France, but the background to his eleventh-hour talks with Paul Reynaud was the steady drumbeat of Marshal Pétain's insistence on surrender.

Between Jacqueline and Anne-Marie Claudel, sitting together at the back of a small bar on the Île St-Louis, there was an evident family likeness. But in contrast to Jacqueline's prettiness, her sister appeared coldly beautiful. Jacqueline's light chestnut hair was piled high on her head in fashionable imitation of American film stars, her lipstick generously applied, her dress the latest from Bon Marché.

Anne-Marie, a few years older, was dressed in a more restrained manner. Her hair was darker than the younger girl's and worn at shoulder length. Under a pale summer coat, she wore a cream shirt and slightly darker skirt. The barman who served them had already decided that Jacqueline was more to his taste. The other girl had something about her; he'd worked in the café long enough to know you didn't risk an intimate remark with a woman like that.

"They say there are still trains running. But there are hundreds of people for every seat," Anne-Marie said. "This morning I was at the Gare de Lyon. They were fighting in the courtyard. But there are still a few places to be had in private cars."

"I'm staying in Paris," Jacqueline said petulantly. "If

anyone should leave it's you. For the first time in my life I have money for clothes, a good job . . . I'm not giving all that up.''

Anne-Marie reached for her glass of aperitif and sipped it slowly. ''A good job at the cinema?'' she said. ''I thought they paid you nothing.''

Her sister shrugged uncomfortably. ''The pay's not that bad,'' she said. ''And sometimes I work a little for Peter Bilescu.''

''For Bilescu?''

''As a showgirl. Nothing more.''

''I've told you, Jacqueline,'' Anne-Marie said gently, ''Paris is full of men like him. They exploit young women.''

Jacqueline stared at her sister angrily. ''You and Litvinov aren't above using Bilescu, why should I be?''

''Litvinov has no wish to associate with someone like Bilescu,'' Anne-Marie said coldly. ''But Bilescu has made a business out of smuggling German Jews into France. Of course the agency does all it can to help once they are here. It's our job, Jacqueline. We can't choose the people we work with. You can. Listen, *ma chérie,* I can get money to you. You can leave Paris tomorrow.''

''And you? You're staying?'' asked Jacqueline.

''Yes, the agency's work must go on, even after the Germans are here.''

''You'll be picked up in the first week,'' said Jacqueline.

''Litvinov is arranging new papers for me. I will have a new name.''

''You think that will help if the Gestapo is after you?'' Jacqueline said. ''And I thought you were the clever one in the family.''

Leaving the café, Anne-Marie Claudel took the métro at Châtelet. Here in the underground world of the subway it was possible, for a few brief moments, to suspend belief in the confusion and panic and the tramp of refugees that for days had been part of the new life in Paris. Here, prim old ladies sat decorously with their hands folded in their laps, impeccably dressed junior officers examined their reflections in the glass of the windows and young lycée students, straphanging in groups, were deprecating about their chances in the coming *baccalauréat* examinations.

At Levallois-Perret Anne-Marie left the subway and walked quickly toward the *mairie*. The double doors of the old building were open, and a chain of clerks was passing documents down to be loaded into a battered green city autobus. Climbing the steps into the cold dark entrance hall, she picked her way through the stacks and bundles of files readied for evacuation. At the *bureau de renseignements* she managed to attract the attention of a clerk long enough to ask him where marriages were conducted.

"Whose marriage?" he asked, emptying drawers of pencils and rubber bands into a packing case.

"Mine," Anne-Marie said impatiently. "The state officer promised to be here at four o'clock."

The clerk shrugged. "First floor," he said. "First door on the right. But don't blame me if he's gone."

"Gone?"

The man stood up straight. "We're being evacuated from Paris," he said importantly. "All essential units of the civil administration are regrouping in the south."

"The Marriage Registry is an essential unit?" she asked incredulously.

"Of course."

Anne-Marie turned away angrily and hurried toward the curving stone staircase. Across the hall a man called to her. In his late sixties, his well-cut suit only partially concealing a heavy paunch, Paul Litvinov threaded his way toward her, gently prodding a clerk aside with a silver-topped cane.

"The clerk said the registrar might already have left," said Anne-Marie anxiously.

Litvinov smiled. "It's all arranged. He's upstairs waiting." He reached into his pocket and took out a fold of franc notes. "You'll need this," he said, handing the money to her. "But it's not too late to change your mind."

"When the Germans come there'll be more work to do than ever," she said gravely. "It will be another kind of battle, in dark alleys and cellars, forging papers and finding rations for the people we have hidden, and the enemy will be the Gestapo."

Litvinov nodded slowly, admiring the spirit in her beautiful eyes.

She put her hand on his. "I'm staying, Paul. No one, not even you, will make me change my mind."

They mounted the stairs. Opening the first door on the right, Litvinov led her through an anteroom. A stench of alcohol and stale garlic rose from a figure in uniform stretched out asleep on a wooden bench. As Litvinov opened the inner door, Anne-Marie glanced down at the soldier, then hurried into the registrar's office.

"You'll forgive me I'm sure in the circumstances if I appear to expedite the proceedings," the middle-aged man behind the desk said. He leaned forward to shake hands perfunctorily with each of them. "My department is due to leave for Orléans later this afternoon. I'm sure you understand, mademoiselle, that only in the very special circumstances am I able to conduct this ceremony."

"I understand the very special circumstances," Anne-Marie's steely glance discomfited the registrar. He bent quickly to open a drawer. Taking out a file, he glanced through it.

"I have all the relevant information here, I think. We lack one thing. A *témoin*, a witness."

"I am the witness," Litvinov said.

"Ah," the registrar squinted through his thick glasses, baffled. "And the bridegroom? The prospective bridegroom?"

"He's outside," Litvinov said. "I'll wake him."

The registrar gave Anne-Marie an uneasy smile. "In these times, mademoiselle . . ." His voice trailed away as Litvinov pushed the soldier into the room. Still half-asleep, the soldier staggered forward and stopped himself with a hand outstretched to the registrar's desk. Red eyed, unshaven, he looked at Anne-Marie. A slow smile showed yellow teeth.

"Delpech," the soldier announced in a thick voice. "Aged twenty-four. Conscript."

"Please stand together," the registrar said.

The soldier took an unsteady step to Anne-Marie's side.

"You, Daniel Georges Delpech, and you, Anne-Marie Claudel, having given due notice to the Marriage Registry at Levallois-Perret . . ."

At the end of the ceremony Anne-Marie counted out five hundred francs and handed the notes to the soldier. There was no attempt to disguise the transaction from the registrar.

"Do I get a kiss too?" asked the soldier, taking the money.

"Perhaps," Anne-Marie said. "On our silver anniversary." She held out her hand. "Goodbye, monsieur." She smiled briefly. "Thank you."

Litvinov ushered the soldier out. The registrar had again taken up his file. Moving rapidly now he quickly checked documents before handing them over. "Marriage certificate, duly signed and stamped. Identity card, revised, authenticated. Ration books. All in the name of Madame Anne-Marie Delpech."

Anne-Marie carefully examined all the papers before putting them in her purse. "And how much do I owe you, monsieur?"

"To take money from such a beautiful girl as yourself seems almost criminal." The registrar beamed.

"It is criminal," said Anne-Marie shortly. "But five hundred francs should assuage your conscience."

Looking down from the window of his private office on the second floor, the graveled expanse of Wewelsburg Castle's inner courtyard seemed to Himmler to have the appearance of a calm, gray sea. From time to time one of the clean-cut young SS officers would cross this triangular sea, moving briskly about his business. Looking up, the solid walls of the castle on all sides gave a sense of impregnable safety.

Himmler would often stand at this window and find the aspect soothing. But today it gave him no such comfort. It was almost 6:00 P.M. and even the faint, appetizing aroma drifting up from the spotless kitchens beside the great dining hall, which usually gave him a pleasing anticipation of ragout and dumplings or beef and sauerkraut, did nothing to shake the Reichsführer's worried frown.

The cause of his concern lay on the desk. Kaltenbrunner had been out of his office all afternoon, and Inspector Krebs had delivered the old shoe box to Himmler in person an hour ago. Now he walked over to view the contents of the box again.

It was spread out across the desk top: a dusty book with what appeared to be wild flowers pressed between the pages, half a dozen unused picture postcards with scenes of North Africa, a small lace fan that had been broken and crudely stuck back together, some cheap imitation jewelry, two French campaign medals, a lock of brown hair tied together with a piece of faded ribbon. Himmler poked around among the rest of the keepsakes. He was sure there was nothing else of significance, except the photograph.

Its deep creases and edges were yellowed, the surface had faded to a faint sepia brown. The Reichsführer-SS pressed the buzzer connected to the office below. By now Kaltenbrunner should have returned. After a few moments a gentle tap sounded on the door.

"Come in," said Himmler, still standing at the desk.

Kaltenbrunner opened the door.

"Come in, Ernst. I have something to show you," Himmler peered over the top of his spectacles, holding out the photograph.

Kaltenbrunner took it.

"Well?" said Himmler.

Kaltenbrunner flinched. In his hand was a postcard-sized front-line photograph such as every squad of German soldiers had had taken during the Great War. But in the center of this one the young man with the Kaiser mustache, his head cocked at an arrogant angle, was clearly Adolf Hitler.

Himmler nodded grimly to himself as if he had just proved some point, then took the photograph from Kaltenbrunner's hand and laid it carefully on the desk.

"So, there we have it," said Himmler in an even tone.

Kaltenbrunner looked up, scanning the items on the desk top. "May I ask where these things were found?" he said.

"In a cupboard under the stairs at the house of the woman Arlette Claudel," replied Himmler.

"The photograph means little or nothing, Reichs-führer," ventured Kaltenbrunner.

"Perhaps, perhaps," mused Himmler. "But consider the possible existence of papers. Consider a certificate of birth."

"We are virtually certain no such document exists," said Kaltenbrunner quickly. "It appears the birth was never registered. The only record our investigation has uncovered is that of the baptism. A simple entry in a book at the church naming only the child. This has already been dealt with."

Himmler thought for a few moments, tapping at his mouth with restless fingers. "Take this trash away and destroy it," he said at last. "Leave the photograph."

Kaltenbrunner began to gather up the items and replace them in the shoe box. "I am sure we can be confident, Reichsführer, there is no written evidence that could be interpreted as proof."

"Which leaves the living proof," said Himmler.

"For the moment," Kaltenbrunner agreed.

Chapter
Three

FROM PARIS THE Great Exodus continued.

In the capital city, the more prosperous districts already presented an empty, plague-stricken air. As the night wore on, the wheels of peasant carts trundled and cracked over the cobbles; the voices of fleeing men and women rose through the streets as the people of Paris, the bakers, grocers, clerks and café owners, joined the exodus. The contagion of rumor swept whole districts onto the road. In the space of a few days, three-fifths of the inhabitants of Paris and the Seine department, three million people in all, had left for the south.

They drove in bakers' vans and expensive long-hooded cars; they led tired, reluctant horses, pulling carts loaded with household chattels; and they hauled, by hand, barrows on which grandmothers and children slept fitfully as another morning touched the rooftops of the city.

The great north-south boulevards were crammed with vehicles of every kind, the bridges clogged, but in other streets, no more than a stone's throw from the slow-moving mass, life continued for those who were determined to remain—or were unable to leave.

As a soft dawn broke slowly over the city, aproned waiters at the corner cafés rearranged chairs around the sidewalk tables. The tricolor fluttered out in a mild breeze above the Eiffel Tower, at the Palais de Justice and over the Foreign Ministry on the Quai d'Orsay. The city rose and stretched. As the sun's rays glanced across the dark courtyards in the poorer quarters, women emerged from doorways, yawning toward the light. In the attic rooms of small hotels lovers untwined their limbs; old *clochards* sleeping over the warm-air grilles of the métro awoke and fumbled for the half-liter bottles in their overcoat pockets; small children sang and cried and rattled the sides of their cribs.

As the day progressed news and rumor, inextricably mixed, filtered through to the city, and in courtyards festooned with clotheslines, Parisians began to speculate on what it would mean to them if the city were to fall.

Yet in the deep well of shadow which was the central courtyard of the crumbling apartments of No. 17 Rue St-Louis, the women gathered around the disused pump had another, more immediately pressing matter to discuss. A gendarme stood in the old coach doorway; another at the foot of the iron staircase. Upstairs, in a top-floor apartment, a girl lay dead.

In the sparsely furnished two-room attic apartment, the four men standing around the body were forced by the sloping ceilings to bend forward in some posture of exaggerated interest.

The two plainclothes policemen watched in silence as the photographer packed up his equipment and the doctor scribbled notes.

Jacqueline Claudel lay dead on the floor between them, her clothes disarranged, a faint idiotic smile on her face, her neck and right cheekbone savagely bruised. Stab wounds had leaked blood across her thighs. A pair of shoes lay near the body, one with a broken heel.

"When can I have the pictures?" Inspector Borel asked.

"I'll deliver them to the commissariat, Inspector. Say,

in two hours," said the photographer. He turned and left.

Borel, broad shouldered, untidily dressed, with a night's growth of beard evident on his dark jaw, stood for a moment preoccupied, caressing the dark fringe of hair on the back of his prematurely bald head. Cases like this, he reflected, were seldom his most difficult. It was usually the boyfriend or lover, or sometimes the man in the next apartment. But in any event it would be someone close to her.

His glance searched the room. Drawers were all neatly closed; bric-a-brac carefully arranged on a tabletop, peasant family photograph, a china ballerina, a child's rag doll. Raped and killed in the bedroom and then dragged in here? By moving his head a little the inspector could see through into the bedroom. He frowned. The peach-colored bedspread was neatly in place. He detached himself from the others and went to stand in the doorway to the bedroom. Again, everything neat and undisturbed. No blood. No sign of a struggle. Raped and killed here in the living room then? Perhaps.

Borel turned to the doctor. "She didn't die from the knife wounds?"

"No," the doctor's eyes roamed again over the blue-black pits in the girl's flesh.

"So?"

The doctor looked up. "Death by strangulation. When?" He asked and answered his own questions. "Within the last twelve hours. Rape? I'd say yes. Sexual interference most certainly. For confirmation we'll need the semen test."

"And the bruise on her face?" Borel asked.

"A disabling blow. Very heavy. Enough to render her unconscious? Almost certainly."

Inspector Borel thanked the doctor and drew a sheet over the body. "Bring in the old woman," he said to his sergeant.

The doctor slipped his notebook into the inside pocket of his old-fashioned tailcoat. "You've heard the news?" he said.

"Yes, the Germans have broken through." The inspector nodded solemnly.

"Worse," said the doctor. "Paris will not be defended."

"I don't believe it," Borel said.

"It's true, I'm afraid. They've declared it an open city," the doctor said.

"They've abandoned Paris?"

"The official announcement is expected later today," said the doctor.

The inspector rubbed his tired eyes. *"Salauds,"* he muttered. "The dirty bastards. My father died in the last war to keep the Germans out of Paris. And now our own damned government opens the city gates for them."

"Our armies are still fighting in the east. Another miracle of the Marne is possible. Just possible." The doctor's voice lacked conviction.

The sergeant returned with a short, fat, elderly woman in carpet slippers. She looked down at the sheeted body on the floor and drew in a deep breath. Her red-rimmed eyes in a gray face remained fixed on a shoeless foot poking from under the cover.

"The poor thing," she said, crossing herself slowly. "The poor, poor thing."

"Madame Bissel." The sergeant announced her to Borel.

"Madame," Borel said with a slight bow. "I have a few questions to put to you. But before I do that I am going to ask you, as concierge of these apartments, to identify the body in the presence of a doctor."

Madame Bissel glanced nervously down.

"The tenant of this apartment was Mademoiselle Anne-Marie Claudel. Correct?" asked Borel.

The old woman's lips worked as she tried to speak.

"Is that correct, madame?"

"Anne-Marie was the tenant, but she hadn't lived here for some time," said the concierge.

Borel glanced at his sergeant, frowning. "You don't mean the apartment was left empty?"

"No, monsieur. Her sister Jacqueline has lived here for several weeks."

"I see." Borel bent and lifted back the sheet. Trembling, the old woman looked down. An involuntary moan escaped from her lips, and she turned her head away.

"Well, madame?" the doctor asked quietly.

"Jacqueline," she whispered. "Jacqueline Claudel."

"Thank you." Borel nodded to the sergeant. "Take her into the other room."

The sergeant led the concierge away. The inspector turned back to the doctor.

"When will the Boches be here?" Borel asked.

"Days . . . hours," the doctor shrugged.

"Even with a German commandant in Paris," Borel said, "a doctor's course is clear. He must go on taking care of the sick. But what does a policeman do?"

Leaning across the body, they shook hands. The doctor walked away shaking his head.

The inspector walked through to the bedroom. The concierge sat on the corner of the single bed. The sergeant had lit a cigarette.

"Close the door," Borel said over his shoulder. He looked down at the old woman, forcing his thoughts back to the murder.

"You're the concierge, madame. You see the comings and goings of your tenants, you see their friends, casual visitors, everybody."

She remained silent, shocked.

Borel placed his hand on her shoulder. "You're going to have to try to answer."

She nodded. "I'm all right," she said. "I'll answer your questions if it's going to help find the swine who did it."

"Mademoiselle Claudel returned home at what time last night?"

"Her usual time, about eleven o'clock. She worked as an usherette in the cinema on the Rue de Rivoli."

"She always returned at the same time?"

"Yes."

"Alone."

"Always."

"She was a pretty girl," Borel said. "She had no fiancé, no young men interested?"

Madame Bissel hesitated.

"If there's something we should know," Borel coaxed her, "it can only help us to find the man."

"On her day off, Sundays, she would go out, all dressed up," Madame Bissel said. "If there was a young man, she met him somewhere else."

"No visitors of any sort?"

"Except last night."

"Ah." The inspector nodded to her to continue.

"A man knocked on my cubicle about ten past eleven. He wanted to see Mademoiselle Claudel."

"You let him in."

"I'm not her mother, Inspector."

"And what time did this man leave?"

"I heard him let himself out about ten minutes later. He wouldn't need a key from the inside."

"You're sure it was this same man who let himself out?"

"I'm sure. The footsteps were the same. In my job, Inspector, footsteps are like faces to other people. It was the same man, ten minutes later."

"And what did this man look like?"

"Not old. A foreigner. He had an accent."

"You don't know what sort of accent?"

Madame Bissel whistled air through her teeth at the sheer impossibility of even guessing. "He had fair hair. English—who knows?"

"Well dressed?"

She grimaced. "In a foreign way."

The inspector glanced around to confirm that his sergeant was taking notes. Satisfied, he turned back to the woman. "Not old, you said. What age? Thirty . . . forty . . . ?"

"Nearer thirty."

"You'd recognize him again?"

"He had a murderer's eyes, close set," the old lady gripped the edge of the bed.

"Leave all that for the concierge next door," Borel said. "For me, just answer the question—would you recognize him again?"

"Yes."

"And he left ten minutes after he arrived?"

"I'd stake my life on it, Inspector," the old lady insisted, "small steps for a tall man."

Borel dug his hands deep into his trouser pockets. "So this was the only visitor you can remember Mademoiselle Claudel ever having?"

"Yes, monsieur."

"And at eleven at night. What did you think?"

The old lady shrugged.

"A concierge likes to know what's going on in her building," the inspector said.

"It's our job, Inspector."

"Of course. And from the courtyard you can see all the way up the staircase to the door of this apartment."

"Since the blackout, there's only a dim blue light allowed on each landing," she said.

"But you watched him all the same?"

"I saw him knock on the door and Mademoiselle Claudel let him in, yes."

"Did she seem to know him?"

"It was dark, monsieur, and my eyes aren't what they were."

"In the ten minutes he was up here, did you hear anything? A struggle?"

"Nothing, monsieur."

"You were standing in the courtyard outside your door?"

"For a minute or two. Perhaps more."

"And you heard nothing?"

She shook her head.

"Voices? A scream?"

"Nothing."

Borel was looking through the open bedroom door

across the living room to the narrow passage leading to
the front door. An oval porcelain plaque of the Virgin and
Child hung slightly askew on the wall. He walked into the
other room and stood in the entrance to the dark passage.
For a few moments he allowed his eyes to become
accustomed to the gloom. Then he knelt to peer at the
frayed linoleum behind the front door.

Stretching out his hand, he picked up a broken high
heel from the deep shadow by the doorjamb. As he stood
he gestured to his sergeant.

"Our murderer was a man of few words," Borel said
quietly.

The sergeant turned his back to Madame Bissel. "You
mean he hit her the moment he stepped through the
door?"

Borel nodded, opening the palm of his hand. "She
went down, snapping the heel as she fell."

"Then he carried her unconscious into the living room,
laid her on the floor, raped her and strangled her?"

Borel sucked at his teeth. "I don't know about you,
Sergeant, but I think I'd prefer to do my raping on a
bed," he said.

The sergeant nodded. "So why didn't he?"

Borel's raised eyebrows showed recognition of the
problem as he returned to the bedroom. "Madame
Bissel," he stopped before her. "You said you saw this
man knock on the door. The blackout light outside was
strong enough for that?"

"Yes," she said hesitantly.

"When Mademoiselle Claudel opened the door, did
they stand talking?"

"I couldn't see her."

"But you saw the door open."

"My eyes, monsieur," the old woman said plaintively.

"I'm not trying to put words into your mouth. Just tell
me exactly what you think you saw after he knocked."

"I think, after a second or two, the door opened and he
walked straight in."

Borel nodded and gestured to the sergeant to follow

him through into the living room. Pushing the door closed behind him, he said, "What sort of rapist climbs five flights of stairs, gains entry to a girl's apartment. Rapes her. Kills her. And calmly returns downstairs to let himself out ten minutes later?"

"The old lady could be wrong," the sergeant said.

"Somehow I doubt it. You heard her describe the footsteps. No. I think we're going to have to believe her."

The inspector held out his hand for a cigarette, was given a crumpled Gauloise, lit it and stood looking down thoughtfully at the outline of the girl's body under the sheet.

"Question number one," he said almost to himself. "Did he know her?"

The sergeant shrugged.

Borel drew on his cigarette, still looking down at the body at his feet.

"You want the old lady for anything else, sir?"

Borel nodded. "One more thing."

The sergeant opened the door, and Madame Bissel came into the room.

Borel walked across to the window and stood for a moment, looking out over the gray, dusty rooftops. Behind him the sergeant and the old woman waited.

"Madame Bissel," Borel turned to face her. "Tell me about the other Mademoiselle Claudel. Anne-Marie. How long had she had this apartment?"

"About two years."

"And why did she decide to leave?"

The old woman shrugged. "She was the one with the real looks."

"You mean perhaps she got an offer?"

"Perhaps."

"When she lived here, what was her job?"

"If she had a job she never told me."

"Men friends?"

"Sometimes one or two would come to the apartment. Serious types."

Borel stuck out his lower lip and grunted. "After her

sister came to live here, did Anne-Marie ever come back?''

Madame Bissel shook her head. ''I never saw her; if the two girls met it was outside.''

''And of course you don't know her new address?''

''No.''

''You give me the feeling, madame, that there was something a little mysterious about Anne-Marie Claudel. Was there?''

Madame Bissel puffed her cheeks. ''Mysterious? I wouldn't say so. Kept to herself. That's all.''

Borel raised an eyebrow in the direction of his sergeant.

''Thank you, madame,'' the sergeant said. ''That's all for the moment.''

The concierge edged her way around the body and stopped. ''Things like this,'' she said, ''shouldn't happen to a nice girl like her. It's not a fair world, is it, Inspector?''

Borel looked up. ''No, madame, it's not a fair world.''

With a last glance down at the shrouded body, Madame Bissel turned and hurried away.

''What now, sir?'' the sergeant said.

''Go through the clothes cupboard—anything unusual in any way.'' Borel dropped on one knee and pulled back the edge of the sheet. Jacqueline Claudel's bruised white face stared up at him. Her lipstick was intact, unsmudged. Both earrings were in place. He pulled the sheet down farther and lifted the dead girl's hand. Not a trace of blood under the fingernails. No marks on the knuckles where they might have been expected if she had flailed out at her assailant.

He pulled at the sheet again. Beneath the skirt she was naked. Bruises blackened the inside of each thigh. Fresh bruises with no trace of yellowing at the edges. And yet the neighbors had heard no sounds of struggle, no screams, no raised voices.

''You know,'' the inspector said, replacing the sheet, ''I don't think you were raped at all, my girl.''

Behind him the sergeant was going through a chest of

drawers. "What do you make of these, sir?" He lifted a mass of peach-colored underwear from a drawer.

Borel turned slowly, swiveling on one knee. "Silk?"

The sergeant nodded. "She didn't buy this with her usherette's tips. This sort of thing costs real money."

"You mean she's been sitting on someone's knee in the back row?"

"A lot of girls do it to make ends meet," the sergeant said, pushing the billowing silk back into the drawer. "It goes on all the time, *patron.*"

Borel ruefully stubbed out his cigarette and sank his hands deep into the pockets of his crumpled suit. In that moment he decided, with the Germans moving relentlessly toward Paris, the only thing he could do was to go on trying, as best he could, to be a good policeman. It would be his own simple act of defiance.

Chapter

Four

BRIGHT CRACKS OF light edged the ill-fitting shutters above Chandler's head. He drew himself away from the warm body beside him and rolled into a sitting position on the side of the bed. Reaching up, he unhooked the nearest shutter and watched it swing open, creaking in the brilliant sunlight.

He stood and turned back toward the half-darkness of the room. The bed was in massive turmoil, sheets and blankets swirling like cloud formations tormented by stratospheric winds. Standing naked by the window, the sun on his back, Chandler watched a brown-skinned leg emerge from under the bedclothes, stretch and be withdrawn into the heaped confusion of the sheets.

"Anelda," he said, "I'm meeting someone for lunch. If you want to stay here and sleep it off it's okay by me."

For an answer a hand reached out across the bed, long fingers felt for a pillow and pulled it down beneath the bedclothes.

Chandler stretched in the sun. He was thirty-two years old. Middle age still felt almost unachievably distant, if by middle age people meant a time when the passions slumbered, the enthusiasms were blunted by skepticism, a time when the world could clearly recognize that a man was midway on the road of life.

To many of his former friends it was the sheer irresponsibility of Chandler's life that guarded his youthfulness. To some of them he simply lacked respectability. But he knew there was a more serious deficiency. He had lived his early life without challenge, and his attempt to create challenge for himself had been seen as irresponsibility. His decision to come to Paris to paint had been seen in just that light. How could he explain that, as he saw it, opting for the life of an artist was accepting a challenge?

Yet he knew he had failed. He padded forward to an unfinished canvas propped on an easel in the middle of the room. The face of Anelda stared out. Her Senegalese features presented a grille effect, the narrow verticality of her head crossed by thin lines of dark eyebrows and long, compressed lips. At least that was how other painters saw her. To Chandler she had large brown breasts and a welcoming smile, and she would sit all day for twenty francs.

"As a model, do I not please the great American painter?"

Chandler turned; Anelda was sitting up in bed, the sheet held up to the level of her nose like a yashmak, her dark eyes fixed on him. She let the sheet drop.

"You please me," Chandler said.

"But not as a model?"

"So Picasso painted you last year and gave you a face like a violin. Why does a genius like that need a model?"

"Why don't you make me your mistress, Theo?" she pouted. "Then all day I will pose for you and all night we can make love."

"And what happens when you get fat and ugly?"

She made a face and slid out of sight under the bedclothes.

Chandler glanced around the studio at his other paintings. As a collection he knew they fell far short of bringing him fame and fortune. Yet something *had* turned up; he had now brought three busloads of Jewish refugees out of Austria to Paris. Three busloads of desperately frightened people, some showing their fear, others concealing everything but their intense relief the moment the French border was crossed. There were real risks for him too, of course. But there was the compensation of Bilescu's payments. Chandler tried to brush the thought of money quickly from his mind; he was getting short again. The rent on the studio was overdue. He thought again of some of the people he'd brought out, Leo and Magda Beckerman somehow always came to mind. He wondered what had happened to them after they had reached Paris and wondered what would happen to them now that, once again, the Gestapo was about to threaten their lives.

Outside on the landing someone rapped on the apartment door.

Chandler picked up a towel and draped it around his waist. If it was the concierge looking for rent, she would have to wait. He walked into the dim hall, so certain that it was the formidable Madame Oberon, he didn't even glance at the shape visible through the thin curtain over the patterned glass pane.

Chandler reached down, slid back the brass catch and pulled open the door.

"Dorothy," he said to his wife standing on the landing. "I—er thought you'd gone back to London."

Dorothy Chandler eyed him coolly from beneath her wide-brimmed straw hat. "Hello, Theo. Aren't you going to invite me in?"

"The place is a shambles," Chandler said. "We could have coffee down at the corner café."

"Which translated," she said in her sharp English accent, "means that you have some floozy in there in a state of undress similar to your own."

He tried what he hoped was a wry smile. "Could be. You still want to come in?"

"Why not?" she said. "I'm beyond being shocked by your choice of tarts."

Chandler led the way into the studio. "That's Anelda under the sheets," he said. "Anelda, say hello to Dorothy."

Anelda's head emerged from the bedclothes. Quickly taking in the heavy gold bracelet and gleaming crocodile bag of the woman looking down at her, she ducked back out of sight.

"The introduction over," Dorothy turned to Chandler, "I'll say what I've come to say."

"What's that?"

"The Germans will soon be in Paris. I've got a car downstairs with full tanks and some reserve cans strapped on the back. Enough petrol to get to Spain. Come with me, Theo."

Chandler reached out and took her hand. "You're English; you've got to get out. I'm an American; I can stay."

"Come all the same."

"Our marriage is over, Dorothy," he said gently, letting her hand fall.

She shook her head. "You've had your fling. You've played the artist in Paris, you've screwed your models." She glanced down at the bed.

Chandler took a cigarette from a paint-stained package and lit it. "I'm a pretty lousy painter, Dorothy."

She smiled. "I'm glad you've realized it."

He stood awkwardly in the middle of the floor, the towel wrapped around him. "I'm not, as you imagine, some kind of natural bohemian," he said. "But I'm not any kind of conformist."

"Nonsense," she said. "Conformity is part of life. Even for romantics like you, Theo. You can't go on playing the juvenile lead forever."

"Jesus," he said. "Did you come all the way to Paris to start lecturing me again?"

"No," she said. "Sorry. I think you bring out the worst in me."

They both smiled.

"How are you off for money?" she asked, reaching into her bag.

"Please, Dorothy."

She took out a slim wad of franc notes bound in a blue wrapper. "I don't imagine they'll be of any use to me in England." She dropped the money casually among the paints and brushes on the table.

"You're always trying to make me feel grateful," said Chandler.

"I used to try," she said, "out of desperation. When I realized it was the only feeling I could elicit."

"Well," said Chandler, "I won't say I don't need it."

She looked at him carefully. "Whether you like it or not, there's a war coming your way, Theo. Isn't it time you started taking sides?"

"America's neutral," said Chandler firmly.

"That's only because Americans are neutral," she said.

Their eyes held for a few moments.

"Go back to England, Dorothy. Sue for divorce. Marry someone you can share your war with," Chandler said.

She nodded slowly. "About the car outside," she said. "I didn't mention it had a driver."

"Who is it?"

"A man—does it matter?" she said. "I came because I thought I should make one last effort with you."

Chandler stepped forward and, ducking below the brim of her hat, kissed her gently on the cheek. "Take care of yourself in London."

"And you in Paris."

Dorothy walked into the hallway, then turned. "Thanks for not coming with me," she said. "Perhaps we will see each other after the war." She turned again and was gone.

Chandler walked back into the studio. Anelda was staring at him reproachfully from the bed.

"Who was that woman?" Anelda asked.

Chandler continued through into the shower, dropped

the towel over the back of a chair and turned on the cold water. Strange, he thought, the idea of Dorothy sleeping with another man. No, not just strange, there was something else there too—an immense sense of relief.

The cinema dated from the days of the old bioscopes. Entering under a drooping awning, Inspector Borel stood for a moment in the sunless lobby, examining the posters ranged along the walls.

"Where's the manager?" Borel held out his police identity card to the thin, balding man who was mopping down the stone steps beyond the ticket desk.

The man straightened up, grunting. "You're talking to him," he said.

From a radio in the ticket office came the voice of an announcer, reporting on the latest position at the front.

"A girl named Jacqueline Claudel," said Borel. "You know her. Correct?"

The man squeezed out the mop. "Yes, I know her."

"Her concierge says she is a country girl," said Borel.

The man nodded. "From the north somewhere." He watched the water from the mop drip into the bucket.

"Goes back to the family on Sundays?"

"Her village is up near the Belgian border somewhere," the manager said. "She'd have to pass through the Boche lines to get home."

"So what does she do with her Sundays?"

"Don't tell me anything about this, will you," the manager scowled at Borel. "I'm not entitled to know, is that it? Well, the Germans will be here by the end of the week. People like you could find yourselves back on traffic duty outside the Gare de l'Est. Or kicked out altogether."

"That's enough," Borel said.

The manager glared at him but was silent.

Then both men turned toward the radio as a roll of drums presaged further news from the front. The announcer's tone was somber: "The Supreme War Council announced at midday today that the counterattack in the direction of German-held Reims continues to inflict heavy losses on the enemy.''

"I was born in Reims," the cinema manager said. "As a boy I worked for all the great champagne houses." He shook his head and turned back to the inspector. "So this girl . . . ?"

"She was found dead in her apartment last night," Borel said. "Murdered."

The cinema manager's face hardly changed expression. "Strange," he said, "she was a nice enough girl, but somehow, at a time like this, you don't feel so much."

"Would you say she was well paid?"

The manager shrugged.

"She was renting an apartment," Borel said. "Cupboard full of clothes, silk underwear . . .''

"I wouldn't claim I paid her a fortune," the manager said warily.

"So on Sunday she made a little on the side. From you?"

"I don't pay myself a fortune either, Inspector. I've a wife, her old mother, three children—I don't have the time or money to chase young skirts like Jacqueline."

"Any idea who did?"

"Monsieur, she worked here for a few months. Jacqueline Claudel is one of a dozen girls in the last year. They all move on."

"You're telling me," Borel said slowly, "that Jacqueline wasn't working here any longer?"

"I thought you knew."

"When did she leave?"

"A week ago. Ten days."

"Why?"

The manager shrugged. "She came in and said she was leaving that evening."

"Think, monsieur. The chances are she said something."

The man leaned his chin on the handle of his mop. "No," he said after a moment. "Just that she'd found somewhere that paid better."

"Another cinema?"

"No. If she was telling the truth the pay was too good for cinema work."

"How much?"

"Enough for me to make a joke about it, I remember."

"The usual sort of joke."

"I suppose so."

"And could you have been right?"

"Perhaps. But she seemed to me to be not that sort of girl."

Borel nodded. Thoughtfully he walked toward the street entrance. One hand on the swinging door, he paused. "I'm sorry about Reims," he said.

Shaved and dressed, Chandler returned to the studio. The sheets were trampled across the floor; paint stained the pillows. Anelda was gone.

Chandler poured a Dubonnet and found himself facing the portrait. Daubs of yellow paint crisscrossed the face. The eyes had been pierced by the thick handle of a brush. He stood for a moment before the ruined portrait. Anelda, he knew, was right. As a critic had once written, his brushwork would not gain him a job sweeping the Place Vendôme. Shrugging, he finished his drink and let himself out onto the landing.

Walking down the winding stone steps from the studio, he stopped at each landing to look out over the sunlit rooftops of Paris. Where the boulevard crossed the Rue Blondel, he could see the plane trees in bright leaf. From the next floor down, he could watch the long columns of refugees fleeing from the battlefields of the north, peasant families mostly, their belongings piled on horse-drawn carts led by weary grandfathers. It had been like this for almost a week now, the bitterly moving spectacle of the dispossessed trudging through the city.

Chandler followed the worn stone steps down to the ground floor. There was more in this stonework, in the cast-iron balustrade, in the heavy ornate coach door out onto the street than in anything he had put on canvas since he arrived in Paris. He was, he decided, neither a painter nor a husband, and he had to admit he found recognition of both facts liberating.

"Monsieur Chandler." The parrot-voiced screech of the concierge from the window caused him to recoil. The old woman who emerged from the doorway was equally parrotlike in appearance.

She stood defiantly, her short, thick arms crossed in front of a straining apron. "No letter from America?" Her sharp beak chopped out the words. "No sign of the money you have been expecting?"

"Could be." Chandler plucked Dorothy's wad of francs from his jacket pocket.

"Yes or no?" Madame Oberon said, moving to block, symbolically, his egress through the twenty-foot-wide doorway.

"Three months in full," Chandler said, peeling off the notes. "Your reputation as a rent collector is saved for another quarter."

Madame Oberon stood squawking new-found confidence in his reliability as he paused for a moment in the shaded courtyard. Outside on the boulevard a spring breeze brushed dust from the trunks of plane trees.

"You've heard about the girl?" Madame Oberon said.

Chandler frowned. "What girl?"

"At Madame Bissel's. Murdered by a maniac."

He pushed the remaining money back into his pocket. "Who was she?"

"It's the young pretty ones," Madame Oberon said darkly, "that get themselves into trouble."

"Have the police got the man?" Chandler asked.

Madame Oberon shrugged dramatically. "They're too busy these days to worry about one working girl. But Madame Bissel saw him. Evil, she said, was written on his face. A foreigner."

"A foreigner?"

"Tall, fair haired," she pointed at Chandler and cackled. "If they weren't so busy with the refugees, the police would be around here asking *you* questions."

"Thanks a lot," Chandler said. With a brief wave he turned for the courtyard door.

"Claudel," Madame Oberon shouted as he stepped through the doorway, "that's her name, Jacqueline Claudel."

He stood transfixed in the bright sunlight of the street. Jacqueline Claudel!

At the corner bar-tabac Borel's sergeant bought himself a pack of Gauloises. "Police," he said to the man behind the zinc counter. "You've heard about the killing?"

"Ten, twenty times already. Don't misunderstand me, monsieur. What I knew of the girl, I liked. She was young, pretty, and to die like that is shocking. But there are lots of other happenings in Paris these days. Perhaps we should be talking about *them*."

"That's all my inspector needs. You knew the girl, you said."

"She came in here most mornings. A pack of cigarettes. A coffee. Sometimes a cognac to settle the stomach. She stood at the bar like a workman."

"Talked?"

"Passed the time of day."

"Did she work?"

"She used to be at the cinema on the Rue de Rivoli."

"Used to be."

"Gave it up, she said, a week or two ago."

"What for?"

"Something better. Why else?"

"You don't know what?"

"No."

"Or where?"

"Across the river somewhere." He turned to a man farther down the bar. "Pierrot, over here a moment."

A man in a black leather cap finished his drink and sauntered toward the sergeant.

"Pierrot drives a taxi," the proprietor said. "Sometimes if she stayed for a second cognac he drove her to work."

"Pierrot," the sergeant said, "this girl we're talking about—the one that was killed last night—where did you drive her?"

"Are you buying me a drink?"

"No. Where was it?" said the sergeant.

The taxi driver raised his eyebrows in the direction of the proprietor. "Two or three mornings I took her to Montparnasse," he said to the sergeant.

"Where did she go when she left the taxi?"

"She turned off down a side street."

"Take me there."

"Do I get paid?"

"Perhaps," the sergeant put two francs on the bar. "Give him a Pernod while I make a phone call."

Chapter

Five

BETH KATELY NEVER rose before noon. The routine was unchangeably rigid. Two glasses of orange juice. One large cup of coffee with her mail. At five minutes to twelve her secretary would run the shower and begin setting out her underwear, stockings, shoes and day dress in the precise order in which she would put them on. The choice of the morning's clothes might well be preceded by ugly threats, made uglier by constant repetition. Her secretary, a tall, stick-dry New Englander whose jacket sleeves never quite covered his wrists, had been seduced by an inflated salary into acting the role of ladies' maid. She had of course never made a sexual approach to him. Rather, she enjoyed his daily humiliation as he laid out her clothes, or endured her middle-aged nakedness or listened to the raw speech she favored after two or three martinis.

At midday he would light a Turkish cigarette for her, and she would smoke it, lying in bed, contemplating the day's appointments, or arranging changes in her schedule. Sometimes she would throw back the bedclothes and get up to stride the room naked, dictating her notes as she drew on the last inch of the scented cigarette. The bell would ring at this time, and the hotel coiffeuse and *femme de maquillage* would arrive to wait nervously in the hall. Beth Kately's levee was a searing experience for all concerned.

This morning in Paris, as the warm water rolled over her short, white, ridged-with-fat body, she was smiling to herself. She stepped out of the shower into the enfolding warm towel held by Martin Upton. Through the half-open door she could see the bedroom. The smile faded. "Martin," she spoke as if her secretary were in the other room, in a loud voice with overlays of her native South, "after fifteen years do you still not know when I say blue I mean *blue?*"

Upton glanced through the door into the bedroom. The day dress he had laid out was draped across the gold leather sofa. "Blue, Miss Kately?" he said anxiously.

"Blue not *turquoise*. Blue."

"I'm sorry, Miss Kately," Upton said. "Truly sorry."

Beth Kately smiled. She prided herself that she had learned to suffer fools gladly. In her profession she had to.

"Just lay out the blue dress, Martin," she said tolerantly. "And telephone the Sappho Club. Find out if Jacqueline is there today."

Wrapped in her towel, she padded barefoot across the room and poured herself a martini Upton had already prepared. She had not yet made up her mind whether or not to stay in Paris. Every newspaper in the United States would be carrying the story of the German Army's triumphal entry into the capital. In the Beth Kately column, she needed something more. The towel fell from her as she stood musing, sipping her martini. Perhaps she should follow the French government south? She shook her head. No, the Germans were the newsmakers today. She would stay on in Paris, at least until they arrived.

The door opened and Martin Upton came into the room. Naked, she handed him her glass to be refilled.

"I telephoned the Sappho Club, Miss Kately." He stood in the middle of the carpet, her empty glass in his hand.

"And?" she turned irritably.

"I have some bad news, I'm afraid."

"Get on with it."

"I spoke to one of the waiters who lives in the same district as Mademoiselle Claudel. He says that she was found dead this morning, murdered."

"Give me another martini." Beth Kately leaned down and picked up her bath towel. "Murdered?" A savage smile spread over her face.

Upton refilled her glass and handed it to her. "The waiter said the police have been at her apartment all morning."

Beth Kately emptied her glass in one gulp. "Could it just be possible," she said to herself, "that the little bitch was telling the truth after all?"

"Wait for us here," Borel said to the taxi driver, as he and the sergeant got out of the back of the cab.

"Waiting's expensive," Pierrot said. "Do I get paid?"

"Handsomely." Borel turned away toward the narrow alley that the driver had indicated. Mostly the buildings were the backs of restaurants. Rotting vegetable peelings overflowed from garbage cans. In one doorway an aproned cook stood in a narrow shaft of sunlight.

"What is interesting about this place?" Borel stopped in front of the cook.

"Monsieur?" the man turned his pale face up toward the heat of the sun. Behind them the click of high heels signaled the entry of two girls into the alley.

"Forget it," Borel said. He stood with the sergeant until the girls had passed them, then slowly followed.

At the end of the alley an archway opened to the right. The girls turned into it.

The two policemen reached the archway as a door was about to close. Borel moved quickly forward and pressed his broad hand against the paneled door. "One moment,'' he said to whoever stood in the darkness of the passage beyond.

The door reopened slowly. A woman of about forty, dressed for the evening rather than the day, looked Borel over carefully. "This is a private club, monsieur," she said. "A *luncheon* club." She used the English word. "The entrance fee alone is very expensive."

"If I pay it, however, I can come in?"

"Not today, monsieur. Regrettably all the tables are reserved."

"Regrettably." Borel nodded. "Show her your cards, Philippe."

The sergeant took out his police identification and held it in front of the woman.

"Ah . . ." She took half a step backward. "And I thought you were an undesirable character," she said to Borel. "How wrong can you be. I'll call the owner."

"No," Borel said. "We'll just go in and occupy one of your reserved tables."

Passing the woman, they continued on down the dark corridor. A thick curtain covered an opening at the far end, and pulling it aside, Borel found himself looking into a small restaurant with a stage at one end. It was some minutes after they had sat down at one of the corner tables that they realized all the other customers were women.

Mostly alone, sometimes in pairs, the women were all middle-aged, all markedly well dressed. In the half-darkness, necklaces and bracelets glinted in the candle-light.

"What do you make of it, Philippe?" Borel signaled the waiter who had been hesitating by the entrance to the kitchen.

"Ask the man," the sergeant said. "I'm new to Paris."

Borel turned to the waiter. "Police officers," he said. "We're having lunch. Bring me two large Pernods."

"Yes, monsieur," the man said without enthusiasm.

"And before you go, my sergeant has a couple of questions to ask you. He's new to Paris."

"Monsieur?" the waiter turned to the sergeant.

"First, I see that all the daylight is shut out. Candles on the tables—more the atmosphere of the evening than midday," the sergeant said.

The waiter turned down the corner of his mouth and nodded. "It's what our customers prefer."

"That leads me to the second question. The customers, they're all women," the sergeant said.

"It's the sort of place women appreciate."

"You have a floor show?"

"Yes."

"During lunch."

"Yes."

"What sort of show?"

"Perhaps monsieur will stay to see it."

Borel shuffled impatiently. "Let's have the drinks," he said to the waiter. "And the menu. And tell your *patron* we want to see him after the show."

When the *carte* had been brought and the Pernod and water jug set down in front of them, both sat smoking, studying the extensive range of dishes. From time to time another customer would arrive, always a woman, usually of early to late middle age, and invariably expensively dressed.

Borel and the sergeant ordered oysters, trout and confit de canard, and a bottle of 1934 La Lagune. Hardly had they finished the oysters when, without any musical preamble, the restaurant's already low lights dimmed and the stage curtains slid aside.

A slender figure stood against a crudely painted backdrop of a Paris skyline. The hair was dyed and cut to stand spikily away from the chalk-white face; the lipstick slashed angrily across the wide mouth. The hips were slim as a boy's, the black trousers tight. There was no visible undulation beneath the white cotton shirt. The air of expectancy in the half-darkness of the restaurant was tangible.

"I think it's a boy," Borel's sergeant said, and was shushed into silence by voices from the dark.

There was a drumroll. A tenor saxophone wailed and was silent. Suddenly a thin, guttural voice hit a note and held it.

The figure on the stage was moving. Hands clasped behind the back, the singer began to gyrate to the drums, which now provided the only backing. Swaying and bucking with some extraordinary ferocity, every now and again hitting a note that was more a scream of agony or sexual satisfaction than part of a song, the slender figure cavorted furiously about the stage.

On the harsh high notes, Borel could hear around him the sharp hiss of indrawn breath as the customers lived their pleasure. Then, as the singer screamed and stamped out the final notes, the ringing tones of childlike frustration died away and the curtains slid silently across the stage.

The low houselights came up. Borel grinned at the sergeant, sitting opposite him. "Well, Philippe, what do you make of that?"

The sergeant looked puzzled. He leaned across to Borel. "I *must* be new to this side of Paris," he said.

"Watch the show," Borel said. "And enjoy your lunch."

The curtains had drawn back again. Show girls filled the stage. Only that they paired and kissed and caressed each other as part of the dance made the performance any different from those in a thousand heterosexual Paris clubs.

"So this was Jacqueline Claudel's job," the sergeant said. "Titillating the perverse instincts of a bunch of rich middle-aged women."

"Is it any worse than doing the same for rich middle-aged men?" Borel asked.

The sergeant sniffed. "It's a good lunch, *patron*," he said. "But I'm not sure it gets us any closer to Jacqueline's killer."

Borel turned toward the tall figure of the man approaching their table.

"Welcome to the Sappho Club, inspector." Peter

Bilescu signaled to a waiter, who came forward with a chair. As Borel showed his police card the sergeant inspected Bilescu with distaste. His bright metallic hair was clearly dyed; his pale gray suit would have cost the sergeant at least a month's pay. Though probably past forty, he had the manner and movements of a much younger man.

"Peter Bilescu," he introduced himself. "What is it brings you here, Inspector?"

"One of your dancers, Jacqueline Claudel."

"Jacqueline." Bilescu smiled a perfect smile. "What's *she* been up to?"

"Getting herself murdered," Borel said. "During the early hours of this morning." He watched Bilescu's smile fade. At just the right speed. This man, he thought, is a consummate actor. Or else he couldn't give a damn about the death of one of his dancers.

"Poor girl," Bilescu murmured. "Murdered, you say. Do you know who did it?"

"We have a description," Borel said. "Tall, fair hair. A foreigner. Where do you come from, Monsieur Bilescu?"

"I'm a Rumanian citizen, Inspector. And my French resident papers are in order."

"How long has Jacqueline worked for you?"

"A little less than a month."

"How did she come to know about the club?"

"Word gets around, Inspector. We pay well."

"She was employed as a dancer?"

Bilescu smiled. "Whatever I am, Inspector, I'm not a hypocrite. She was employed because she was very attractive to my customers."

"She was a lesbian tart."

"It's not against the law."

"Did she have any special clients?"

"If she had," Bilescu said easily, "their names are not known to me."

Borel nodded slowly. "So you can't help us in this matter?"

"I can offer you lunch on the house. But I can't help in identifying your murderer."

"The lunch we accept," Borel said briskly. "I have a witness, someone who saw this tall, fair-haired foreigner. Come down to the station at four this afternoon. The address is on my card."

Leaving the Sappho Club, Borel walked morosely back down the alley.

"You don't think he's our man?" his sergeant asked him as they reached the street corner.

"He can get what he wants from any of those girls."

"But you said yourself, *patron*, that it might not have been rape. Perhaps Jacqueline was blackmailing one of the customers."

"Perhaps," Borel grunted as he climbed into the back of the taxi.

"Two hours, Inspector," the taxi driver protested. "Two hours' business lost on a day anybody will pay anything for a cab. Even while I was waiting I've had six offers to take fares as far as Orléans."

"Did you ever pick up Jacqueline at any other place but the bar-tabac?" Borel asked, ignoring Pierrot's complaints.

"No." He paused. "Yes, once," the driver growled resentfully. "Once I picked her up here. She was with an old lady, dripping diamonds."

"How old?"

"Fifty. More, even. An American. Giggled like a schoolgirl all the way to the Hôtel Crillon."

"Jacqueline?"

"The American."

"How long ago?"

"Two or three days."

"Where to now, *patron*?" the sergeant asked.

Borel smiled. "Lunch at the Sappho Club must be followed by five o'clock tea at the Hôtel Crillon."

Beth Kately fixed Borel with a look of unmixed hatred. "What are you suggesting, Inspector?"

Standing in the middle of the room, Borel lifted his hands and let them drop. The barman downstairs had told him Miss Kately was a woman with formidable connections. "Madame," he said, "I am suggesting nothing. I am investigating a murder."

"What are you suggesting?" She stabbed out the words, standing, her feet wide apart, her head down as if she were about to charge.

For Borel it had been a long day. It had been a day in which he had been forced to accept that the government which he served had deserted the people of Paris, whom he also served. Suddenly he had no more patience to expend on this influential foreigner. "If you prefer girls to boys, madame," he snapped, "it's no concern of mine. As I said, I'm investigating a murder, not a touch up the garter in the back of the taxi."

"Martin," she screamed, purple faced, "get me the Minister of the Interior on the phone."

Upton came running into the room and stopped at the confrontation before him.

"This man is making all sorts of wild accusations. You heard them."

"Yes, Miss Kately."

"Then tell the minister that if he ever wants a favorable mention in the American press again, he'll take this bum off my back immediately."

"The Minister of the Interior," Borel said wearily, "is in Tours, or Beaugency or for all I know on the road to Bordeaux. If you can get him on the telephone in the next week, you'll be doing better than any civil servant in France."

The color slowly faded from her cheeks. "Get out," she said to Upton. "I'll handle this alone."

For seconds they stood staring at each other. Then she grimaced, gesturing with a ringed hand. "You're not a polite man, Borel. But then I'm not a polite woman."

"No."

She grunted. "I was at the Sappho Club on Thursday. I

brought Jacqueline Claudel back here after lunch. She stayed a couple of hours. What else did you want to know?''

"It was the first time you met her?''

"Yes."

"Did you plan to meet her again?''

She shrugged. "There are lots of other girls at the Sappho Club, Borel."

"Did you speak of another meeting?''

"In these circumstances you always do. It improves performance.''

"But you arranged no particular day."

"No. She was a pretty enough girl. Not particularly bright. Not particularly inventive. I didn't commit myself, no.''

Borel pulled his cigarettes from his jacket pocket and lit one. "How long have you known Bilescu?" he asked, blowing smoke out into a shaft of sunlight.

"A year or more. I go to the Sappho once or twice every time I'm in Paris.''

"What do you know about him?''

"Rumanian émigré. Knows how to please ladies of a certain taste. Art dealer on the side. Quite a good one, I hear.''

"What about his own tastes?''

She laughed. "You don't mean in painting," she said mock-ruminatively. "I think Peter Bilescu's tastes run off the board.''

"Did Jacqueline talk of any men in her life?''

"Hardly.''

"Did she talk about anything?''

"She wasn't here to discuss Flaubert, Inspector. Now why don't you pour us both a drink and recognize that you're barking up the wrong tree?''

"I don't drink," Borel said, picking up his hat. "I signed the Salvation Army temperance pledge on my seventh birthday. Since then I haven't touched a drop.''

* * *

The cinema manager, now dressed in striped trousers and a black jacket, emerged from behind the ticket grille as Borel approached.

"I should cuff you around the ear," Borel said amiably.

The manager shot a quick glance over his shoulder to the middle-aged usherette standing at the entrance to the hall. "My wife," he said, his voice lowered.

"Very good, monsieur," Borel put one arm around his shoulder and walked him toward the glass doors. "Jacqueline," he said, "was a first-class tart. Men, women too."

"Ah." The manager tried an unsuccessful expression of surprise.

"No games this time, monsieur. Or I ask your wife to step over here and corroborate your statements."

"There's no need for that," the manager said hurriedly. "If there's anything I can do to help, just ask."

"She used the cinema, the back row?" Borel removed his arm from the man's shoulder.

"It's strictly against the company's rules," the manager said.

"Of course. The sort of thing a girl could lose her job for. But Jacqueline didn't."

"No."

"Because you had a little arrangement with her."

The man was sweating. Checking again over his shoulder to make sure his wife was still in position, he nodded quickly.

"Money?"

"No, monsieur. Never money . . ."

"She paid in kind. After the last customer had left."

The manager bubbled air between his lips. "Once or twice."

"You're lucky you're not tall, fair haired and speak French with a foreign accent, monsieur," Borel said.

"The murderer was a foreigner?"

"Possibly. Did Jacqueline have any foreign friends?"

"There are a lot of foreigners in Paris, Inspector. Or there were until recently. English officers on leave enjoyed coming here."

"Anyone special?"

"I wouldn't know, Inspector. That's the truth. Anybody special she took to the hotel around the corner. Sunday afternoon was her time."

"The hotel around the corner?"

"The Hôtel Clemenceau, Inspector. For her very special customers only."

In the faded lobby of the Hôtel Clemenceau Borel's sergeant leafed slowly through the hotel register. Borel sat in a cane armchair, a cigarette in his mouth. The small middle-aged woman in the straight-backed chair opposite him pursed her lips. "Dead, you said."

Borel removed the cigarette from his mouth. "Murdered, I said. In a very nasty way, madame. Neck broken, clothes ripped off, thighs badly bruised . . ."

"Thank you, Inspector," she said. "I can do without the details." She paused. "As far as I know I never heard of this girl. Of course it's possible that she stayed here as the wife of someone. I fill in my night forms and hand them to the police like a law-abiding hotel keeper. Don't expect us to do your job as well, Inspector."

"You lying old bitch," Borel said evenly. "You had a deal on for that girl's Sunday clients, didn't you?"

"If I've ever met Jacqueline Claudel, I don't know it," the woman said firmly.

"Saturday and Sunday are her busiest nights," the sergeant closed the book. "No singles. A couple in every room."

"And afternoons, with clean sheets naturally, you're rented out to the after-lunch trade, is that it? Cash. No questions asked."

"I keep to the rules," the woman said, her lips hardly moving. But as she finished speaking her tongue moistened the black down on her upper lip.

Borel drew on his cigarette, exhaled the smoke through his nose, nodding. "Show her a few pictures," he said to the sergeant.

The sergeant opened the chafed leather case on the desk top and took out a handful of curling, newly printed photographs. He passed them to the woman.

Borel watched her mouth fall open. "Go on, look through them. You don't remember her like *that*, do you?"

"They're disgusting," the woman said.

"The man who did it," Borel said, "was almost certainly one of her boyfriends. Someone she brought here on Sunday afternoons. He could do it again. To another of the girls. I'm not interested in your financial arrangements, madame. But I want the name of any man she came here with. Otherwise I apply for an order from the préfecture to close you down today."

The woman handed the photographs back to the sergeant. "Jacqueline came here most Sunday afternoons," she said. "She took the big bedroom at the back for a couple of hours after lunch. I always insisted on identification for the man. If you don't, I find sometimes they can turn nasty and think they'll get away with it."

"A different man every Sunday?"

"No," she got up and crossed to a cupboard behind the desk. "Five or six altogether."

She took out a black notebook, opened and handed it to the sergeant. "She wasn't on the street. Usually she came with the same man for a few weeks running. Then there'd be someone else. She wasn't a professional."

The sergeant copied names into his own notebook.

"You were," Borel said. "A professional."

"A long time ago now, Inspector." Her face relaxed.

"That's how you bought the hotel."

She was silent, assenting.

"How long had Jacqueline been in Paris?"

"A few months. Her sister, Anne-Marie, was already here. They come from the north somewhere."

"Her sister was in the same line of business?"

"If she was," the woman said, "she wouldn't have troubled herself with a place like this. She's got the looks for a big hotel. Or an apartment in the Bois de Boulogne."

The sergeant handed the black book back to the woman.

"All right," Borel said. "Let's see what we've got." He stood up.

"One thing, Inspector," the woman said. "This man that killed her. If he could pay for what he wanted, why should he kill her for it?"

"You ought to have joined the police, madame," Borel said. "We could do with minds like yours."

At the all-American lunch at the Café Lipp, the talk was entirely about who was staying, who was leaving Paris. The newsmen, of course, would stay to report the German entry, which they now knew was inevitable. The diplomats would be moving south as soon as the French government established its final resting place. The others —the writers, painters, the wealthy and not-so-wealthy young men who were just there to enjoy the city—were still undecided.

It was a notably more somber gathering than was usual at Sunday lunchtime at the Café Lipp. During these days in Paris, it was impossible to escape the catastrophe that was overtaking France and, by extension, the whole of European civilization. The latest reports of Nazi treatment of Jews in Poland were seeping through to diplomats and newspapermen, unconfirmed accounts of whole communities being herded into new ghettoes, of the requisition of property and assets, and even more sinister, mass recruitment for forced labor.

Usually Chandler would be among those who stayed on drinking and talking after most of the working Americans had left, but today he felt no great wish to sit and speculate about the disaster to come, or the disaster that was already happening all around them. Leaving his share of the bill, he waved goodbye around the table and walked off in the bright sunlight toward the Île St-Louis. Perhaps, he thought, Dorothy was right after all; it was time to take sides. Something more than smuggling out refugees for Peter Bilescu for a few thousand francs. He had no problem, of course, in feeling anti-Nazi. But anti-German was more difficult. His father's family, the Kandlers, had come from Germany. Theo Chandler himself had cousins at this moment in the German Army, ordinary, decent Germans whom he had skied and visited with before the war. And yet he had seen something of Nazi Germany himself, something beyond the Berlin Olympic Games and the new autobahns. He had heard stories from refugee families, and the stories coming out of Poland were different only in scale and a new, more confident, edge to the brutality.

He had already turned into the Rue de Rivoli before his thoughts again returned to Jacqueline. The cinema where he had first met her was opposite, on the corner. He tried to think of her lying dead but found the idea impossible to entertain for more than a few seconds. With less difficulty he remembered her flushed face, below him on the vast, musty pillow of the Hôtel Clemenceau.

He crossed onto the island at the Pont St-Louis and walked the length of the street he found the most beautiful in all Paris. Perhaps, he thought, he was still suffering from shock. How else to describe the strange distance he felt between himself and the fugitive idea of Jacqueline lying dead.

At his apartment building he ducked instinctively to enter the low doorway in the porte cochère, passed into the cobbled courtyard and stopped.

The two men standing before him exchanged a quick glance. On the brisk nod from one, the other blocked Chandler's path.

"Monsieur Theodore Chandler?" the sergeant said.

"Yes."

"Monsieur." Borel came forward. "I am Inspector Borel. I'm told at the Hôtel Clemenceau that you're a foreigner. English."

"American."

Borel nodded. "I'm also told at the hotel that from time to time you entertained a certain Mademoiselle Jacqueline Claudel there."

"That's true," Chandler said warily. "May I ask why you should be asking all these questions at the Hôtel Clemenceau?"

"Certainly," Borel said, his eyes never leaving Chandler's face. "Because last night in her apartment Jacqueline Claudei was brutally murdered."

"Murdered?"

Borel stood silently watching the American's reaction. "Well, monsieur," he said, "have you no questions to ask me?"

"Of course I've questions to ask you," Chandler said.

"I too have questions," Borel said. "With luck we shall be able to provide each other with some answers. Such as to why you should pretend not to know Jacqueline Claudel was murdered when your concierge, Madame Oberon, told you less than two hours ago."

Chandler said nothing.

"A bad question, monsieur?"

"Am I under arrest?" Chandler asked him.

Borel smiled briefly. "No. Not yet, Monsieur Chandler."

Chapter

Six

ON THE ROADS of France the madness continued. Funneled through Paris, the unending column of refugees stumbled on toward Orléans, a hundred kilometers distant. There, with orders to blow up the George-V bridge at the approach of the Germans, a Lieutenant Marchand waited through unending Luftwaffe attacks. Because the young lieutenant knew that when the moment came there would be no possibility of first clearing the bridge of civilians with his sixteen-man squad, he dreaded the arrival of the order.

As the cities and countryside of northern France emptied, the townships and villages south of Paris were engulfed by the great wave of fleeing people; hungry, thirsty and desperate, 70,000 refugees surged into the small Corrèze country town of Brive-la-Gaillarde; in two days 40,000 passed through the Rue Baron-Duprat reception center in Lourdes; in the second week of June, Cahors, on the river Lot, population 13,000, was swamped by a vast refugee army marching on the town. While thousands drifted on south, 40,000 people, exhausted, many sick, all at the limit of their endurance, camped in the market squares and on the steep hillsides that ran down to the river.

No town in the Dordogne, the Lot or the Gers escaped the tide. French reinforcements struggling toward the battle in the north found every road and bridge blocked. Among the unending columns of civilians marched schoolchildren in the charge of distraught teachers, convents, homes for the aged, the staffs and patients of whole hospitals, all struggling toward the asylum they imagined existed somewhere south of the Loire, south of the Dordogne, south of the river Lot.

Afterward, to those with a will to remember those days under a blue sky without pity, it was as though a whole people was on the move through the roads and fields and woods of the countryside, swarming through the alleys and squares of the towns. It was, of course, far short of a whole people. But if the French Army, overwhelmed as much by French civilians as by the German invader, is included, it is probable that in those early June days close to one-third of the population of France was on the road to a destination, known or unknown.

Anne-Marie Claudel was nineteen when she first came to Paris. At that time, almost three years before its present humiliations, Paris had seemed to her, as to millions of more traveled visitors, the city of attainable dreams. To most Parisians it was perhaps something sadly less. It was, like any other big city, a place where laundry had to be done, tables waited on, roads dug, windows cleaned, and it would be in occupations like this that most of its people would be engaged. But Anne-Marie possessed an asset that might raise and maintain her above the mass of Parisians who served and cleaned and labored: she was a markedly beautiful young woman.

She knew this as a casually sober fact. The knowledge came slowly. From watching her widowed mother, Arlette, as she held court in the family café in the small northern village of St-Eloi. A tall, well-built woman with red-blond hair pulled back from her fine features, Arlette would move among the card players at the Café de la Paix, resting a hand on someone's shoulder as she served drinks, allowing, encouraging small intimacies, a brief touch of her thigh, an arm around the waist. Shortly after Anne-Marie's fifteenth birthday her mother had begun to instruct her openly. "Men," she had said, "are born fools for women to take advantage of. When you serve a drink, bend forward over the table. Let them take a look at what you've got; it costs you nothing. Then straighten up, let them see your line. And when you carry your tray back to the bar, walk like this." She demonstrated a free, swinging walk, the tray held easily in one hand. "They'll be watching, whoever they are, whatever their age. They don't come here just to play cards and drink Pernod."

She had not, however, been an apt pupil, this fifteen-year-old girl, already almost as tall as her mother. It's true that her appearance had pleased the customers of the café, but as she reached the age of sixteen, then seventeen, the peasant farmers of the village saw her as too reserved, too self-contained for them to banter with. She lacked, they all agreed, the easy manner of her mother.

To Arlette it was a family asset wasted. To Anne-Marie the demand that she should swing her hips or allow old Junot's hand to brush her thigh was deeply degrading. So too were her mother's boasts of past conquests, her crude hints of an amorous present, her nightly efforts before the peasants of St-Eloi to demonstrate her *availability*. She was not promiscuous, at least not in the conventional sense. But it made little difference to her daughter. Throughout Anne-Marie's eighteenth year the arguments grew in frequency. On her nineteenth birthday she told her mother she wanted to leave for Paris.

It was late one evening after the last of the cardplayers had left. Arlette had paused over a table she was wiping. Very slowly, cloth in hand, she had turned to face her daughter. "Paris," she said. "You want to go to Paris."

Anne-Marie stood, her back to the bar. "I've thought about it for a long time. A girl can earn three hundred and fifty francs a month there waiting on tables."

"Paris," Arlette repeated, her face set. "The only way a girl can earn good money there is on her back."

"Three hundred and fifty francs is good money, *maman*," Anne-Marie said quietly.

Arlette hurled the cloth she was holding into the basin behind the bar. "It upsets you, does it, when old Junot's hand strays a little? Or some passing salesman wants to give you a bit of a squeeze?"

The girl said nothing.

"And you're happy to go to Paris, are you? To share a bed with some fat café owner while his wife's at the market. *That's* what they pay three hundred and fifty francs for."

"No." Anne-Marie shook her head vehemently. "If I share anybody's bed it will not be some fat café owner's."

"Ah, you see yourself set up in an apartment in the Bois de Boulogne, do you? The woman of a reserve colonel or a politician, even? Let me tell you, Anne-Marie," she said. "I've known girls who've gone to Paris. They end up one place only—on the streets."

"I've enough money for the train fare," Anne-Marie said. "Do you want me to stay until the end of the week?"

"If you're leaving, leave tomorrow," her mother said bitterly. "Within a month you'll be servicing Arab workmen at the Gare St-Lazare."

Now thoughts of her mother came flooding back to her as Anne-Marie stood trembling with shock in the lobby of the cinema on the Rue de Rivoli.

The manager, shuffling uncomfortably out from the ticket office, stopped in front of her. "I'm sorry, mademoiselle. It was the police that told me. They were here earlier today. They wanted to know all about her."

Anne-Marie nodded, fighting to regain control of her body. "Do you know what happened?" She framed the sentence with effort. "Do you know where?"

"She was killed in her apartment; that's all I know," the manager said. "They ask more than they tell, the

police. Perhaps they thought she had a rich boyfriend.
Something about expensive silk underwear they found in
her commode.''

''Last night?''

''Or early this morning.''

''Did the police think she knew the man?''

''Mademoiselle,'' the manager said patiently, ''if the
police think *anything*, if they've got time to think anything these days, they'll tell you. Go and see them, they'll
want to speak to you anyway.''

Anne-Marie nodded absently. Thanking the man, she
turned away. Out on the sunlit street she found herself
standing, not moving, holding close to her the bag that
contained the thousand francs she'd intended to give
Jacqueline to make her escape from Paris. Now, of
course, she would never escape. Slowly Anne-Marie
began to walk along the almost deserted Rue de Rivoli. It
was no secret to her that her sister had used the cinema to
pick up lovers for Sunday afternoons at the Hôtel Clemenceau. She knew that Jacqueline had met the American
there. But as she walked slowly through the shade of the
plane trees in the Place d'Autriche, she found, in shock,
that her mind veered away from images of Jacqueline,
resisting the picture of her lying dead in the familiar Île
St-Louis apartment. Instead, in her mind's eye, she began
to roll back the years, and her thoughts turned more and
more to Arlette, her mother, in St-Eloi.

Last week it had been Inspector Borel's office, a large
high-ceilinged room with long narrow windows overlooking the barges on the Seine. Today it was a room into
which three extra desks had been jammed, along with the
complete files of fifteen evacuated police commissariats
from the occupied north. Papers were piled high on trestle
tables and packed in cartons lining the walls. Above the
din of clattering typewriters and ringing telephones,
police officers in shirt-sleeves, their foreheads dripping
sweat as the temperature rose toward noon, shouted
inquiries to each other across the room. A distraught

refugee family was trying to trace a missing daughter; a large, frightened black dog roped to the handle of a battered suitcase, yelped incessantly.

Borel stood in the doorway, stricken by the chaos in the room. He turned to the sergeant at his shoulder.

"*Putain!*" he swore under his breath. "Take him across to the café. We'll interview him there."

In the corridor outside, Chandler watched trolley-loads of blue files being stacked in a curtained alcove.

"Monsieur Chandler," the sergeant said sardonically, "you're in luck. The inspector has decided to buy you a drink."

The café opposite the commissariat was one of the most fashionable in Paris. In other days the tourist could expect to see under its red-and-gold awning at least one well-known politician lunching at the Café Anschel; models from the small couture houses along the boulevard chattered like brightly plumaged birds at its terrace tables; from time to time Sartre would appear with Simone de Beauvoir on his arm, or for some, an even more memorable event: Picasso himself would occupy a corner seat, tearing paper napkins into incredible shapes, the dark eyes in the monkey face fixed with openly challenging lust on a woman three or four tables away.

Inspector Borel indicated to Chandler a shaded table in the corner of the terrace and dismissed his sergeant with a few whispered instructions.

"So," he said, seating himself opposite, "since the city of Paris can no longer provide an office in which to interview suspects, it can at least pay for their refreshments. What will it be, monsieur?"

When Chandler had ordered a vin blanc and Borel a demi of beer, the two men sat for a second staring at each other.

"Let's begin then, Monsieur Chandler," Borel said at length. He took out a notebook. "Tell me about Jacqueline Claudel."

"There's not a lot to tell, Inspector. A few weekends I took her to the Hôtel Clemenceau. That's all."

The inspector removed his hat and ran his hand across the red welt on his forehead. "How long ago did you first meet her?"

"Three or four months."

Borel sipped his beer. Beyond the packed café tables, beyond the laughing girls, the wine bottles and the dishes of grilled langoustines, a column of French infantry trudged along the cobbled streets. The young lieutenant on horseback refused even to glance down; his men, in heavy overcoats, glared bitterly at the customers of the café, as they led their pack mules past.

The inspector turned back to face Chandler.

"Were you in love with Jacqueline Claudel, monsieur?"

"No."

"You were attracted to her, then."

"She was an attractive girl, yes."

"You are avoiding the issue, monsieur. I am trying to discover what sort of emotional connection there was between you."

Chandler looked at him blankly. "Inspector, I was sleeping with her. I liked her. But that's all." He paused for a moment and drained his glass. "I met Jacqueline while she was working as an usherette at a cinema on the Rue de Rivoli. The next day I took her to lunch at the Hôtel Clemenceau. I booked a room."

"She had already made it clear you would not be wasting your money."

"I don't have to tell you the score, Inspector," Chandler said. "There are a lot of girls in Paris like Jacqueline. She wasn't a street girl; she still kept a job. But weekends she tried to make something on the side."

Borel ran his hand around the fringe of dark hair at the back of his head. "Let's go back to your first meeting," he said. "Tell me how it happened."

"I'm sure you know. There are some cinemas in this area . . ." Chandler's voice trailed off uncomfortably.

"I know nothing," Borel said, signaling the waiter to renew the drinks.

The American shrugged. "Okay, Inspector, you know nothing. Nothing about a cinema like Jacqueline's. Well, the system's straightforward enough. If a man goes into the cinema alone, an usherette approaches and asks where he prefers to sit. If he says at the back, she shows him to a seat, sits down with him for a while, and he gives her a few francs tip. If he likes her, he takes her to lunch on her day off. And afterward to a cheap hotel."

"What bad luck," Borel mused.

"Bad luck?"

The inspector nodded. "If one of the men Jacqueline approached in the darkness, one of the men she sat with in the back row, was her murderer."

"I wasn't the first man she took to the Hôtel Clemenceau."

"No. But you were the last."

"I haven't seen Jacqueline for nearly a month," Chandler said.

"Why is that?"

"This sort of affair runs its course."

"You were happy to let things drift."

"Sure."

"No other man came on the scene?"

"Not as far as I know."

Borel grunted to himself. "Tell me, Monsieur Chandler, did you ever meet Jacqueline anywhere else but at the Hôtel Clemenceau?"

"No."

"Did you meet her at any other time but Sunday for lunch and bed?"

"No."

"Did you never meet her perhaps after work, when the cinema closed, for a coffee or a beer?"

"No, Inspector," Chandler said tensely. "I see what you're trying to suggest, but you're wrong. In nearly four months I saw her as many times. I was *not* involved with Jacqueline in any way."

"Except carnally."

"Yes."

"Did you ever go to her apartment?"

"The apartment was only loaned to her, by her sister I think she said. She didn't want the concierge to know she was receiving the occasional friend."

The inspector sat back, his eyes disconcertingly searching Chandler's face. "Did she ever mention the name of any other of her men friends?"

Chandler raised his glass and drank casually, but his mind was racing. Did the inspector know that Jacqueline had introduced him to Peter Bilescu? If not, Chandler had no wish to bring his connection with the smooth Rumanian into the open. Smuggling Jewish refugees into France might be considered admirable by some, but in French bureaucratic terms they were still illegal immigrants.

"Well, monsieur?" said Borel.

Chandler shook his head. "No, I don't think she ever did."

Borel rubbed his chin thoughtfully. "You never met the sister?"

"No," said Chandler.

"Did Jacqueline ever talk about her?"

Chandler shrugged. "The sister was older. I got the impression she moved in a different circle."

"Go on."

"I seem to remember Jacqueline suggesting she had done quite well for herself," said Chandler.

"Do you know how?"

"No."

"Perhaps a more successful Jacqueline?"

"I don't know," said Chandler. "She'd been in Paris longer. I also got the idea she was an unusually good-looking girl. So you may be right, Inspector."

Borel grunted. "One thing worries me about you, Monsieur Chandler. True, you don't look like a murderer to me. But there is a sense in which you act like one."

"There is?"

Borel nodded. "A girl is dead. Someone you knew well. But you're not at all curious about who might have killed her."

The thunder of aircraft engines lifted every head on the café forecourt. Six Heinkel bombers, the black crosses clear on the pale undersides of their wings, roared across the rooftops and disappeared in the direction of the eastern suburbs.

Morosely, Borel watched a peasant family trail along the boulevard: an old man leading a horse-drawn cart piled with belongings, children skipping beside it; a teenage boy driving two balky black-and-white cows; three or four middle-aged women in flowered aprons, black kerchiefs around their heads, each leading a sheep by a rope halter.

Chandler watched the inspector and was struck by an overwhelming sympathy for the French as this vast national tragedy unfolded before their eyes. At that moment, as the peasants' cows snorted at the café tables and the women urged the sheep forward with sharp cries in a language that seemed barely French, *who* had killed Jacqueline Claudel hardly seemed to matter. She was another victim, yet another, of the crisis rapidly enveloping them all. How to explain that to Borel?

Raised voices caused the customers at the Café Anschel to pause in their conversation and look toward the road. Two uniformed gendarmes were pushing an elegantly dressed figure in the direction of the inspector's table.

Peter Bilescu flailed about him. "I have eyes. I can see. The inspector is drinking wine with one of the principal suspects. How very French! How very civilized!"

He stopped before the table in the corner of the terrace. Ignoring the inspector, he bowed to Chandler. "Peter Bilescu," he said. "Suspect number two." His eyes flickered a warning.

"Sit down," the inspector said curtly. "Wait over there," he said, dismissing the hovering gendarmes.

Bilescu drew up a chair and sat down. "So you," he pointed a long finger, "are the American, Chandler. I've never bought one of your paintings, Mr. Chandler, but then I have a reputation to consider. Too photographic for my taste, and my clients'. The faultless painter."

"So was Andrea del Sarto," Chandler said.

"That was before photography devalued the importance of the pure likeness."

"Monsieur Bilescu"—the inspector leaned across the table—"we're not here to discuss art."

"We're here, I believe, to discuss murder, are we not?" Bilescu turned with an even-toothed smile to the group at the next table, including them in his performance.

"If you prefer it, I can have you questioned in a cell," the inspector said.

"God forbid. Ask your questions, Inspector."

"I want to know when you first met Jacqueline Claudel."

"When she came to work at my club."

"You're lying," Borel said flatly.

Bilescu sighed. "It becomes a habit, Inspector," he said easily. "In Bucharest it was essential to protect one's reputation. In Paris the whole world laughs at the idea of a reputation. I'd known Jacqueline for five or six months."

"Where did you meet her?"

"At a party. To celebrate the outbreak of war. We were all convinced it would be over in a few months. We neutrals were all convinced—" He turned toward Chandler. "I'm a Rumanian citizen, you see."

"You've an application for French citizenship under review," the inspector said sharply.

"No longer," Bilescu's smile dropped. "At least I'm in process of withdrawing it, if only I could find where the relevant government department has evacuated itself."

"Is it not a little early," Borel said, eyeing Bilescu from beneath his thick eyebrows, "for the rats to be deserting the sinking ship?"

"The ship has sunk, Inspector. You must be as aware of it as anyone."

"After the celebration party," Borel said, "when did you next meet Jacqueline?"

Bilescu shrugged his slender shoulders. "Oh, we made some arrangements for lunch. I offered the choice of the best restaurants in Paris, but she insisted it should be the Hôtel Clemenceau. No doubt the manager compensated her. We went there once or twice, but it proved less than interesting.''

A police car had drawn up at the curb. Chandler watched as Borel's sergeant got out and opened the door for an old woman.

At the crowded tables around them people stopped talking, sensing further drama as the old woman was escorted from the police car.

"Madame Bissel," Borel drew her forward, "do you recognize either of these men as the man who called on Jacqueline Claudel last night?"

The concierge looked from Bilescu to Chandler.

Bilescu smiled broadly at her. "You've never seen me in your life before, madame. Admit it."

"Silence," Borel snapped. Then turning to Madame Bissel, "Just take your time," he said. "We're in no hurry."

"The monsieur is right," Madame Bissel said. "It wasn't him."

"And the other gentleman. Have you seen him before somewhere?"

Madame Bissel stood before the café table, sucking at her teeth. Chandler's heart was hammering in his chest but he tried as calmly as possible to return her stare. Once or twice she moved a hand to scratch at her chin, or cocked her head to focus better, and he felt himself blink involuntarily.

"Would the monsieur walk up and down a few steps?" she said at length to Borel.

The inspector hesitated. "No, madame," he smiled. "I don't believe that would be the sort of evidence any judge would welcome."

"Ah."

"You don't have to answer, madame. If you do you must remember that a great deal of importance will be attached to your opinion."

The old lady shook her head.

"You mean he is not the man?"

"I mean I can't be sure, Inspector." She grimaced unhappily. "Thirty years as a concierge, and I can't be sure!"

Chandler felt his shoulders droop with relief.

Borel nodded to his sergeant to take Madame Bissel back to the car.

"And where does that leave me?" Bilescu asked.

"It leaves you free to go," Borel said shortly.

"What about me?" asked Chandler.

"You too are at liberty to leave. It happens all the time in my work, Monsieur Chandler. A witness swears he or she can make a positive identification. But the memory plays sad tricks. So we are now looking for a man who may or may not be a foreigner. Who may or may not be you or Monsieur Bilescu."

"I'll leave you to ponder the problem, Inspector," Bilescu said, rising from his seat.

"And yet," Borel said, "I still think my man is tall, fair headed and not French."

"In the circumstances, this may be one of those mysteries without a solution," Bilescu said. Adjusting the angle of the brim of his straw hat, the Rumanian nodded to them both and began to thread his way through the tables.

"That was a close call for you, Monsieur Chandler," Borel said as they walked together across the café terrace and stopped on the sidewalk.

"Do you really think I killed Jacqueline?" asked Chandler.

Borel regarded him carefully. "If you did, what was your motive?"

"You're asking me?"

"Yes," said Borel gravely.

Chandler shrugged. "Jealousy maybe. I can't think of anything else."

Borel shook his head. "Our killer tried to rape her. Or made it appear he tried to rape her."

"I don't follow you," said Chandler.

"The semen test proved negative."

"She wasn't raped?"

"She was bruised. The killer even attempted penetration. Possibly by hand. But she was not raped, monsieur."

"You mean he couldn't make it?" said Chandler.

"No; I'm beginning to believe he didn't even try. But he wanted me to think he had."

"So why was Jacqueline Claudel killed?" asked Chandler.

"Perhaps," said Borel casually, "it was all a mistake."

"A mistake?" said Chandler. "You can't believe that."

"It makes a motive unnecessary."

"Very convenient when you don't have one."

"If I had a motive for you," Borel said lazily, "I would arrest you on the spot, monsieur."

"Despite the fact that the concierge failed to identify me."

Borel smiled. "That's all she did. She *failed* to identify you. She did not confirm that it was *not* you."

They stood together on the sidewalk, eyeing each other.

"What's your next step, Inspector?"

"Who knows," Borel said. "Perhaps Bilescu is right. Perhaps this is a murder that will never progress from the unsolved file. In these circumstances"—he waved his arm to encompass the whole agony of the city—"how could anyone expect otherwise?"

For a moment they stood in silence.

"Will you send her body back to her village for the funeral?" Chandler asked after a few moments.

Borel looked at him wearily. "We are at war, my friend. Jacqueline Claudel came from a village near the Belgian border. A hundred kilometers or more behind the present German lines."

Chandler nodded apologetically. "I'm sorry. I haven't taken it in yet. So she'll be buried here in Paris?"

"We'll try to locate her sister. In all this confusion I

doubt if we'll succeed. In any case the city will give her a simple burial—she seems to have died with no more than a few francs to her name.''

''Inspector,'' Chandler said, ''I'd like to pay for the funeral. Can that be arranged?''

The inspector looked at him. ''It's a generous gesture, monsieur.''

''Is there any reason I shouldn't? It won't implicate me further?''

''No.'' He paused. ''Will you be staying in Paris for the funeral?''

''If I'm not in danger of arrest for a murder I didn't commit.''

Hands thrust deep in his trouser pockets, Borel eyed the American from under his heavy eyebrows. ''No, monsieur,'' he said evenly, ''no danger of arrest for a murder you *didn't* commit.''

Slowly Borel crossed the road toward the commissariat, slapping his hat against his leg at every other step. Somewhere on the roads south, his wife and their six-month-old daughter were struggling toward her parents' home in the Auvergne. He had thought it best for family men like himself to be alone in Paris for the bitter street fighting he had imagined would take place as the Germans entered the northern suburbs. Never for a moment had he considered the possibility that Paris would be declared an open city. Some people were already talking about calling on Marshal Pétain to lead France through her agony. But Pétain was in his eighties, an open supporter of at least Franco, if not Hitler. Where would he lead the people of France?

Borel mounted the steps of the commissariat, moving heavily under the hot, low sun. His sergeant was standing on the top step with a yellow file in his hand and a broad smile on his face.

Borel stopped in front of him and gestured to the file. ''What's that, a crime sheet?''

The sergeant smiled his pleasure. ''You know what you

say, *patron*. All a good policeman really needs is a memory like an elephant and a lot of good luck.''

Borel closed his eyes against the bright sunlight, the world and the self-satisfaction of his young sergeant. ''So it's a crime sheet you dug out of the files.''

''Not ours, Inspector Triboulet's files,'' the sergeant said in triumph. ''The Germans have occupied his district. It's taken him days to reach Paris; the roads are complete chaos. He arrived this morning with all his files. What luck. You see, I remembered—''

Borel held up his hand to stop this flood of words. ''Wait. Sergeant, I've had a hard day. Please explain in simple terms whatever it is you're trying to tell me.''

''I remembered Inspector Triboulet is from the north, Amiens. St-Eloi is in his area.''

Borel's eyes opened wide. ''St-Eloi. Where Jacqueline Claudel was born?''

''Yes, *patron*,'' the sergeant said.

Borel snatched the file from his sergeant's hand, flipped open the cover and read the title.

''My God, Philippe,'' he said, ''you'll make a policeman yet.''

Chapter
Seven

DURING THE MORNING of June 13, the government of France had begun to move yet again, ministers, civil servants, deputies and military liaison staff evacuating Tours in chaotic flight to the city of Bordeaux.

There, in the great southwestern sea port, hundreds of thousands of refugees fought for hotel rooms and clamored for the most elementary shelter in lobbies and garages. Restaurants and food shops were besieged; thousands of trucks and cars blocked side streets and main boulevards. During the preceding nights the city had come to resemble the encampment of some vast rabble army. In the parks and squares blankets strung from the sides of cars formed rough tents, and camp fires glowed among the trees in defiance of the blackout regulations. At those cafés still open, desperate men, known intellectuals and—most desperate of all—those Jews who had fled Germany in the years before the war, bargained for sufficient gasoline to get to Spain.

Into this infernal confusion the government of France was decanted. Haggard and unshaven, Premier Paul Reynaud still struggled against the insistent, defeatist demands of Marshal Pétain. The war could and should be continued, Reynaud argued, if not in France itself, then from the French North African colonies.

Continued resistance, Pétain insisted, was both ''ignoble and cowardly.'' The Supreme Commander, General Weygand, supported him; members of the cabinet plotted to deliver the government to him. In the moral confusion of those June days, no one thought to ask how resistance to the invader could possibly be cowardly. It was a moral confusion that Pétainism would carry with it throughout the war.

Somehow the very enigma that was Marshal Pétain seemed to support his view that France must ask for an armistice. Elegant even in his ninth decade, the only surviving Marshal of France and her most respected citizen, Pétain was a man in whom the arteries of pride had hardened. He now saw himself as the savior of a defeated France, as the single link in the chain of honor between the country's past and its uncertain future. In a more sinister vein he personified a military distaste for French democracy and a covert anti-Semitism that would lead him down the stony path of collaboration with Hitler's Reich.

In Bordeaux he established his headquarters in private apartments on the Boulevard Président-Wilson. A military man poised to profit from the defeat of the army he had created, he was sure he had not long to wait.

In Paris it was another brilliant day. Among the gravel paths and shining black marble monuments of the vast Père-Lachaise cemetery, Theo Chandler stood next to the open grave, listening to the priest, feeling the full blast of the sun on the back of his dark suit and wondering whether the Germans would arrive in Paris that day.

The memory of the dead girl had faded disturbingly quickly. A few moments spent wrestling in the large old-fashioned bed at the Hôtel Clemenceau was not enough, he found to his distress, to compete against the involvement of being an onlooker in Paris during these strange, unreal days. Distantly, to the north, he could hear the unhurried reverberations of heavy explosions. Over the eastern suburbs, two black columns of smoke rose almost vertically in the still, hot air.

Mesmerized by the murmurings of the priest, by the warmth on his back and the strong scent of fresh-dug earth from the grave, Chandler stood, his hands banging at his sides, his head lowered. Until he heard the soft crunch of gravel, he had supposed he would be the only mourner.

Looking up, he saw the tall girl in black standing opposite him across the grave. He had an impression of blue eyes under dark-brown hair. Anne-Marie's lips moved in acknowledgment of his presence and as dust and small stones rattled on the coffin, she turned her attention to the priest.

As the service ended Chandler watched the girl drop on one knee at the edge of the grave. For a few moments he hesitated as the priest approached and helped her to her feet. Then Chandler turned and walked slowly back along the gravel path to wait for her at the gate.

On this June midafternoon the little square outside the cemetery was as silent as at midnight. Not a baker's van or delivery boy's bicycle passed across the gleaming, gray-black cobbles; the apartments above the shuttered shops gave no sign of life. There was no one on the narrow sidewalk; only the hotel café on the far corner, and the post office behind him were open. Sheltering from the sun, Chandler stepped back into the cool hallway of the post office and watched the girl talking to the priest.

Anne-Marie paused at the cemetery gate and then came out into the square. She had already seen Chandler in the doorway and now came forward and extended her hand.

"I'm Anne-Marie Claudel," she said, "Jacqueline's sister."

"Someone managed to contact you?" Chandler asked.

Anne-Marie nodded. "You were a friend of Jacqueline's?"

"For a short time. My name's Theo Chandler."

"I'm grateful to you, monsieur, for arranging the funeral. But the costs are my responsibility." She opened her shoulder bag and began to search for her wallet.

"Please forget it," said Chandler hurriedly.

"I want to repay you," she said firmly.

"We'll talk about it over a café cognac," he pointed across the square to the crumbling front of the small hotel. "We could both use a drink."

Anne-Marie hesitated, then nodded reluctant agreement, and together they began to cross the deserted square. She walked with slow steps, her high heels clicking on the cobbles like a metronome, her hands in the pockets of her black raincoat, her head down.

"It doesn't help to say I'm sorry," said Chandler. "Nothing helps in a senseless tragedy like this."

"No," she said distantly. "Nothing helps."

They entered the hotel and sat at a table by the window in the bar.

"You were not only a friend of Jacqueline's," Anne-Marie said. "I also know your connection with Peter Bilescu."

Chandler looked at her silently.

"I'm aware of your business arrangements with that man," she said with an edge of contempt in her voice.

"The people he helped were desperate to leave Germany," he said.

"So were many others without the ability to pay for their lives," Anne-Marie retorted.

Chandler drew in a deep breath. "I'm not sure of the morality of the whole thing. But I know there are many here in France today who are very happy they are not in Nazi Germany."

She shrugged.

"How do you know about Bilescu?" Chandler asked.

"I work for the Jewish Resettlement Agency. We received the people you and others brought out, applied for French citizenship on their behalf, arranged for them to travel on to London or New York, if that's what they wanted."

"And for all this, of course, you charged nothing," said Chandler.

"It's no secret where the money came from," she said. "Paul Litvinov, the financier."

"But it's the reason you despise Bilescu?" Chandler said.

"I despise Bilescu for many reasons."

For a few moments they sat in silence.

"What will you and Litvinov do now?" said Chandler at last. "What will happen to the agency now the Germans are about to enter Paris?"

"You would not expect me to tell you," she said coldly.

"I don't believe we're really on different sides of the fence, mademoiselle. I hope not."

Her nostrils flared. She lowered her eyes to her hands, clasped on the table before her.

An old woman waddled out of the rear room, and Chandler ordered coffee and two large cognacs.

"Did you know any of Jacqueline's friends in Paris?" he asked.

Anne-Marie shook her head. "She hadn't been here that long. I doubt if she had many. Not many friends, monsieur. She told me how she met you. And others like you."

"Jacqueline made her own choice," said Chandler. "I just happened to be there at the time."

"To take advantage," said Anne-Marie flatly.

"If you like," he said. "But I don't accept any blame for Jacqueline's death."

"No," she said slowly. "Why should you?"

"Could it have been one of these other friends? Jealousy perhaps?"

Anne-Marie shrugged. "It's possible."

In the long pauses between question and answer Chandler studied her face. It was drawn flat between the high cheekbones by shock and whatever she felt for her murdered sister. Her lips were pursed and trembling slightly. Suddenly Chandler had the overwhelming feeling that this beautiful, white-faced girl was terrified. He watched her as she took a cigarette and lit it. The curling smoke seemed to soften the line of her lips.

Chandler handed her the cognac and she sipped it quickly. "Are you leaving Paris?" he asked gently.

"Perhaps."

Chandler looked down at her hands. The long fingers clasping the glass of cognac were shaking.

Anne-Marie placed her shoulder bag on the table. "Please tell me how much I owe you for the funeral."

"Nothing," he said as she fumbled in her bag. "I *mean* nothing." Chandler reached forward and put a hand on hers, preventing her from taking out the money. "Just leave things as they are."

She lifted her head quickly. Again the nostrils flared in anger or fear. Then the tightness around her eyes slowly relaxed. "Thank you," she said.

She stood up and held out her hand. "Goodbye, monsieur."

"You haven't finished your cognac," Chandler said.

"I'm sorry, I must go."

"Why would anyone want to kill your sister?" Chandler threw the question at her.

Anne-Marie crushed her cigarette out in the tin ashtray. "Some passing maniac."

"No. Whoever it was who came to the apartment asked for her by name."

It was the flicker of fear that showed in her eyes that made him realize. Of course. That was what Borel had meant.

"Came to the apartment," Chandler said slowly. "Asked for Mademoiselle Claudel."

Anne-Marie stood immobile. Very slowly she reached down and picked up her shoulder bag.

"It was your apartment. It was Mademoiselle Claudel the killer asked for. You." Chandler stared up at her.

She turned away and walked toward the doorway.

"Goodbye, monsieur," she said over her shoulder.

He reached the door before her. "I'd like to see you again."

"Please let me go," her face blazed with something close to open panic.

Chandler stepped back.

She turned quickly and passed through the swinging doors out into the sunlight of the square. For a few moments he stood at the window, watching her until she reached the far corner, until she disappeared into the deep shadow cast by a relentless June sun.

For a second or two longer he stood staring into the emptiness of the square, then he barged through the doors and ran for the corner around which she had disappeared.

He had no clear idea what impelled him other than an overwhelming sense of some exchange uncompleted, of a dozen unformed questions he felt driven to put to her. As he reached the shadowed corner of the square he saw that a long and narrow alley led upward to a patch of sunlight where it joined a wider street. He fancied, even, that he could hear the receding click of high heels. As he started up the cobbled alley a man emerged from a doorway, shouldering him brutally against the wall. It was Inspector Borel.

"I almost missed you, monsieur," he gripped Chandler's arm. "I have a few additional questions to put to you."

Chandler was gasping for breath. "The girl that just passed you."

"Passed me? Here? Nobody passed me, monsieur," he was pushing Chandler back toward the square.

"She was only seconds ahead of me," Chandler said. "You must have seen her."

"You were following this girl?"

"Yes. It was Anne-Marie Claudel."

"Why were you following her?"

The host of unshaped questions whirled in Chandler's brain as they stepped back out into the brightness of the square. "I had things to ask her," he said lamely.

Borel nodded, releasing his hold on Chandler's arm. "And I have things to ask you," he said.

Chandler brushed a sheen of sweat from his forehead. "Suddenly you're no longer interested in Anne-Marie, Inspector?"

"At the moment, Monsieur Chandler, I am much more interested in you."

Borel indicated a plain concrete bench shaded by a shuttered kiosk. They sat in silence, at opposite ends of the bench, angled to face each other.

"I've been making a few inquiries about you," Borel said. His tone was flat and unfriendly.

"If there was something you wanted to know, why didn't you ask me? You know where I live."

Borel grunted. Unhurriedly he took out a pack of Gauloises and tapped out a cigarette on the back of the bench. "I'm told you're a painter."

"Not a good one," Chandler said.

"Been in Paris, how long? A year?"

"I came to Paris just before war was declared. About ten months ago."

"About ten months ago," Borel said thoughtfully as if making a mental note.

"Yes."

Borel shaped his lip and wet the end of his cigarette. "Where from?"

"What?"

"Where did you come from?" Borel's voice was calm but unrelenting.

"I'd been living in England with my wife. We decided to separate. She stayed in London. I came here."

"Your *carte de séjour* shows that you entered France from Germany. Not England."

Chandler shrugged in exasperation. "I took a short holiday there. After I left London, before I came to Paris."

"Your first visit to Germany?"

"No, for Christ's sake, about my fifth. I have distant cousins there. What's all this about?"

Borel lit his cigarette. "Chandler—is that a German name?"

"No. When my grandfather went to America at the end of the last century, his name was Kandler. He changed it, anglicized it to Chandler."

"So you're what is known as a German American."

"No. I'm what is known as an American. Plain and simple," Chandler said, beginning to lose his patience.

"Tell me about your visits to Germany."

"There's nothing much to tell. My cousins live just outside Munich. I went there a couple of times to ski. The other visits—I don't know—because I got along with them." He watched Borel's face as the cigarette smoke curled up into the sunlight above the inspector's balding head. There was something almost oriental in the eyes, screwed up against the brightness. He waited while Borel stared at the dark shape of the kiosk.

"The German Army is perhaps a few hours away," Borel said. "They will be in Paris by tomorrow at the latest."

"So the radio says."

"Does the prospect please you, Monsieur Chandler?"

"No, it doesn't please me. And if the real question is, am I a Nazi sympathizer, the answer's no."

"And your cousins in Germany?"

"Some of them are German officers. But a year ago they hoped there would be no war."

Borel nodded and flicked his cigarette out across the cobbles. Slowly he removed his hat and ran his hand around the dark hair that fringed his glistening, bald pate.

"I hope you don't think," said Chandler slowly, "that I came to Paris to spy for Germany."

"An interesting idea, but no, that is not exactly what I had in mind."

"Then what *did* you have in mind?"

Borel turned his head to fix Chandler with his look. "Have you ever been to St-Eloi, monsieur?"

"St-Eloi?"

"A village near the Belgian border where both Jacqueline and Anne-Marie Claudel were born.''

"Never."

"Not at any time for any reason?"

"No. Why should I go there?"

"That is for you to tell me.''

"You're talking in riddles, Borel." Chandler stood up from the bench.

"Sit down," Borel said fiercely.

Chandler sat, surprised by the venom in Borel's tone.

"The doctor's report on Jacqueline Claudel—'' Borel's voice was calmer now. "The knife wounds were comparatively minor but would have been particularly painful.''

"I don't understand," said Chandler.

"I have concluded that it must have given the killer some form of sadistic pleasure to inflict pain before he finally dispatched his victim.''

The two men held each other's look for a few moments. The chime of a church clock in the distance broke the silence.

"Am I free to go or am I under arrest?" Chandler said at last.

"I'm not sure," Borel said. He fumbled inside the heavy, double-breasted jacket of his suit. When he withdrew his hand, a small pistol lay in the large, open palm.

"If I were sure, Monsieur Chandler," Borel said quietly, "I would leave you dead, here, alone in this empty square.''

Chapter
Eight

As CHANDLER OPENED the wrought-iron gate the sound of music and raucous shouts and laughter drifted out from the elegant facade of No. 25 Avenue Foch. It was almost dark, and splits of light showed through the roughly drawn curtains over the windows. He wondered again why Bilescu wanted to see him. The note, delivered by hand, had been left with Madame Oberon, the concierge: Come to a party tonight. You know the address. It's important. Peter.

Now high-heeled, silk-stockinged legs stepped over and danced around him. Sitting cross-legged on the thick-piled carpet, a bottle of brandy between his knees, Chandler watched the dancing, the erupting champagne bottles and the spluttering aggressions of the strange gathering.

Some of the younger girls had begun to remove their clothes; an older woman danced shamelessly wrist-deep in a young man's fly. Men fondled men in deep sofas, girls kissed girls, with darting tongues. A black jazz band from Martinique blasted the "Beale Street Blues" across the spacious room.

Peter Bilescu's party was in full, uncontrollable swing.

A plump, bare female arm slid around Chandler's neck. "That man over there, in the gray suit," a woman's voice whispered huskily in his ear, "is my very respectable husband."

Chandler tried to focus through the clouds of tobacco smoke. "What's he doing?"

The still unseen woman brought her cheek closer. Expensive perfume wafted over him.

"The gray suit," she said again. "On the sofa there."

A break in the passing legs and trailing dresses showed Chandler a large man apparently lying face down on the deep-cushioned sofa.

"There's a girl underneath him," the husky voice said in his ear. "I swear to you she's barely more than sixteen. It's Götterdämmerung, darling. The Germans will be here in the morning."

Chandler passed the brandy bottle to the woman behind him.

She took the bottle and slid around to sit beside him. "How would you like to take me upstairs and do the same thing to me?"

She was in her late fifties. Not beautiful.

Chandler smiled. "I'm already spoken for," he lied.

"Ah." She got unsteadily to her feet. Fluttering her fingers to Chandler in a dismissive gesture she made her way across the room to where the members of the jazz band were preparing for another set. When he lost sight of her in the crowd she had her arm around the neck of a slender, zoot-suited saxophonist, her ringed fingers pointing to the sofa where the fat man sprawled on the girl.

What was he doing here? He stood and lit a cigarette. In the two hours he'd been at the party he had seen no sign of Bilescu.

Earlier, at his apartment, he had begun to pack. After his bizarre confrontation with Borel outside the cemetery he had decided to leave Paris immediately. But on the phone Jack Grossmith at the U.S. embassy had told him that the next transportation for U.S. citizens wishing to leave the city would not be available until tomorrow morning, at 9:00 A.M. at the embassy. If he was late, his place would be assigned to someone else.

He had considered briefly asking Anelda to come over for the night, but the idea of a hassle about the daubed portrait had no appeal. Similarly the thought of an evening with any remaining American friends somehow seemed too remote from the events of the last few days. From the events of today: this afternoon, Borel with the pistol nestling in his huge hand; Anne-Marie, her nostrils flaring in fear as she faced him in the hotel café.

As the level in the brandy bottle went down, the party, to Chandler, began to assume a strange patchy aspect. It was as if he had ceased to exist in the periods between minor incident. From time to time he was aware of himself reeling about the room, sometimes dancing with a girl, at one point singing with the band. At another moment in seamless time he accosted the fat husband who had earlier been active on the sofa. "If I were you," Chandler told him gravely, ignoring the disheveled girl in his arms, "I should take my wife home. What's sauce for the gander is sauce for the goose, or something."

The man looked at him in astonishment. "My wife, monsieur, is at this moment in Lisbon, where I sent her last week."

"Oh. Very wise move," said Chandler.

"I myself am remaining in Paris at the specific request of the government."

"Duty is duty," agreed Chandler as he turned away. Peter Bilescu was approaching across the room. With him was a middle-aged American woman.

"Somebody wants to meet you, Chandler," Bilescu said.

Chandler eyed the matronly figure, the overly made-up face.

"I'm sure you've got a lot in common," Bilescu said, and drifted away into the throng.

"You're drunk, Mr. Chandler," Beth Kately said.

"Yes, afraid I am."

"Too drunk?"

Chandler's eyes opened. "For what?"

"Too drunk to talk a little business?"

"Never."

"My name's Beth Kately," she said. "And I'm not asking you to take me upstairs."

"Beth Kately?" Swaying, Chandler lit a cigarette.

She nodded. Linking an arm through his, she walked him out onto the balcony. She leaned forward onto the stone balustrade overlooking a formal garden. "I'm told you're a painter."

"Sure, I'm a painter." Chandler's hopes rose. Perhaps a portrait was what she wanted. Something slightly flattering, something to peel off eight or nine years of time from her face.

"Do you make money?"

"A little," Chandler said. "Enough to keep going."

"You're lying," she said easily. "Bilescu tells me you've hardly sold a picture since you've been in Paris."

His hopes of a commission fell. "I can't even give them away," he said. "And I've decided I'm not a painter."

"Good." She nodded without interest. "And you know who I am?"

"Of course. Your gossip column's syndicated throughout the States."

Even before she stiffened he knew he had made a mistake.

"I do not have a gossip column. I report. I do not retail gossip."

"I'm sorry," he said.

She cut him off with a sudden smile. "You're a womanizer," she said. "Correct?"

"A womanizer?" He was beyond puzzlement.

"You also like to put yourself across as something of an adventurer."

"Bilescu told you that?"

"He told me a story or two, yes."

"I'm older now," Chandler said cautiously.

"Still running Jewish refugees into France?"

He looked at her as she turned from the balcony. "With the Germans banging on the city gates, I don't think this is the time to talk about such things," he said.

"So you have plans to stay in Paris?"

"Maybe not. I haven't made up my mind."

"Let me help make it up for you. I'll pay you two thousand dollars to leave tomorrow. The S.S. *Washington* is berthed at Bordeaux under orders to evacuate United States citizens."

"Let's get this straight, Miss Kately. You are prepared to pay me two thousand dollars for what I might be planning to do anyway?"

"That's right."

"There's something you haven't told me."

She nodded. "I want you to take someone with you."

"A refugee?"

"The girl you met at the funeral today—Anne-Marie Claudel."

Below them in the garden a group of revelers was carrying things out to pile on a circular flower bed. In the half-light Chandler could see mattresses, bedding, gleaming pieces of furniture.

"They're setting it on fire," Chandler said in amazement as someone threw gasoline from a can and set a match to it.

The flame leaped almost to the level of the balcony. "What does Bilescu care?" Beth Kately said. "He's leaving Paris tonight, and he sure can't take it all with him."

Chandler watched for a few moments, sickened, as Louis XV consoles and Empire *tables de chevet* were hurled onto the fire by guests reeling with drunken laughter.

"Well?" Beth Kately said, impatient now. "Will you do it?"

"I'd need to know a lot more about it," Chandler said.

"You leave tonight. You take with you a personal letter

from me to the captain of the S.S. *Washington* requesting
him to take Anne-Marie aboard. What else do you need to
know?''

''When I saw Mademoiselle Claudel at the funeral this
afternoon she didn't seem to be going anywhere. What
changed her mind?''

The leaping flames from the courtyard below reddened
her face. ''This is *my* story, Chandler, understand me.
Take the money and do the job without questions. Try to
edge me over and I'll bite your ass—that you wouldn't
like.''

Chandler shook his head slowly. ''You're right,'' he
said. *''That* I wouldn't like.''

''Yes or no? What's the answer?''

''The answer is I'm leaving Paris in a convoy from the
U.S. embassy at nine o'clock tomorrow morning.
Alone.''

''You're passing up two thousand dollars.''

''I could also be passing up a spell in jail as a murder
suspect.'' He shook his head. ''Thanks a lot, Miss
Kately. Get Bilescu to find you someone else.''

She turned away without a word and walked through
the glass doors into the salon. For a moment or two
Chandler stood there, drink in hand, watching priceless
pieces of furniture being hurled onto the fire below. Why
would Beth Kately want to get Anne-Marie to the United
States, he wondered drunkenly. Altruism could be ruled
out without difficulty. Some story that Anne-Marie could
help her with then. Perhaps about a distinguished refugee
the Jewish Resettlement Agency had helped escape. He
went into the salon and poured himself a drink. Vaguely
he felt he had made the right decision, to leave tomorrow
morning. The interview with Inspector Borel on the
concrete bench outside the cemetery had shaken him. The
Frenchman's tone had changed dramatically since their
previous encounter. Whoever had murdered Jacqueline
had intended to kill Anne-Marie; he was fairly sure of that
now. And of course that's what Borel himself had hinted

at during their earlier interview.

He leaned against the wall and lit himself a cigarette. The party was developing a new frenzy. If Borel already suspected that he might have killed Jacqueline, *and* believed that it was a mistake—that Anne-Marie was the intended victim—Chandler knew he would be mad to have anything to do with Beth Kately's proposition. No, he would take a place in the nine o'clock embassy convoy. The times in Europe were strangely out of joint. The sooner he was on board the S.S. *Washington* the better.

Peter Bilescu was coming toward him, oblivious of the chaos and damage around him.

"I hope you're enjoying yourself, Chandler."

"I'm getting drunk."

"How drunk?"

"Very."

"Come with me then, my dear fellow. You'll enjoy this."

He led the way out of the main salon into the black-and-white tiled hall. Here too there were people, but less frenetic than in the salon. Here the atmosphere was more the quiet desperation of a railway station. People drifted back and forth across the expanse of tiled floor as if waiting the arrival of their train; a young couple stood together in the corner, the girl sobbing quietly; on the cold tiles, a man slept like a station *clochard,* his hand supporting his head.

Peter Bilescu paused at the foot of the curving staircase and surveyed his guests. Drunk as Chandler was he recognized the contempt on Bilescu's face.

"If you hate them all that much, why invite them in the first place?"

"They have their uses," Bilescu said dismissively.

"Me too?" Chandler said.

"Of course. You're an American."

"I nearly didn't come tonight."

"I'm glad you did." He turned to face Chandler. "I

need a visa," he said. "Do you have friends at the U.S. embassy?"

"Half of Europe wants a U.S. visa. What makes you so different?"

"Don't be superior with me, my friend," Bilescu snapped. "You already have a visa in your hip pocket. Or even better, a passport."

Then suddenly, like an actor, he let the tension drain from his face. "I don't think you Americans realize how desperate Europeans have become in the last twenty years," he said. "Individually, I mean. We are prepared to take courses that Americans could not yet envisage. When the belief in the *possibility* of a stable life crashes, its *desirability* goes with it. You don't understand me, of course. Americans are rich and smug and safe over there across the Atlantic. The fools still believe in the essential goodness of man, the noble savage. I believe in the savage savage, Chandler. And I will be proved right. Come," he said, beginning to climb the stairs, "let's see the way *your* tastes are inclined."

On the upper floor they entered a large room. Even before Bilescu opened the door Chandler could hear the pandemonium inside. His first impression was of the floor of the New York stock exchange. Men—women too—pushed and jostled, arms waving, shouting bids.

In the center of the room, on an improvised catwalk, a line of bodies stood—sullen, contemptuous young girls and adolescent boys, old women—the sweepings of the Bastille area where the most grotesque sex in Paris was to be had. The auctioneer lashed them with a soft leather whip as he repeated the bids.

"Christ!" Chandler exploded. He was watching a woman in her sixties, the skin flaccid on her stomach, the legs thin and hard with sinew, as she pirouetted and cavorted, offering her buttocks to the whip. "Jesus Christ!"

"I want that visa, Chandler," Bilescu said in his ear. "I've got a car ready to leave tonight. Come with me to

Bordeaux and arrange a visa at the U.S. consulate there.''

"You wanted to be French—be French!''

"All Europe's sick,'' Bilescu said urgently. "The night's coming. I can see the darkness creeping over us all.''

"You can keep your goddam visions to yourself.'' He grabbed Bilescu's arm. "Out of here, I want to talk to you.''

On the landing, couples drifted uncertainly by them.

"You think I killed her,'' Bilescu said, smoothing his sleeve.

"Did you? Did you torture her first?''

"It might have been fun. But the answer's no.''

"You bastard.''

"You're so shockable, Chandler. So *tempting*. If I *had* killed her, give me the credit for a little more style. And a more leisurely manner. It was all over in a matter of minutes the police told me.''

"Why is an American journalist like Beth Kately interested in Anne-Marie Claudel?''

"In business, my dear fellow, the art is to know when to ask questions—and when to keep silent.''

"I'm prepared to tell the police what she said to me tonight.''

"The Germans will be here tomorrow—do you really think the French police will be interested in continuing to investigate the murder of a minor Paris tart?''

"I know one policeman who will.''

"Listen to me, Chandler. I have no idea who killed Jacqueline Claudel, and I have no interest in discovering who it was. If you did it, you had your own good reasons. I'm interested in Bordeaux. And a U.S. visa.''

A wave of drunken revulsion swept like nausea over Chandler. His fist came from waist height and hit Bilescu just below the ribs. He turned for the stairs with barely a glance at the long figure of the Rumanian curled up by the doorway, his hand slapping at the floor as he groaned his pain out to vague, incomprehending guests.

Barely keeping his balance down the wide staircase, Chandler made for the front door.

Since Paris had been declared an open city, the street lamps had come on again at night. Though it was still not late, hardly a soul was to be seen on the streets. The cafés were closed; there were no taxis in the empty boulevard. Chandler's footsteps rang on the granite flagstones as he walked beside the river.

Again he seemed to lose the pockets of time between events. At one moment he was walking, watching the street lamps play their light among the broad leaves of the plane trees. At the next, he was slumped across the coping of the embankment, retching.

When he looked up, he felt he too was fighting visions. A small figure in a tattered coat stood before him, in his hand a pole with a twist of flaming tar-cloth on the end.

"Can I help you, monsieur?" the man said.

"God knows," Chandler squinted at him. "It depends who you are."

The man looked toward the burning flambeau and smiled. "Ah, no cause for alarm, monsieur. I am the river lamplighter. One of them, that's to say. For thirty years I have been responsible for the warning lights on the water's edge between the Louvre and the Palais Royal."

"The warning lights?"

"Gaslights. For the barges, monsieur." He pointed to the opposite bank. For the first time since he'd come to Paris Chandler was aware of a string of faintly guttering red lights, low on the water's edge.

"Germans or no Germans, the barges will need their lights." The man rolled the burning tip of his pole on the paving stones, extinguishing the flame. "Evidently my colleague decided the same."

"Your colleague?"

"On the other bank, monsieur," he pointed again to the lights.

"You didn't discuss it together?"

"How could we? For thirty years we have worked opposite banks. We have never yet met."

Chandler straightened up. How could Bilescu be right about a society collapsing when two lamplighters independently decided to work tonight of all nights?

"Which way are you walking, monsieur?" the Frenchman asked.

Chandler indicated the direction of the Pont St-Louis.

"Me too." The man put his pole on his shoulder and they set off together along the embankment.

"You're a foreigner, monsieur," the man offered.

"American."

"Ah, what good fortune."

"Somebody else said that to me tonight, more or less. He had a nightmare vision of the future."

"For France?"

"For Europe."

"For Europe, yes." The lamplighter nodded. He lifted his head, his eyes scanning the rooftops. "Can you feel it?" he said. "As if the whole city's waiting for them to arrive."

They walked on toward the lights of the Pont St-Louis and their wavering reflection on the surface of the river.

"Whichever way it goes," said Chandler, his eyes following the course of a lone dog padding homeward along the sidewalk opposite, "tomorrow will see a very different world."

The lamplighter's lips moved without speaking. His hand reached out and touched the American's arm. He was staring past Chandler's shoulder across the wide boulevard.

Chandler turned his head. Nosing slowly from out of the side street was a motorcycle and sidecar combination. The outline of the German steel helmet was clearly visible above the rider's goggled eyes. The long barrel of a light machine gun moved slowly back and forth in the hands of the hunched figure in the sidecar.

With a touch of the accelerator, the driver steered the

motorcycle out into the boulevard. A second and third *Zundapp* combination cautiously followed.

"They're here," the lamplighter whispered, drawing Chandler back into the shadows. "Tomorrow has already come."

Chapter
Nine

BUCKLING THE LEATHER belt around his suitcase, Chandler glanced again at the clock. Seven-thirty. Carrying the bag it would take him half an hour to walk to the U.S. embassy. His eyes moved from the clock to the canvases stacked against the wall. He crossed to them and flipped them back one by one against his knee. Crude, trivial pieces they now seemed. Amateurist Utrillos or Sunday-painter portraits. He was not reluctant to leave them all behind. Yet he had enjoyed Paris—the restaurants, the company and of course the girls. An image of Anne-Marie flooded his mind, and he thought briefly of painting her. Perhaps when he got back to America he would become a photographer. His painting had often been likened to photography. He pushed the stack back against the wall and, without venom, drove his toe deep into the canvases.

The clock again. Time enough for another cup of coffee before he left. He crossed to the bed and again tested the weight of the suitcase. Half an hour to the embassy, he recalculated, should be ample.

He crossed to the stove and lit the gas under the coffeepot. Last night's drinking had left him shaky, in desperate need of coffee. There would be little to be had on the drive to Bordeaux. The coffee heated, he turned off the gas. Standing, coffeepot in hand, he listened to footsteps mounting the stone staircase outside the apartment. He replaced the coffeepot on the stove and walked into the narrow hall. Through the flowered curtain covering the glass pane he could make out the shape of men.

The knock rattled twice on the loose glass. He opened the door immediately. The two young men on the landing were hatless, their dark double-breasted suits fitting just a little too tightly.

"Monsieur Chandler?"

"Yes."

"We're from the police, monsieur."

"You don't sound French to me," Chandler said.

"Our forces began the occupation of the city in the early hours of this morning."

"We are members of the Occupation Police Authority," the second man added.

Chandler looked from one young fresh face to the other as they alternately spoke their piece.

"I'm an American citizen," he said.

"Yes, we know that."

"What is it you want?"

"We have been instructed to ask you to accompany us."

"I imagine it's a formality in connection with your neutral status, monsieur," the second man said.

"I'm due at the United States embassy at nine o'clock. I have transportation arranged for Bordeaux."

"I'm sure this will not take long. We have a car waiting."

"I'm sorry. It can't be done. I'm a neutral citizen. I'm leaving Paris today."

The two young men stepped back and gestured for him to move out onto the landing.

"Our instructions are that you accompany us," the first said smiling. "We are naturally bound to obey our instructions."

"I can refuse to accompany you."

The smile disappeared from the young man's face. "No, monsieur. That is out of the question."

In the car the young men had waiting outside, Chandler was accorded the passenger seat next to the driver. The second man climbed into the back.

They sped through what seemed a dazed Paris. There were no civilian cars visible between the Île St-Louis and the Quai d'Orsay. German military trucks rumbled along the cobbled street, German military police directed the convoys with maps and pointed instructions to the drivers. A few groups of civilians, mostly women, gathered on street corners and watched the trucks, the half-tracks and the powerful step of marching troops.

At each intersection they were waved down by military police units, but the driver's identity document rapidly disposed of all problems. No one could fail to be impressed by the apparent maturity of an organization only a few hours old.

On the Avenue Rapp they stopped, and the car door was opened for Chandler to get out. An armed trooper stood outside the fin-de-siècle entrance to the Hôtel Belfort. As he passed, Chandler had just time enough to notice that the soldier's collar carried the black flashes of the SS.

Inside, the two men conducted him by an elevator up to the restaurant on the top floor. The tables had been replaced by a large desk and deep armchairs, which were now arranged in the center of the room. Two men in shirt-sleeves stood at the window looking out across the rooftops of Paris.

Without turning, Reichenau beckoned. "Herr Chandler, come quickly. This is a story to recount to your grandchildren."

As Chandler crossed the room toward him, the man

had half turned from the window.

"I'm Colonel Hans-Peter Reichenau," he said, extending his hand rapidly. "This is Inspector Krebs, one of my senior executive assistants."

Krebs turned from the window and bowed formally. His moon-shaped face remained expressionless.

Placing a hand on Chandler's shoulder, Reichenau drew him forward to stand at the window. "Now," he said, "we should note the time—" He checked his watch. "Just eight-ten."

The American followed Reichenau's glance as his head rose from his watch. Four or five hundred meters away the Eiffel Tower rose on its massive latticework of cast iron. At the top small figures were drawing in the billowing folds of the tricolor flag of France's Third Republic. As the three men stood silently watching, a thick bundle of red cloth broke from the flagpole and was run upward, snapping out fold after fold in the stiff breeze until the swastika of Nazi Germany was flying over the highest point in Paris.

Reichenau was beaming. Krebs's moon-face had still not changed expression.

"I know you're a neutral in this great conflict, Herr Chandler, but history is history," Reichenau said. "We can none of us turn our faces from it."

He gestured Chandler to one of the armchairs and himself took the seat behind the desk. Krebs remained standing unobtrusively by the window.

"A day to remember," Reichenau said. "Do you realize that today the German Occupation forces have taken charge of not only a massive city of two million people, but the world's most felicitous assemblage of buildings, medieval Europe's greatest historical archives and the finest art collections in the history of the world? What a responsibility!" he breathed.

Chandler watched him without answering.

"Your family is German, I understand." Reichenau changed gear quickly.

Chandler lit a cigarette and inhaled slowly. "Was it my German antecedents you wanted to see me about?" he asked Reichenau.

"No . . . no, that was purely conversational." He paused. "Inspector Krebs is a criminal investigation officer. He has assumed responsibility for criminal matters in your arrondissement. It appears there are one or two points outstanding on the file of a case in which you were marginally involved."

"I pointed out to your two officers that I am expected at the U.S. embassy at nine o'clock."

"Quite so," Reichenau said. He nodded to Krebs, who came forward from the window.

"The case concerns the death of a woman named Jacqueline Claudel, Herr Chandler," Krebs said.

Chandler remained silent.

"I've studied the French police file," Krebs continued. "It seems complete as far as it goes. For an unsolved crime, that is."

"Unsolved?" Chandler said. "It only took place less than a week ago."

Krebs shrugged his plump shoulders.

"I think that was Inspector Krebs's point," Reichenau came in easily. "He felt that not enough effort had been made to trace certain key witnesses."

"The dossier shows you paid for the funeral," Krebs said.

"I did."

"Why?"

"It seemed the least I could do. The dossier also no doubt shows I was having a mild affair with Jacqueline Claudel shortly before her death."

"It does. It also lists Monsieur Peter Bilescu, an art dealer of Rumanian origin. Did this," his lip curled, "gentleman offer money for the funeral?"

"No."

"Were there no members of the girl's family who could have contributed?"

Chandler felt the trickle of sweat run down inside his shirt. "No," he said carefully. "I spoke to the French police inspector on the case. He said her family was within German occupied territory. Now that we all are, it's probably different."

Reichenau smiled encouragingly.

Krebs slid his hands down his thighs. "Yet there *is* one member of the family in Paris, I understand."

"A young woman turned up at the funeral, yes," Chandler said.

Krebs nodded. "Anne-Marie Claudel. The sister of the murdered girl."

"Yes."

"What did she have to tell you?" Krebs asked.

"Just who she was. She offered to repay me for the funeral costs. I refused."

"Why?" Krebs's eyes never left him.

Chandler shrugged. "I don't know. Bravado in front of a very pretty girl."

"You think she's a very pretty girl?" Krebs said.

"Yes."

"Did you arrange to meet again?"

"No."

"Why not, if she is that attractive?"

Chandler turned to appeal to Reichenau. "The funeral of your murdered girl friend isn't the place where even I would think of making a date with her sister."

"Quite so," agreed Reichenau primly.

"I'm sorry, Herr Chandler," Krebs accepted the rebuke. "My professional enthusiasm ran ahead of me. Nevertheless I feel that to clear up this matter Mademoiselle Anne-Marie Claudel must be interviewed at the earliest possible moment. It was, after all, her apartment in which Jacqueline Claudel was murdered."

"I can't help you," Chandler said. "She's dark haired and attractive, but so are fifty thousand other Parisian girls."

Krebs nodded thoughtfully. "What can you tell us

about the Rumanian, Bilescu?''

"He was a friend of Jacqueline's," said Chandler carefully.

"He never bought pictures from you?"

"No. He claimed he had once seen some of my work. He was pretty insulting about it, so maybe he had."

Reichenau smiled. Krebs's lips remained pressed together in his round, smooth face.

"Where is Bilescu now?" Krebs asked.

"On the way south, I imagine. He told me last night he had a car ready to leave." Chandler realized too late he should not have volunteered the information he had seen Bilescu as recently as the previous evening.

"Why should he wish to leave?" Krebs said.

Chandler glanced up at Krebs and wondered if the brute knew about his and Bilescu's connection with the Jewish Resettlement Agency. "You may be able to answer that question better than I can, Inspector."

Krebs smiled. It was a sight as sinister as any Chandler would want to see again.

"Had he remained in Paris, as an applicant for French citizenship, he would be within the jurisdiction of the Occupation authorities," Krebs mused.

"I'm not," Chandler said, as steadily as the memory of that smile allowed.

Krebs shook his head. "No. But we nevertheless expect, I would go as far as to say demand, your cooperation. In particular we would insist on the answer to this question: Did you ever meet Anne-Marie Claudel before the funeral?"

"Never."

"Jacqueline Claudel must at least have mentioned the existence of a sister?"

"Possibly; I don't recall."

Krebs glanced across at Reichenau who responded with a brief nod.

"Herr Chandler," Krebs said slowly, "I have the impression that you are being less than cooperative."

"I have told you all I know."

"I am still not satisfied," Krebs said.

"There's nothing I can do about that." Chandler went to stand up.

"Stay where you are, Herr Chandler," Krebs said sharply. "I see I must acquaint you more clearly with your present position. As the Occupation police officer in charge of the case, I consider that you are the principal suspect."

Chandler could feel his heart hammering. He turned to Reichenau. "A few moments ago you talked about my being marginally involved in this case."

Reichenau smiled apologetically. "Inspector Krebs is the investigating officer. He must draw his own conclusions from the evidence presented."

Chandler turned uneasily back to Krebs. "On the evidence available," he said carefully, "what conclusions do you draw?"

His plump face in shadow, his broad, round shoulders silhouetted against the window, Krebs stood silently looking down at the American. "Last night," he said at length, "fresh evidence was revealed. The French police decided to carry out a further examination of the Claudel apartment. A wine glass was discovered, bearing a clear set of your fingerprints, Herr Chandler."

"I don't believe you," Chandler exploded. "I was never in that apartment in my life."

"Then explain the glass," said Krebs.

Chandler stood, tense with fear and anger. "I don't have to because the glass doesn't exist." He appealed to Reichenau once more. "What the hell is he trying to do to me?"

Reichenau passed a hand through his thick gray hair. "Inspector Krebs believes that for some reason you have been less than frank about your knowledge of Anne-Marie Claudel."

"Why? Why should I be?"

"Face the facts, Herr Chandler," Krebs said. "You know the murder victim over a period of perhaps four months. Your relationship develops rapidly until she becomes your mistress. During this time the said Jacqueline Claudel was living at her sister's apartment. She must have talked about Anne-Marie—why she wasn't living at the flat, what she was doing for a living, where she was staying.''

Chandler stood in the middle of the room looking from Reichenau to Krebs. "Just why is it so important for you to find Anne-Marie?"

"I have a murder case to resolve," said Krebs evenly. "She's a possible witness. Until she is traced, you must remain the principal suspect. As such, naturally the Occupation authorities will retain your passport for such time as is necessary to establish your innocence." He paused. "Or prove your guilt."

"I'm not to be allowed to leave?"

"You will not leave the German-occupied area."

"Until you find Anne-Marie Claudel, is that it?"

"We hope you'll be able to help us do that," said Reichenau smoothly. "Indeed, we think you can."

"How, for God's sake?"

"By telling us all you know about her," said Krebs.

Chandler stood at bay in the middle of the room. "Okay, I'll tell you my guess," he said. "My guess is that she left Paris yesterday, right after the funeral."

"Why would she do that? Paris had already been declared an open city. She was safe here." Reichenau rubbed his chin thoughtfully.

Chandler spread his hands wide. "Safe! With a killer looking for her. Surely it must have occurred to you that Jacqueline was murdered by mistake."

The two Germans exchanged a quick glance.

"You mean that Anne-Marie was the intended victim?" said Reichenau.

Krebs's hand went to his pocket. Chandler had no way of knowing it contained a coiled length of piano wire.

"She as good as told me at the funeral that she thought so."

"Then all the more reason for us to trace her," Krebs said.

"Maybe. But if that's the case it leaves me with no role in this murder," Chandler said. "I can't be suspected of wanting to kill a girl I didn't know."

"You forget," Krebs said, with the stretching of his pale lips that passed for a smile, "that we here in Gestapo headquarters are not yet satisfied you did *not* know her."

Chandler wiped away the sweat, which was now forming freely on his cheek.

"Did you ever meet Monsieur Paul Litvinov?" Reichenau asked.

"Never."

"You've heard of him?"

"Most people in Paris have heard of him. He must be one of the richest men in France."

"A Jew," Krebs said.

"Probably."

"Certainly. He financed the so-called Jewish Resettlement Agency."

"So the newspapers reported." Chandler tried to keep the panic out of his voice.

"The organization did a great deal of anti-German publicity on behalf of immigrant Jews from Germany."

Chandler shrugged. "What else would you expect?"

Krebs's eyes narrowed. "I would expect you to be more forthcoming with your information, Herr Chandler. Are you going to tell me that you were unaware that Anne-Marie Claudel was one of the Jew Litvinov's principal assistants?"

"Why should I have known that? It was Litvinov the press mentioned. Not his assistants."

"Why should he have known that, Krebs?" Reichenau asked amiably.

For the second time Krebs smiled. "There could be many things Herr Chandler knows that he has not yet confided to us, Colonel."

"True." Reichenau nodded.

Chandler looked from one to the other in near desperation. Emboldened by his American origins, he made one attempt to put the interview on what he could recognize as a sane basis. "I believe you're looking for one particular Jewish refugee," he said. "And I think you believe Anne-Marie Claudel could lead you to him. If that's the case, there's nothing I can do to help."

"Inspector Krebs is investigating the murder of an acquaintance of yours, Jacqueline Claudel," Reichenau said. "His favored form of questioning is often discursive; I've noticed that in the past. But Inspector Krebs is one of our most talented investigating officers. And he, I'm afraid, believes there's reason to require you not to leave occupied France until this case is solved."

Theo Chandler stood staring at his open suitcase, aware of a tension that was an entirely new experience in his life. It was after 9:30, and he had certainly missed the morning's embassy transportation south.

The two young Gestapo men had returned with him to his apartment and, the veneer of politeness dropped, had unbuckled his bag and spread the contents across the bed until they found his passport, *carte de séjour* and ration cards. Then they had turned to the rest of the room, collecting old letters, bills, any scrap of paper, depriving him, he felt as he watched helplessly, of his official existence.

He had never felt fear like this, even in Nazi Germany itself. He had never, before today, realized how much his outlook, as an American in Europe, depended on the backing—the guarantee—that a U.S. passport provided. In a brief hour he had seen himself reduced to a new vulnerability. When the young men left without a word, he poured himself a large Glen Morangie malt whisky and, taking a canvas shoulder bag that he had used for paints and brushes, he packed a few essentials from the pile of clothing on the bed. Then, adding two or three packs of cigarettes and the almost full bottle of Glen Morangie to the bag, he made for the door. The U.S. embassy was going to have to get him onto the next transportation to Bordeaux, even if it meant unseating widows and grandmothers to find him a place.

Descending the winding staircase, he reached a point where he could see down into the courtyard. Madame Oberon was scrubbing a piece of worn carpet with a stiff, long-handled broom and a bucket of soapy water. There was no sign of anyone else beside the porte cochère.

Chandler continued on down to ground level. The sound of his descending footsteps had caused Madame Oberon to stop work. She turned as the American stopped in the entrance to the courtyard.

"Monsieur Chandler," she said, her voice lower than her habitual screech, "already the gentlemen have taken an interest in you."

He took two hundred francs from his pocket and pressed the notes into Madame Oberon's still-damp palm.

"You're leaving Paris, monsieur?"

"I've no choice, madame."

She folded the notes and stowed them under her apron, nodding, repeating his words. "No, no choice."

He extended his hand. "Goodbye, madame."

She offered her forearm so that he could avoid her soapy right hand. Awkwardly he grasped her thin wrist.

"After the war . . ." he said.

Her eyes had filled with tears. "There's only one man can save us now," she said. "Only one who can stand up to the Boches."

He released her arm, and quickly, unexpectedly, she crossed herself. He knew she was thinking of Marshal Pétain.

"Perhaps you're right. Who knows?" He began to move toward the courtyard door.

"Not that way, monsieur," she said. "There's a German car outside. They're watching the house."

He stopped and came slowly back toward her.

"There's a back door in the old cellars," she said. "The alley takes you onto the Rue Fontaine."

She stood the broom in the bucket of water and led the way across the courtyard to a small arched entrance that Chandler had seen a thousand times before but had never

thought to ask where it led. She opened the door and
started down a short flight of stone steps. Dusty circular
windows at pavement level allowed light into the long,
gray-flagged cellar. Following Madame Oberon between
empty wooden crates and rusting bicycles from another
age, he saw before them a low grilled door.

The old lady took a bunch of keys from her pocket and
fitted one into the lock. *"Au revoir,* monsieur,*"* she said,
and swinging the door open, she stood back to let him
pass.

He emerged into a narrow alley enclosed by the backs
of nineteenth-century apartment buildings. Behind him
the door slammed shut, and he heard Madame Oberon's
key turn with difficulty in the disused lock. A few yards
down the alley in the general direction of the Quai
d'Anjou, he came into a narrow street and from there
zigzagged toward the river. He passed no one in the tiny
ruelles, although from time to time he could hear motor-
cycles or heavy supply trucks moving across the island
from the Left Bank through the Rue des Deux-Ponts.

He was already some distance from his apartment
building but, until he had left the Île St-Louis altogether
and was heading toward the Place de la Concorde and the
U.S. embassy beyond it, he continued to cast glances over
his shoulder.

In the main streets there were German military vehicles
everywhere and armored columns moving south. But it
was the lone black Opel Chandler was looking for and the
zealous young Gestapo men in the slightly overtight suits.

Reaching the Avenue Gabriel, he could see the usual
single French policeman on duty outside the American
embassy. Idly shifting his position, the gendarme
watched the columns of German trucks rumbling past the
Élysée Palace.

One final glance over his shoulder, and Chandler
stopped before the gendarme. There was something
immensely reassuring about the familiar embassy building, about the U.S. flag fluttering from the white staff. He
glanced up. With a sense of mounting apprehension, he

saw that today there was no flag flying from the immaculate white pole.

"Yes, monsieur?" The gendarme saluted perfunctorily.

"I'm an American citizen." Chandler made to move past him.

The gendarme stretched out an arm to block his way. "You can't go in, monsieur."

Chandler faced him tensely. "Can't go in? Why not? I'm an American."

"I'm sure," the gendarme said. "But it's locked. They've all gone."

"Gone?"

"Evacuated to Bordeaux, monsieur. The last convoy left this morning at nine o'clock."

Chapter
Ten

OPPOSITE THE SILENT, shuttered American embassy, the entrance to the sumptuous Hôtel Crillon clattered with military activity. Motorcycle messengers roared to a halt and stamped through the great doors into the lobby beyond; field officers' cars decanted generals and their staff; machine-gun units took up guard positions on the flat roof overlooking the Place de la Concorde. On this first morning of the occupation of Paris, the Hôtel Crillon had been selected as one of the Wehrmacht's principal headquarters buildings.

Inside, a dozen large tables covered with red cloth had been set up in the Crillon's magnificent lobby, and administrative officers were working on the allocation of subsidiary headquarters buildings to army staffs as they arrived in Paris.

Chandler's American accent had gotten him assigned without difficulty to a young lieutenant, who rapidly flipped through typewritten lists.

"Miss Beth Kately. I remember the lady," he said. "She has been assigned to another hotel. She wasn't pleased."

"I don't imagine she was."

The lieutenant grinned. "No details on this list. Let me make inquiries. There may be a later list." He left Chandler in the middle of the lobby and crossed to one of the red-topped tables.

While he waited, Chandler lit a cigarette. When a waiter passed, he signaled to him. "Can you get me a scotch and soda?"

"Of course, sir."

When the waiter returned, Chandler paid him and, glass in hand, leaned against an ornate column to watch the swirl of activity in front of him. Field officers of the Wehrmacht and Luftwaffe milled around in the middle of the lobby and received directions to their new quarters from youthful junior officers carrying maps of Paris neatly clipped to millboard. The atmosphere was relaxed yet bustling. Voices were raised in congratulations for a Place Pigalle quartering or mock commiseration for an assignment that would take an officer out of the city center.

Chandler felt himself begin to relax. These were the sort of Germans he was familiar with, the sort of Germans he had encountered on his visits to Bavaria. To Theo Chandler, who had met them in their homes, in restaurants, on the ski slopes and the tennis courts, it was impossible to fit someone like Gestapo Inspector Krebs into the same mold. Leaning against the marble pillar, he found himself shuddering at the thought of the man's softly rounded cheeks and the dead stare of his disbelieving eyes. Yet here, in the Crillon lobby, he found a part of himself curiously identified with the sheer exhilaration of victory that these German officers were experiencing. From time to time a captain or major would enter, thick dust outlining the white goggle marks around his eyes, his legs unsteady from the sleepless nights of advance, boots mud covered, a steel helmet dangling from his hand. Invariably one of a group of generals would catch the arm of a waiter, calling: "Give that young officer a glass of champagne." And the general would raise his own glass to the dust-covered newcomer: "Prosit!"

The young lieutenant returned with a new sheaf of typed lists. He removed a pale-green printed form from his clipboard. "You'll also need this." He handed the form to Chandler.

"What is it?"

"It's a Wehrmacht *laissez-passer*. A pass to let you move around Paris. Without it, civilians will be obliged to observe the curfew."

"Curfew?"

"It begins at midday. Don't worry, it won't last long. It's just to give us time to catch our breath. Things will be working normally in no time."

Chandler finished his whisky and put down the glass on a table beside them. "Thanks for the pass," he said.

The lieutenant handed him a pen and offered the back of his clipboard to write on. "Just fill in your name and address. It's already signed."

Chandler hesitated for a moment, then filled in the pass.

"You've lived in Paris for some time, Herr Chandler."

"Nearly a year." He handed back the pen and clipboard.

"And is it all it's supposed to be?" the lieutenant raised his eyebrows.

"It was."

The young German's face hardened. "You mean until the Wehrmacht arrived."

"It may be the same again," Chandler said. "God knows. I guess it's up to people like you."

The lieutenant's smile reappeared. "I see what you're saying, Herr Chandler. But I think you've no need to worry. It's the Wehrmacht that controls Paris, not the Gestapo."

Chandler shook hands with him. "I hope you're right," he said fervently.

Twenty minutes later Chandler was shown into the drawing room of Beth Kately's suite at the Ritz. She stood by the flower-decked fireplace, martini in one hand, wearing the gloss of the very rich and confident.

"Come in, Theo," she said. "Help yourself to a martini."

"Thank you." He crossed the room and poured a martini from a silver jug glistening with condensation.

"You've decided we can do business after all, have you?" She crossed to an armchair and sat down.

"More or less decided," he agreed cautiously.

"What changed your mind?"

"The Gestapo."

Her lips twisted in a heavily lipsticked smile. "You're not afraid of the Gestapo."

"Terrified," he said shortly. "They pulled me in this morning with a bunch of questions about Jacqueline Claudel. What they were really asking about was Anne-Marie. I thought you'd tell me why."

She stared at him, her face impassive. Then she smiled again, the same smile whose very meaninglessness seemed to require an additional muscular effort. "So the Gestapo is interested in Anne-Marie. Good. And you have decided to take my offer of a job."

"I'll be frank with you, Miss Kately," Chandler said. "I'm accepting because the way I see it even the Gestapo isn't going up against the writer of the Beth Kately column. And by getting this girl out of France, I get myself out."

"I'm touched," she sneered. "You're putting yourself under my protection. Is that the way it is, Theo?"

"The Gestapo has withdrawn my passport. The U.S. embassy's closed."

"Poor boy," she said. "You're mixed up in something you don't understand. And you're afraid."

He finished his martini. "When do I leave for Bordeaux?"

She stretched out her hand and gave him her glass to refill. "First we have to find the girl."

Chandler rode the elevator down to the ground floor and ordered himself a White Lady in the Ritz's main bar.

Beth Kately, he had no difficulty deciding, was the most repulsive woman he had ever met in his life. He had no doubt she would be a formidable enemy. One that even the Gestapo could not afford to make. He had read her column in the past and knew she took a fairly neutral view of nazism. What the Nazi press chiefs called ''fair-minded.'' There were not too many neutral columnists in the U.S. newspaper world today. Berlin, he was sure, could not afford to offend Beth Kately.

He had seen how she operated and it was, he had to admit, impressive. To find Anne-Marie Claudel, now that Litvinov's Jewish Resettlement Agency had disbanded, was not going to be easy. She might have left Paris; she might have gone underground with Litvinov. Perhaps she had gone back to St-Eloi, where Borel said she had been born; it would be a natural thing to do. And if anyone knew her address in Paris it could well be someone in her home village. So Chandler would go to St-Eloi.

Within ten minutes of that decision, Beth Kately had been talking to General Heinz Remick, senior administration officer in the new Occupation Authority, and had secured an *Ausweis* for Chandler to travel to the Belgian border. Less than an hour later the pass had been delivered to the Ritz.

Chandler paid the barman for his drink from the wad of dollar bills Upton had given him. Memories of Jacqueline moved patchily through his mind as if he were chasing her apparition in some fogbound dream. Could Beth Kately have any interest in her murder? Was one of Jacqueline's former lovers, some minister or general, tied up with the disaster the war had now become? A scandal for Beth Kately's column. But Jacqueline didn't have that kind of lover, she had near-penniless artists like himself. No, for whatever reason, it was Anne-Marie that Beth Kately was really interested in. And the Gestapo too.

Chapter

Eleven

At MIDDAY ON June 17, the sky, a brilliant blue for so many uninterrupted weeks, took on a leaden hue. Across the battlefields, from Brittany to the Alps, the sound of distant thunder mingled with the roll of gunfire.

In Bordeaux, the government of Paul Reynaud had fallen in a confusion of rhetoric and defeatism. The venerable Marshal Pétain had "offered himself to France." The midday storm broke as Pétain's car nosed its way through the swollen mass of people on the Boulevard Président-Wilson. In the backseat the old man sat upright, impeccable in his marshal's pale tan uniform, the peak of his gold-braided kepi shadowing the drooping white mustache. Once before, twenty-four years ago, France had called him in her hour of need, as the only man capable of extracting the French Army from the inferno of Verdun. Victory had been his means then. Now he was again called to save the French people from another military cauldron. But today the means must be different; the acceptance of defeat was the only road ahead. The marshal closed his eyes to the drenched crowds on the boulevard. He, not they, epitomized

France. He and perhaps a small group of senior army officers were the repository of France's honor. Never for a moment did it enter the old man's mind that they were also responsible for her defeat.

The car turned right and continued down the Rue Croix-Blanche in the direction of the Garonne.

At the Lycée Longchamps the car drew to a halt. An aide from a following car opened an umbrella over the marshal's head and conducted him up the steps worn by the feet of generations of French children.

In a ground-floor classroom, technicians had installed equipment capable of broadcasting to the whole of France.

The marshal stepped toward the microphone. In towns and villages, in army encampments and makeshift shelters across the country the people waited for his words.

"I have made a gift of my person to France . . ." he announced. "With a heavy heart, I tell you today that it is necessary to stop fighting."

With a few ill-considered words from an old man, the dam broke. That afternoon, whole regiments began to withdraw from the front lines. Weapons were abandoned; explosive charges were removed from bridges, roadblocks dismantled. German planes dropped thousands of leaflets proclaiming the end of the war; at the front, German loudspeaker vans broadcasted the news to French troops: Marshal Pétain has ordered you to stop fighting. General Rommel, attacking Cherbourg with his 7th Panzer Division, mounted a white flag on his tank and drove through the outskirts of the town calling through a loudspeaker that the war was over. In Bordeaux, the 18th Military District, charged with the defense of the government, ordered officers to disarm all troops and peacefully await the arrival of the Germans. In one short broadcast, a French general said bitterly, Marshal Pétain had broken the last resistance of the French Army.

He was right. After the midday broadcast of June 17, there could be no more than scattered pockets of resistance among the battered French armies; France's premier soldier had announced her defeat before even asking how harsh Hitler's peace terms might be.

The *Kübelwagen* slowed to walking pace as the long column of marching men approached. In the driver's seat, the stocky, gray-haired German sergeant major turned to Chandler.

"The village of St-Eloi is just over the hill," he said.

Chandler watched the column of infantry as it swung toward them, the seemingly inexhaustible reserves of the Wehrmacht on their way to occupy France.

"I wonder if those boys know the fighting is over?" the sergeant major said.

"If they don't, they soon will," Chandler said without enthusiasm.

The sergeant major waved through the windshield to the young men in green uniforms as they began to pass. "It'll be the invasion of England next," he said. "That'll be a real war."

Chandler looked at the sergeant major, at his ruddy, farmer's face and open expression, and wondered if he was right.

The *Kübelwagen* had picked him up outside the Ritz in Paris. Beth Kately's influence was apparently limitless. Now they drove on and reached the top of a low hill as the last of the infantry passed. Along the ridge to their right, line after line of neat, white crosses followed the undulation of the ground. A green signboard at the gate of the cemetery read: BRITISH WAR GRAVES COMMISSION 1918. St-Eloi, below them, was a church, a small railway station and a drab huddle of houses.

The sergeant major accelerated down the hill and pulled into the small gray square. A line of French women had formed outside the *boulangerie*. The door to the café, with its net-curtained windows, was ajar.

The German braked the vehicle and Chandler climbed out, swinging his bag from the backseat. "Thanks for the ride," he said. "Can you pick me up on the way back?"

The sergeant major lit a cigarette. "Field mail HQ is

about half an hour from here, if the road's clear. I'll find myself something to eat, get the latest news from my friend Genschler and collect the mail. I should be back here in about three hours. Good enough?''

"That should be fine." Chandler reached inside his bag, took out the bottle of malt whisky and tossed it across the seat to the sergeant major. "Have a drink with Genschler, on me."

The German grinned, crashed into gear and drove off. Outside the café, a uniformed Frenchman watched impassively.

Chandler watched the *Kübelwagen* climb the hill, then he walked across the square toward the café. The man at the entrance withdrew inside as he approached, but left the door ajar. The eyes of the women in the bread line followed every step.

The church, Chandler noticed as he came closer, was badly damaged by fire. An old priest, emerging from the porch, raised a hand in salute.

"Good morning, Father." Chandler stopped.

"Monsieur," the priest said, coming out into the sunlight.

"I'm sorry to see the church suffered in the fighting." Chandler gestured to the blackened tower and the remnant of stained glass hanging in the melted leading of the windows.

"You're a foreigner," the priest said. "Not a German, I would guess."

"American. My name's Chandler. I'm looking for the Claudel family."

"Then the café is the place," the priest said. "Ask for Monsieur Murville, the station master." He turned back to look at the ruined church. "No, it wasn't the fighting. It was a fire. An accident, monsieur, despite what you will hear to the contrary."

Chandler frowned. "What am I likely to hear to the contrary?"

"People in a village like this, monsieur, lack romance in their lives. Sometimes their imaginations are called on to provide it.'' The priest's gentle, blue eyes blinked in the light.

"How does a fire in a church supply romance?" Chandler asked.

"Look at these hills around you, monsieur. A great battle was fought here in 1918," he said. "Lost, of course, in the annals of even greater battles in that most terrible of wars." He pointed. "Up there is the German cemetery. Next to it, the French—another ten thousand crosses. Beyond that wood the Canadian cemetery, thousands more. This village should be named St-Eloi le cimetière."

"What has this to do with the church?" asked Chandler.

"Some human bones were found near the altar when the fire had burned itself out. A skull too." The priest shrugged.

"Someone was killed in the fire?"

"A death in the church? Perhaps a human sacrifice? No. You are a romantic too, monsieur. The fields and woods around here are full of bones. For every soldier's body buried in a marked grave another lies in the ground where he fell. Some of the village lads, drunk I dare say, threw the bones in among the smoldering ruins. I'm sure of it. I don't think we have to look further than that for an explanation."

The priest brushed some dust from his cassock, then looked up and smiled quickly at Chandler. "Of course," he added, "the village is full of stories about witchcraft. Their world is full of devils."

Chandler said goodbye to the priest and went on across the square. Strange, he thought, how amid all the confusion and turmoil of the present, with the Germans in occupation, an old priest could still be concerned with the reputation of his parish, could still worry that accusations of witchcraft might be attached to his flock.

As Chandler pushed open the café door the bottom scraped across the floorboards. It had been damaged and roughly repaired with lengths of unpainted wood. He was in a small room with half a dozen tables set for lunch with white paper tablecloths. The uniformed Frenchman, the only occupant of the room, stood at the bar.

"Monsieur." Chandler nodded as he walked toward him. The Frenchman, he saw, had an empty right sleeve neatly sewed to the side of his station master's uniform.

Chandler looked toward the curtained door behind the bar. "Can I get a drink here?" he asked the Frenchman.

"The old ladies are busy in the kitchen," the station master said, moving around behind the bar. "What can I get you, monsieur."

"A Pernod. And one for yourself."

"You're a German?"

"Won't you drink with Germans?"

The Frenchman looked at him and smiled slowly. "So far, why not?"

"I'm American," Chandler said.

"I thought the accent sounded not quite German. And what brings you to our poor village, monsieur?" He grinned wryly. "Not tourism, I'll bet."

"No, I'm looking for the Claudel family."

The station master grunted. "Monsieur, almost half the village people are Claudels. The rest are Murvilles, like myself. We've hardly had a new name appear in St-Eloi this century. How can I help you?"

"I'm trying to trace the relatives of a girl named Jacqueline Claudel."

"Jacqueline?" He set two Pernods deftly between them.

"You know her?"

"Of course. She's my niece. She's in Paris."

Chandler hesitated, searching for the right words. He could feel the station master's gaze. A means of softening the blow eluded him.

"Jacqueline's dead," he said in the end. "She died last week."

The station master nodded his head gently, absorbing the shock. Raising his drink to his lips, he emptied the glass.

"The bombing?"

"Not the bombing," Chandler said quietly. "She was attacked in her apartment."

"Attacked?" The station master's face screwed up in incredulity. "You mean murdered?"

"Yes. The police haven't yet succeeded in finding the man responsible."

For a few seconds the station master stood with his head sagging from his shoulders. Then he straightened up and went behind the bar to refill his glass. Coming back slowly, he stood beside Chandler. The movement had given him time to control the muscles in his face. When he spoke it was almost to himself. "In times of war you expect death. You expect men to die." He gestured toward his empty sleeve. "I myself almost died once. But women—to be attacked, murdered." He shook his head. What are we to make of that, monsieur? As God-fearing Christians, what are we to make of that?"

"I don't know," said Chandler.

They stood together in silence.

"You were a friend of Jacqueline's, monsieur?"

"For a few months," Chandler said.

"Tell me how it happened."

"There's not much to tell," said Chandler. "Jacqueline worked in a cinema. She came home alone one evening. A few minutes later, the concierge told the police, she had a visitor. He stayed no more than ten minutes. The next morning she was found dead. Strangled."

"Strangled?" The look of total disbelief was back, contorting the station master's face.

"Yes."

"Her neck broken. Her body . . ." Murville's voice trailed off.

"How did you know?" asked Chandler.

The station master remained silent, staring down at his glass. Whatever thoughts absorbed him, he had no intention of communicating them now.

Chandler put the question he had to ask: "Her sister

Anne-Marie, is she here? Did she come home?''

Murville seemed to gather himself a little. ''Anne-Marie? No, she is not here. We have lost touch with her, here in St-Eloi.'' He pushed his drink aside. ''It was kind of you to come all this way, monsieur. Now I will go to my wife, to Jacqueline's aunt.''

''Will you come back?'' Chandler asked. ''I must talk to you again.''

''If you can wait an hour.'' The station master's eyes were tired, heavy with grief.

''I'm sorry,'' Chandler said. ''And I'm sorry I couldn't find a better way to tell you.''

''There is no better way. I should know, monsieur. It was me who broke the news last time.''

''Last time?''

''The other murder.'' The station master said it as if Chandler already knew. ''When their mother, Arlette, was killed.''

In his office at the Hôtel Belfort, Gestapo Inspector Krebs examined the folded card in his hand before placing it on the desk beside him.

Fists clenched deep in his jacket pockets, Borel watched the German as he stared angrily down at the card.

''And this is all the documentary evidence you are able to find?'' Krebs turned his attention to Borel.

''Yes.''

Krebs nodded grimly. ''Between professional policemen, it would be fair to agree that it's not much.''

''I doubt if you realize the chaotic state our files are in,'' Borel said evenly. ''Half of them have been taken by the government to Bordeaux. Others are buried under thousands of documents brought from the evacuated towns in the north.''

''You're telling me I'm lucky to get even this,'' Krebs rapped the document on the desk with the back of his powerful hand.

''You could say that, yes.''

"And what does it tell us, this document?"

"It's, as you can see, a ration card. Made out to Anne-Marie Claudel at the address on the Île St-Louis where her sister was murdered. Partly used, and then canceled on June 8th."

"In what circumstances would it have been canceled?" Krebs asked.

"The most obvious circumstance is death."

Krebs stared at Borel with unconcealed malevolence. "She was reported to have been alive two days ago at the funeral of her sister."

Borel shrugged easily. "That report came from one man, the American, Chandler, your chief suspect, who it seems has now disappeared into thin air. How far are you ready to believe him?"

"You give up too easily," Krebs snapped. "What other circumstances might account for the cancellation of this card?"

Borel took a pack of Gauloises from his pocket and drew one out. Hooking it into his lower lip, he rubbed at his dark chin. "If she left Paris for another district, it would have been cancelled and reissued there."

"Unlikely. What other circumstances?" Krebs demanded.

"I can't think of any." Borel lit his cigarette.

"You're looking for an easy life," Krebs said. "Believe me, there will be no easy life from now on. What other circumstances?"

"I told you, I can't think of any."

"I can."

Borel drew on his cigarette; screwing up his eyes against the smoke, he watched Krebs's moon-face move into its parody of a smile.

"What if Anne-Marie Claudel were married?"

Borel nodded slowly.

"Would that not mean," Krebs said triumphantly, "that her single person's ration card would be cancelled?"

"Yes."

"And one issued in another name, her married name?"

"Yes."

"And since we have the precise date, would it not be a simple matter to check the Marriage Registry for the name of the husband and thus the new name of Anne-Marie Claudel?"

Borel crushed out his cigarette in an ashtray on the desk. "It would indeed be a simple matter, if the registry were still in Paris. As I tried to indicate, the official documents of the French government are spread between here and Bordeaux. I have a report that thousands of documents are sitting in a schoolhouse in Souillac."

Krebs's eyes narrowed, but Borel ignored the threat.

"What sort of documents?" Borel continued. "Police files, identity data, marriage certificates? Who knows? South of Paris there are a hundred schoolhouses like the one in Souillac. There are trucks full of official papers burning at the roadside. Don't tell me it's a simple matter to check for Anne-Marie Claudel's new name."

Borel held his look without flinching, but Krebs's eyes had turned to flint.

In just over an hour, as he had said, the station master was back in the café. He sat with Chandler at a table apart from a group of French workmen eating lunch.

"She owned this café," Murville said. "Both the girls were born upstairs." He pointed to the ceiling. "You'd have been surprised to see the place then, when Arlette was in her prime. She was different, you see, monsieur. Not like myself, old Junot, the rest of the villagers —we're all peasants at heart. But Arlette was different."

"How was she different?" Chandler asked.

"She didn't come from here, not even from the district. Brussels, she used to say, but she was such a storyteller it could have been anywhere."

"She married a Claudel?"

"Yes, Jean-Pierre, a soldier, a professional. Did very well for himself. He was in Morocco, Algeria, all over.

Somewhere, he met Arlette. God knows where, they didn't talk much about it.''

"He's dead?"

The station master nodded. "For many years. He was wounded on the Somme. At the end of the war he came home, but he died soon after Jacqueline was born. The wagging tongues didn't help.''

"What do you mean?''

Murville shrugged. "Her husband away at the front. She was a handsome woman, monsieur. Arlette was a very handsome woman.''

"I can believe it," Chandler said. "I've seen Anne-Marie.''

"Just so.'' The station master fell silent.

Chandler waited but knew he must ask. "The murder. How did it happen?''

"It was a bad night, raining, but Arlette still took her dog out for a walk. I was here in the café with Junot and a few others, playing cards. Half an hour later the dog came back alone. Scratching at the door, terrified; cringing under the table there, whimpering. I think we all knew something bad had happened.'' The station master paused, his memory sharpening.

"You went out to look for her?" Chandler asked.

"Yes, the cardplayers and a few others at the bar. We lit some farm lanterns and started searching. It was night, you see. Old Junot took some of them to the east. I went with the rest, past the church, the way she usually took the dog. It was our group that found her. Just outside the village, near the crossroads. Thrown into a hedge like a bundle of rags.'' The station master drew his breath in sharply through his teeth.

"And the murderer?''

"There was some talk of a stranger. Some children said they'd seen a stranger pass through the village early in the evening. Who knows? Perhaps they did.''

"This stranger, did you try to find him?''

"A police inspector came over from Amiens, took statements for his report. But the stranger was never traced. Perhaps he never existed.''

"I must ask you," Chandler said. "Had she been sexually assaulted?''

Murville shrugged.

"Why was Arlette Claudel murdered?''

"You ask me for a motive. Now I ask myself if this can really be a coincidence. Arlette and now her daughter Jacqueline, both strangled in the same way. Who knows why? Perhaps the others are right.''

"What do they believe?''

"Village talk,'' Murville shrugged again. "Women's talk, mostly. But I've traveled, monsieur. During the last war. All villages are the same.''

"What do the women say?'' Chandler pressed him.

"The devil at the crossroads,'' Murville said dismissively. "You know what they say.''

"No, I don't.''

"It's where the body was found. At the crossroads. On dark nights the devil waits at the crossroads. Sometimes on horseback. He waits for a woman alone. It's a story to frighten young girls with, monsieur. And now Jacqueline, she too met her devil at the crossroads.''

Chandler was silent, watching the grief rise on the station master's face.

"There's something I must tell you,'' Chandler said. "Jacqueline was living in Anne-Marie's apartment. Anne-Marie's name was still on the door. When I saw her at the funeral, she was terrified. She believed the murderer made a mistake, that it was her he intended to kill.''

"Why did you come here, monsieur?'' said Murville, his voice hardening.

"I'm trying to find Anne-Marie. I thought she might have come back here, or that someone in St-Eloi could tell me where she lives in Paris.''

"Why do you want to find her?'' the station master's tone was now suspicious.

"To warn her. The Gestapo is looking for her. You know what that means?''

"I know what it means, but I can't help you.'' The

station master got to his feet. "Go back to Paris, monsieur," he said, raising his voice.

The group of workmen at the other table stopped eating. Chandler could feel their silent, aggressive stares. He stood. "Thank you for all you have told me."

The station master followed as Chandler walked to the door. As he pulled it open, it scraped and creaked in its broken frame.

"What happened to the door?" Chandler asked.

"It was smashed in. The same night the church caught fire."

"A break-in. What was taken?"

"What is there of value in a poor café like this?" Murville gestured around with his arm. "But the place was ransacked, every room, every cupboard."

"Who did it?" Chandler asked.

"Strangers, monsieur. It must have been strangers."

Chapter
Twelve

THIS WAS THE honeymoon period between the people of Paris and the Occupation Authority. The curfew had been lifted, and Parisians, now returning to the city at the rate of 100,000 a day, had begun to take up their old habits. Along the Boulevard St-Michel the cafés were again full, now with a colorful mix of civilians and German Army and Luftwaffe personnel.

The struggle to come between the Wehrmacht and the Gestapo had not yet reached the surface. To most Parisians, except a few in the Fresnes or Romainville prisons, the police were still the French gendarmes they saw sharing checkpoint duty with the German military. The Gestapo, at this stage, remained in the shadows.

"Put your trust in the German soldier," the Occupation Authority poster proclaimed. Instructions to the Wehrmacht backed and reinforced this idea. Behavior of the military was to be *korrekt* at all times. There was to be no confiscation; goods and services were to be paid for at the admittedly highly favorable reichmark exchange rate.

It sometimes has been said that during these summer days the whores of Paris were the most enthusiastic

supporters of Franco-German cooperation. For the rest of
the population the attitude was perhaps more that they
should wait and see. But in the meantime, unaware of the
Gestapo's determination to exercise final police authority
in occupied France, the people of Paris viewed the
green-uniformed soldiers, with some relief, as a massive
tourist army, sitting at the cafés, visiting the monuments,
being photographed with their arms around French girls.

Once through the revolving door on the Vendôme side
of the Ritz, Chandler felt safer. He made his way quickly
to the paneled Little Bar and ordered a scotch and soda.
There were only three other customers, well-dressed,
aging Frenchmen who looked as if they had been there all
day.

He had failed to discover Anne-Marie's whereabouts.
But he still needed Beth Kately's protection. Somehow
he was going to have to persuade her to extend that
protection to him until he reached Bordeaux. What he
needed most of all from her was another pass to travel
south.

He finished his whisky and ordered another. Anne-
Marie's mother had been murdered in St-Eloi. Jacqueline
had died in Paris in what seemed to be a bungled attempt
to kill Anne-Marie. Beth Kately was interested enough to
spend time and money discovering the whereabouts of
Anne-Marie. The Gestapo, as almost its first act in the
newly occupied capital, was investigating the murder of
an obscure French girl. And somehow he, Chandler, was
in the middle.

"We haven't seen many Americans here in the last few
days." One of the old Frenchmen leaned toward him. "I
ask myself," the Frenchman said in a low, confidential
tone, "whether this is the end of the Ritz as an international meeting place."

"I wouldn't know," Chandler said indifferently.

"In the old days," the Frenchman said, "you could
look across at the banquettes there—Hemingway would
be having a drink with Coco Chanel, Winston Churchill
would be holding court in the corner. Picasso would be

seducing a new South American lady.''

"Those were the days.''

The old man nodded. "And now one solitary American painter sits nursing his scotch and soda.''

Chandler frowned. "What makes you think I'm a painter?''

"Ah, perhaps I'm wrong.'' The Frenchman played with the gold bracelet on his wrist. "Perhaps you're a businessman selling armaments to the highest bidder.''

"No.''

"You have the air of an artist, monsieur. You're a painter or a writer, I'm sure.''

Chandler regarded him uneasily.

"Are you staying on in Paris, monsieur?'' the Frenchman asked.

"I could be. I haven't decided yet.''

"These young German officers with their pockets full of francs will be excellent buyers.''

"Buyers?''

"Of paintings, monsieur.''

"I've never painted a picture in my life,'' Chandler said. "The artistic inclinations of the Wehrmacht won't help me any.''

The Frenchman nodded. He pushed a handful of francs across the bar. "Bonjour, monsieur,'' he inclined his head. "Paintings or armaments,'' he said thinly, "I'm sure the Wehrmacht will have great need of both.''

Chandler sat for a few moments, finishing his drink and contemplating the idea of ordering another. According to the latest reports, the Germans were already far south of Paris, pushing on to Orléans and the Loire. Even with an *Ausweis* arranged by Beth Kately, to reach Bordeaux he would still somehow have to cross the front line. Unless, of course, Pétain's broadcast brought the quick armistice he so clearly seemed to wish.

In the mirror behind the bar, Chandler registered movement, and then recognized the old Frenchman of the strange conversation. He was pointing across the room toward Chandler. Beside the old man, two men in long, brown leather coats nodded and began to walk to the bar.

Chandler half turned on the stool, but this time there were no formalities, no veneer of politeness as had been offered by the young Gestapo officers in his apartment. These were older, tougher men. They gripped Chandler by the arms and yanked him off the stool to his feet.

"Who are you? What do you want?" Chandler protested.

Ignoring the questions, they dragged him out into the lobby. A few people stopped and watched in puzzlement rather than concern. A pimp or petty thief. Well, the efficient Germans could handle him.

Martin Upton, emerging from the small elevator, stepped back quickly into the car. Watching, just long enough before the doors slid closed, to see Chandler frog-marched away, he pressed the button for the floor of Beth Kately's suite.

In the Ritz dining room, Inspector Krebs was uneasy. Colonel Reichenau had made it clear that this woman had influence in the highest Berlin circles. To Krebs she seemed like any other jeweled matron of the sort he had despised and pandered to in his early days as a Munich shop clerk. To Emil Krebs, nazism was a working-class creed: the National Socialist German Workers' Party. He had believed Gregor Strasser who, when asked what nazism stood for, had replied, "As great a difference as possible from today."

And yet here in German-controlled Paris, fat, beringed women could still summon a Gestapo inspector to dinner. And Reichenau had made it clear he should obey. Where was the socialism in all this? He passed his eyes over the tables of elegantly dressed guests. Where was the workers' party when it was agreed to let all this continue?

In the last resort, Gestapo Inspector Emil Krebs was an idealist. In some uncertain way he believed that *rightness* and *justice* were embodied in the working class. Others, even aristocrats, could associate themselves with this rectitude. But they could never be part of it. Adolf Hitler had expressed it simply in his early Munich speeches. There could be no upper-class workers, as there could be no working-class Jews. Whatever the facade any of them presented, it was ideologically impossible. The task of the shock troops of the Third Reich—the Gestapo and SS—was, they had been told, to burst the bag of blood that obscured this fact from the eyes of the rest of the world.

"Have you ever eaten foie gras, Inspector?" Beth Kately inquired, her tongue scavenging morsels from her richly daubed lips.

"It's all the same to me," Krebs muttered.

"Sad for you," she said. "I'm told Colonel Reichenau adores it."

Krebs knew that tomorrow's world would never belong to upper-class exploiters like Reichenau. Tomorrow belonged to people like himself, Emil Krebs. Tomorrow the swastika banner of nazism would sweep away all these bowing waiters and bejeweled guests in the Ritz dining room. Into the Gestapo and SS, Reichsführer Himmler was recruiting some of the most energetic working-class activists in Germany. They were the advance guard of a national socialism that would astonish the world in its cleanliness and incorruptible honesty. In the meantime Emil Krebs was forced, as he saw it, to compromise with present reality. And that reality was the woman opposite him, with the undulating silk dress and the marks of her diamond necklace etched purple in her fat neck.

"Since you don't appreciate foie gras, asparagus, salmon or lobster, there's no point in pretending we're having lunch together," Beth Kately said. "We're merely eating together, Inspector. Or at least at the same table."

The anger rose in Krebs as he felt the familiar need to apologize when well-dressed women insulted him. He stayed silent, his eyes sullenly on his food.

Beth Kately leaned across the table. Her varnished fingernail tapped imperiously on Krebs's plate. "You have arrested one of my employees," she snapped. "I want to know why."

He was on surer ground now. "The legal government of Paris is the German Occupation Authority," he said. "It has the power and the right to arrest anybody in the city."

She waved her hand dismissively. "Why did you arrest Theo Chandler?"

He wondered how this terrible American woman had even discovered it. His agents at the Ritz had taken the American out discreetly. The whole thing, they had assured Krebs, had been over in a few moments.

"You may not be aware that Mr. Chandler is involved in a criminal investigation." He knew she was aware.

"Why did you arrest him?" she persisted. "Equally important, how did you know to find him at the Ritz?"

Krebs drew from his inside pocket a copy of a travel *Ausweis*. "Issued to Mr. Chandler," he said. "The applicant is yourself. I assumed that if he was traveling on your behalf he would report back to you. At the Ritz."

"He was traveling with a *legal* travel pass." She paused. "I've always reported, Inspector Krebs," she said menacingly, "that the reputation of the Gestapo had been misunderstood to a degree. I've always said *so far* that its methods were perhaps harsh, but fair."

Krebs pushed his plate aside. "It is an accurate description of our methods," he said stiffly. "Reichsführer Himmler himself has described our methods in this manner."

"That's exactly where the phrase comes from, Inspector," she said. "Last month when I had dinner with him in Berlin."

Krebs knew he had lost.

"Harsh but fair," Beth Kately mused. "Now, am I going to continue describing your methods that way in the future?"

The long steel galleries of Fresnes prison, netted against suicide attempts, seemed to Theo Chandler to echo unendingly with the clatter of the prisoners' *sabots*. From the little he had actually seen since being dragged from the Gestapo car and hustled across the dreary stone courtyard, the German authorities had taken over the basement cells, while the civil prison continued to function above. From the galleries, the warders' shouts were all in French; but in the long passages of the basement level, German military police patrolled outside the empty cells.

The almost empty cells. As night fell he began to hear other prison noises. The angry screaming questions from an interrogation room at the end of the corridor. The eerie sound of a man sobbing in despair in a cell on the other side of the enclosed courtyard. Sudden shouts of fear and pain.

It was, in fact, almost the shortest night of the year. But to Theo Chandler no night had seemed longer. Lying on the bare mattress, he had slept an hour or two after midnight, fitfully, awakened constantly by the clang of steel doors, the strange formless shouts, the footsteps on gray-flagged floors. Beyond the small grilled window a night bird sang in pointed incongruity with the grim prison sounds.

At three o'clock he was awakened by one of the men who had arrested him, wrenched by the shoulder out into the corridor and propelled forward with punches in the lower part of his back. Dazed, he had arrived in a room bright with interrogation lights. A second Gestapo man threw Chandler's coat across the desk. "Sign this," he said, pushing a sheet of paper toward him.

"What is it?" Chandler turned the buff form in order to read it.

"You're being released. Sign this statement that you've no complaints about your treatment." He threw a pen down onto the form. "Quickly, before someone changes his mind."

Chandler signed the form and picked up his coat. On the first man's gesture, he followed him out of the room. Five minutes later he was standing in the cool night air before the huge prison doors.

Mist hung below the street lamps before him. He

walked forward, pulling on his coat. Fatigue made him
stumble on the granite cobbles. He was hungry for a
cigarette. Perhaps above all for a drink. When Martin
Upton stepped from the shadows into the pool of light
beneath a street lamp, Chandler found he lacked the
energy to express surprise.

"I hope they didn't treat you badly," Upton said.

"No," Chandler rocked on his heels. "Do you have a
cigarette?"

Upton took out a pack and handed it to him. Removing
one from the package, he put it in his mouth and waited
for the secretary to light it. He realized that he had never
felt as tired in his life.

"Miss Kately arranged your release, of course,"
Upton said.

Chandler nodded, drawing on the cigarette.

"She's flying to Bordeaux as soon as the armistice is
signed," Upton said. "Courtesy of the Gestapo. Inspector Krebs offered to arrange an aircraft."

"Good. I'll go with her."

Upton looked at him from under his craggy New
England brows. "I don't think you understand, Mr.
Chandler. Miss Kately needs you to take Anne-Marie
Claudel to Bordeaux. Even she could not persuade
Inspector Krebs to cooperate in that."

"Why not, for God's sake? Why is Krebs so interested
in Anne-Marie?"

Upton's face was impassive. "It's Miss Kately's story,
Chandler. She made that clear to you."

"Okay. I'll make this clear to her. I want nothing to do
with Anne-Marie. I'm finished with the whole business. I
want a seat on that plane. I believe I'm as good as dead if I
don't get it. She won't refuse me."

Upton nodded slowly. "She will, Chandler. She has
no interest in you outside of Anne-Marie. And when Miss
Kately has no interest in someone, he might as well not
exist."

"She'd leave me to Krebs's tender mercies?"

"Without another thought."

Chandler stretched out a hand to lean against the lamp post. "Son of a bitch," he said. "Is she really like that?"

"Yes." Upton paused. "Did you discover where to find Anne-Marie?"

"No," Chandler almost shouted. "I couldn't take Anne-Marie down to Bordeaux even if I wanted."

"All the same, Miss Kately must be *told* that is what you are doing."

Chandler pushed himself off the lamp post. "Do I detect a trace of disloyalty, Upton?"

"I'm beyond being sneered at," Upton said. "I'm trying to arrange a few hours' liberty for you."

Chandler looked at the sad figure of the New Englander. "I'm sorry," he said.

"I will tell her that you will bring the girl down to Bordeaux," Upton said. "That way you'll be free of Krebs's attentions until the moment Miss Kately leaves Paris. After that you're on your own."

"You won't tell me what this is all about?" Chandler asked.

"I daren't. For your sake too. Leave Paris tonight. Join the refugees."

"Without a car I'll never make Bordeaux in time to catch the *Washington*."

"I can't help any more. The moment the armistice is signed Miss Kately will be leaving for Bordeaux. From that moment Inspector Krebs will be looking for you. Disappear now."

It was 4:00 A.M. when Upton dropped him at Les Halles. The chaos of porters, vegetable trucks and late-night revelers was much reduced from a month ago, but there were still enough handcarts to delay the Opel that had followed them from Fresnes, and the maze of alleys surrounding the market were well enough known to Chandler to make him confident that he had slipped any Gestapo tail. In the back room of a small café in the Rue Rambuteau, he ordered croissants and coffee and a large cognac—the market-workers' breakfast. He had no inclination to delve into the mystery of Arlette and Jacqueline.

Or perhaps the even greater mystery of Anne-Marie. In the café everybody was saying that the armistice would be signed tomorrow. Marshal Pétain, they said, had promised. He hadn't, of course, but he had already made it certain that there would be an armistice, and that was enough. For Chandler the impossible problem was to guess what the terms of such an armistice might be. Would the victorious Germans occupy the whole of France? Or just part of it? Would the Gestapo's writ run in the German part only? Or in the whole of France? Would Bordeaux be France or Germany? Or would it make no difference? Should he leave Paris now and join the refugees on the roads, or try to hole up in a small hotel for a few days?

He was incapable of coherent thought. Above all he knew he needed some sleep. His mind ranged over the names of Americans who had intended to stay on in Paris. None of his close friends were among them. Would an acquaintance risk his journalist's accreditation with the Occupation Authority to put him up for a few hours? Would it be safe even to chance going to an American journalist's house?

He thought of the Beckermans only on the second large brandy. After he had brought them out of Germany last month they had been lodged in a small, overpriced apartment a few streets from Les Halles. He had no doubt that they had already moved on south but he knew the concierge was willing to take a few hundred extra francs and ask no questions. All he wanted was a room and sleep.

He paid the bill at the café bar and went out into the street. Unshaven, stumbling from fatigue, he was just another of the drunks who had always haunted the Les Halles district.

Himmler scratched his head with one hand, resting the other lightly on his stomach. He was standing, barefoot, wrapped in a long woolen dressing gown that almost touched the floor, trying to clear the sleep from his mind.

The Reichsführer-SS was seldom at his best in the small hours.

Kaltenbrunner stood, stiff in full uniform and topcoat, near the door. Himmler waved him to a seat; he could do without this long-faced hulk looming over him.

"Tell me again, Ernst. Why does Krebs want to use more men?"

"To widen the search, Reichsführer, and to—"

"Yes, yes. So you said," Himmler interrupted. "This affair seems to be getting out of hand," he mused. "Killing the wrong girl. And was it necessary to burn down a church?"

"Most certainly, Reichsführer. For two reasons," Kaltenbrunner said eagerly. "Firstly, to distract the attention of the villagers while the café was entered and searched. Secondly, to destroy the baptism record, which, even though it was by no means conclusive, did give the date of birth. And if you consider that this record was the only one that—"

"Yes, yes. I remember now," Himmler interrupted again.

Kaltenbrunner waited in silence, sitting on the edge of a chair.

Suddenly Himmler turned to him, his voice much more authoritative now. "I cannot impress upon you too strongly the need for total security, absolute discretion in this matter."

"Of course, Reichsführer."

Himmler rubbed the bridge of his nose where his glasses usually sat. "So, these additional men Krebs wants?"

Kaltenbrunner now thought he knew the cause of Himmler's concern. "I can assure you that they will be told nothing; they will simply follow orders."

"Total security," Himmler yawned.

"Absolute discretion, Reichsführer."

Himmler nodded slowly and then stood very still, his eyes closing for long moments, as if the urge to sleep had become irresistible.

Kaltenbrunner waited.

Himmler was swaying gently on his feet, then his head slumped to one side and he jolted awake. He turned to stare at Kaltenbrunner. "Krebs can have his extra men," he said, "as many as he requires. Tell the inspector he has my authority to do whatever is necessary to resolve this unfortunate affair as quickly as possible."

"Yes, Reichsführer," said Kaltenbrunner, rising from the chair. "I am sorry to have disturbed you."

"No need for apologies," said Himmler. "We must be ready to concern ourselves with the Führer's well-being at any hour of the day or night. Heil Hitler."

"Heil Hitler." Kaltenbrunner returned the salute.

Himmler yawned again, then padded off to the bedroom.

As Kaltenbrunner came out of the hotel past the armed SS guards into the cool night air, he made a mental note to have Krebs's letter of authority typed up first thing in the morning. He wanted the Reichsführer himself to sign it as soon as possible. He considered it a wise precaution. An authorization to "do whatever is necessary" could be a dangerous instrument in the hands of a man like Krebs.

For over an hour Chandler had taken elaborate precautions to make sure he wasn't followed. Waiting in doorways, tracking back through the ancient *ruelles* that surrounded the market, he had made his cautious way to the crumbling row of houses where the Beckermans had stayed.

It was light now, the first early morning brightness of another day. When he tapped gently on the door of the back kitchen, he saw the concierge look up at him with infinite suspicion.

She opened the door a crack and Chandler pushed a dozen ten franc notes into the gap. "Who is it?" she hissed.

"Please, I want a room. For twenty-four hours, no more."

The concierge opened the door a little farther. Chandler slid into the kitchen. "I brought the Beckermans here," he said.

"A hundred and twenty francs," she said. "Have you papers?"

"Nobody has papers anymore, madame. They get lost on the road, stolen, burned in air attacks—"

"You're not French," she said.

"I'm American."

"Or English." The concierge eyed him warily.

"I'm American, madame. Neutral."

"You look English."

Chandler let the silence fall between them.

"In the first war," she said, "I worked in an English hospital in Bapaume."

"You were a nurse?"

"I washed the floors, monsieur. Every day I washed the blood from the floors. We were all young then. Mostly they laughed at their wounds. To lose a hand—the right hand was best—was joked about. A Blighty, they called it."

"A Blighty?"

"It meant with such a wound you would never go back to the front. One man I remember," she said. "A sergeant. When he was better we used to walk in the gardens. You could hear the guns in the distance. Rumbling, rumbling," she said, her eyes misting, "like a thunderstorm that never ends. Sergeant Smith, his name was." She pronounced it *Smiss*. "Sergeant Smith, did you ever know him in England, monsieur?"

Chandler shook his head. "No," he said. "I'm afraid not."

The concierge nodded. "In England, Sergeant Smith said it was a well-known family. Wellborn."

"It is," Chandler said. "I just don't happen to know them."

She composed her face. "For one night? A hundred and twenty francs for one night." She riffled the notes together and held them in her hand. "You brought the Beckermans here, you say."

"Don't you remember me?"

She shrugged. "Perhaps."

"You gave them a room on the top floor."

"It's not illegal."

"They had no papers either," Chandler said a little desperately.

"The Germans say everyone who rents a room must immediately report it to the Kommandeur." Already she had learned to work her tongue around the German word.

Chandler took another fifty francs from his pocket and proffered the note across the table.

She pushed his hand away. "Wait here," she said, then got up and waddled from the room.

When the heavy footsteps of a man sounded on the staircase a few minutes later, Chandler had already braced himself for the worst. He was too exhausted to make a run for it.

"Herr Chandler." Leo Beckerman stood, tall in the doorway, his wife Magda behind him. "We thought it must be you. Even though the concierge insisted you were an Englishman."

He clasped Chandler in a bear hug.

"It's good to see you again," Magda said, taking her turn to embrace him. "Very good."

"I didn't expect to see you both here," Chandler said. "I just thought of this as a safe house. I assumed you'd already be on your way south."

"We tried," said Leo Beckerman, "but the roads were clogged, blocked with refugees. We had to turn back. We are too old to run anymore."

Magda had slipped away and now returned with a liter bottle of wine and glasses. "Madame has allowed us the use of her kitchen to entertain the Englishman." She smiled quickly, glancing at her husband. "It's perhaps a little early to be drinking, but no matter."

Chandler slumped heavily in a chair, his face drained by fatigue.

"Are you all right, Herr Chandler?" asked Beckerman.

"I just need somewhere to stay."

"If I may ask, why would you, an American, need a safe house?"

"I'm on the run too, the Gestapo has taken my passport."

A sudden rattle of the door as it opened made them all start. It was the concierge.

"At six o'clock in the morning one should not be drinking red wine, monsieur." She bustled over to a cupboard and produced a half bottle of brandy. "If you must drink, it must be spirit."

The concierge placed the cognac in the middle of the table. "When you get back to England, monsieur, remember me to Sergeant Smiss."

They lifted their glasses and toasted the sergeant. Beckerman placed a hand on Chandler's shoulder and leaned close.

"Do not worry, Herr Chandler," Beckerman whispered. "This time I believe *we* can help *you*. Magda and I have decided to stay in Paris."

At just before one o'clock Beth Kately stood, dressed, a martini in one hand, a cigarette in the other, before the flower-filled chimneypiece. She was feeling inordinately pleased with herself. She had bent even the Gestapo to her will. Chandler had been released from Fresnes prison and was, Upton had just informed her, even now on his way to Bordeaux with Anne-Marie. Although she had been in the newspaper business since her teens, she preferred not to talk of scoops. They were for the cheap daily journalists whom she had risen so much above, yet this story gave the term a new meaning. If she could return to New York with Anne-Marie, it would be the scoop of the decade.

The adrenaline ran fast in her veins. Outside in the anteroom to her suite, Inspector Krebs was, for a second time, in attendance. Well, she knew she could deal with any problem he might care to raise.

She finished her martini and rang the bell for Upton to show the Gestapo man in.

Refilling her glass, she caught a glimpse of her image in the full-length mirror. Perhaps a little overweight, if she was honest, but then the flame-red dress suited her. She straightened up, smoothing the dress where it wrinkled at the top of her thighs. Where was Upton? She rang the bell again.

Crossing to the fireplace, she positioned herself. It was a bore not to be able to sit down. She would have much preferred to receive a visitor seated, but it was a problem of the dress riding up, always in the same place, where the thighs bulged beneath the girdle.

The door opened and, to her surprise, Inspector Krebs entered unattended by Martin Upton.

Angrily she looked past the German into the anteroom but could see nothing through the half-closed door. "Where is he?" she flared. "Where is Upton?"

Krebs smiled grotesquely. "I believe he's busy."

"What d'you want to see me about?" she snapped, her good mood totally evaporated. As she stormed past Krebs, she raised her voice. "Martin, get in here."

Krebs turned to watch her push open the door, then silently moved forward. She stood gasping, transfixed, staring into the anteroom.

"Miss Kately," Krebs whispered, now immediately behind her.

Beth Kately spun around, her face ashen, tight with fear. "You fool," she said. "I've cabled everything, I've sent the whole story to New York. It's already done."

Krebs shook his close-cropped head. "I've had all cables checked for the last five days. The mail for the United States is still in the sorting offices; my men are going through it at this moment. The transatlantic telephone, as I'm sure you know, has not been operating for over a week." Krebs smiled again, a terrible, mirthless grin. "There is nothing in New York."

Beth Kately trembled violently. "It's madness," she blurted. "Madness."

Krebs nodded silent agreement, his eyes wandering curiously down over the flame-red dress.

"Please," she begged, trembling uncontrollably.

After he hit her, Krebs stood back a moment savoring the pleasure of the soft, plump cheek under the hard edge of his massive hand. She had fallen in a heap on the carpet, then rolled onto her back, stunned, fighting for breath.

Krebs took a small knife from his pocket and opened the blade. Kneeling down, he cut the red dress free and tore it aside. He would take his special pleasure now, but first he must stuff a handkerchief in the mouth to stifle the screams of pain. Beth Kately's eyes stared up at him. He touched the side of her painted face with the blade. The head flopped sideways. Krebs felt for a pulse; she was dead, her neck broken by the blow meant to stun.

As he got to his feet and started to leave, the words of his report were already forming in his mind.

In the anteroom the Gestapo inspector paused a moment and glanced up at the hanging body of Martin Upton, doubting if the gaunt New Englander had had time to contemplate the thinness of the noose.

Chapter

Thirteen

IT WAS A part of Paris Chandler had never seen before. Leaving the metro at Porte St-Denis, he found himself in an area of long, cobbled streets lined with garages and decaying factory buildings. In the bright moonlight every stone, every house, every factory wall was a deep shade of gray. There were few corner cafés and even fewer shops. The only building that stood out from the industrial slum was an occasional school or a branch of the Crédit Lyonnais.

He had studied the map before leaving the Beckermans. Turning off the boulevard, he walked for a few minutes along the length of the canal. On both sides, ancient warehouses loomed over the glistening black water. From time to time he paused, standing in deep shadow, listening for the sound of following footsteps. But there was nothing. The area seemed devoid of people.

He knew now that he was almost there. On his right a small hump-backed bridge crossed the canal. Opposite, a row of workers' houses, low, peeling and mostly empty; on the street corner ahead, the rusting gates of an old factory.

He moved forward quickly now. There in the wall was the small iron gate as described. Beside it a poster advertised for the unemployed of Paris to join in the construction of anti-panzer barricades. A poster already from another world.

Chandler pushed the iron gate. It creaked open. Entering the cobbled courtyard, he saw that the inscription FORGES LITVINOV was still just legible in pale blue lettering across the factory's facade.

From his bag he took a flashlight Beckerman had given him and walked across the courtyard to a pair of sagging coach doors. Set in one of them was a smaller door, standing slightly ajar.

He pressed his hand against it, swinging it wider. Stepping over the sill, Chandler found himself in a cold, complete blackness. There was a smell of musty stone and perhaps a trace of motor oil. He pressed the button on the flashlight. The light leaped out and splayed across a scarred, yellow wall. He moved the beam along the wall. A broken door, a pile of heavy cast-iron machinery, a notice board barely hanging from a bent nail in crumbling plaster.

He played the beam out in the other direction. His spine tingled with the sudden certainty that he was not alone.

Chandler moved cautiously forward. The smell of motor oil was stronger but mixed incongruously with something else. The moving flashlight beam picked out the stripped-down chassis of an old truck and, farther left, a narrow staircase leading to the basement.

In the silence the faint click as he extinguished the flashlight sounded loud in his ear. As he listened, in total darkness, he could just hear a human being breathing close to him.

Chandler aimed the flashlight and switched it on. The beam hit the girl full in the face.

It was Anne-Marie Claudel.

"Who's there," she said, flinching away, her hand rising to shield her face from the light.

"It's Chandler. Theo Chandler."

"Take that light away."

Chandler lowered the beam to the floor.

Anne-Marie looked at him coldly. "What are you doing here?"

"For Christ's sake," said Chandler, suddenly full of anger. "I'm here because of you, because of the Gestapo. You must know that?"

The light, bouncing off the floor, flickered on their faces.

For a moment Anne-Marie was silent. "This way," she said, guiding the flashlight in his hand toward a flight of concrete steps. He led the way down, the light probing before them. At the last turn of the stairs they entered a wide, steel-joisted cellar.

Two couples lay sleeping on bedding rolls in the far corner. One of the men looked up, an old kerosene lamp lighting his startled face.

"It's all right," said Anne-Marie with a reassuring gesture. "This man is known to me."

Professor Mendel stood up from his wife's side. "He is also known to me, mademoiselle."

He came forward to Chandler's side, touching his arm lightly as a greeting. "Mr. Chandler, we meet again."

Mendel was dressed in a coarse shirt, rough trousers and jacket—peasant's clothing that hung loosely on his small frame. He was shoeless.

"I hardly recognized you in your finery," said Chandler.

Mendel smiled, his brown eyes shining in the soft light. "Golda says I look like a circus clown. Come," he said, leading Chandler across to his family.

"Golda, look who's here."

Frau Mendel's eyes opened sleepily as her husband's hand touched her shoulder. She looked up, then smiled in recognition.

"Felix, Sarah, you remember our fearless driver," said Mendel.

Felix and Sarah said quiet hellos, but to Chandler, their

young faces seemed to have developed the fixed, haunted look he had come to recognize on so many faces in Nazi Europe.

Mendel sat on his bedroll. Beside him, Chandler crouched down on his haunches. "The Beckermans have decided to stay in Paris," Chandler said.

"Yes, we know," said Mendel.

"They have given me their place."

"So, you are going south," said Mendel, pulling on a pair of hand-tooled leather shoes of obvious quality.

"Yes," said Chandler. "What are the arrangements?"

"We leave for a place called the Château d'Arblay as soon as the gasoline arrives," Mendel said. "Two cars, there's plenty of room. Perhaps my wife and I will have the pleasure of your company on the journey."

"I'd like that," Chandler said.

"We have one planned stop on the way down," said Mendel, "at a hotel owned by an uncle of Mademoiselle Claudel's."

The professor stood up, raising his arms to shoulder height. "So, what do you think of Mendel the French garlic farmer?" he said.

Chandler smiled. "Perhaps the footwear is not entirely in the spirit of the rest of the disguise. But apart from that, bravo, monsieur."

"These shoes stay with me," said Mendel firmly.

Chandler became aware that Anne-Marie had moved away. Glancing over his shoulder, he saw her disappearing up the concrete steps to the factory above. "And Anne-Marie?" he asked. "What does she plan to do?"

"She is staying in Paris. She and Monsieur Litvinov still feel they can be of use here."

"Where is Litvinov?"

"We are waiting for him now. He is arranging for the gasoline," Mendel said, taking a gold pocket watch from his jacket. A tiny chime tinkled as he opened the cover. "But he is late. Very late."

Chandler mounted the steps to the disused factory. The

large coach doors were open. He walked to the entrance.

In the cold, silvery light of the moon, Anne-Marie stood immobile in the courtyard, her arms folded, drawing her shoulders tight. She turned slowly as Chandler came forward to her side.

"What time is it?" she asked in a low voice.

"Almost two."

She lowered her head, pressing her lips together.

"Where is Litvinov getting the gasoline?"

"I don't know," she said. "All I know is that if it is still possible to find a few liters in Paris, Paul will find them."

"You've decided not to leave?"

"Not yet."

"You know the Gestapo is hunting for you?"

"They're looking for anyone who worked for Jewish resettlement."

"So, after all that's happened, you're going to stay on?"

"After Jacqueline's death, you mean?"

"After Jacqueline's murder and your mother's," Chandler said deliberately.

Her face, in the moonlight, was as if etched in stone. "How did you know about my mother?" She had taken a step away from him.

"I went to St-Eloi," Chandler said. "Trying to find you for an American woman journalist who thought she had a story. The Gestapo also seems to think there's a story. Maybe it's the same one." Chandler paused. "What's it all about, for God's sake? Do you know who killed your mother and Jacqueline?"

For a long time she was silent. "Yes," she said at length. "I know the Boche swine who killed them."

"Are you saying it was the Gestapo?" Chandler asked slowly.

For a moment Anne-Marie seemed about to reply. Then she checked herself, shaking her head angrily. "You are mad to ask me these questions," she said. "Aren't you in enough trouble? Travel south with the others and cross into Spain. Go back to America and forget all this ever happened.''

Chandler stepped forward and took her arm. ''I have a right to some answers.''

The anger seemed to drain from her. ''Perhaps, but I have no right to give them to you.''

Chandler's hand dropped from her arm. Anne-Marie turned and walked back toward the factory.

''Don't ask me, monsieur,'' she said, pausing in the doorway. ''It's a death sentence for you to know.''

Downstairs in the cellar they could hear the Mendels talking in low voices. In the partitioned office on the factory floor Chandler had lit an oil lamp. Anne-Marie sat on an old wooden chair against the wall. As the minutes ticked away the lamp guttered and smoked between them. From time to time she would hold up her wrist at an angle to catch the light and peer at the face of her watch. But she no longer spoke. Mostly she sat, her legs crossed, on the straight-backed chair, staring through the open doorway of the office into the darkness of the factory floor beyond.

Suddenly she stood. Chandler crossed the office to join her. Together they strained to hear. Outside the factory an engine was idling. As it died they heard the outside gate creak open and footsteps cross the courtyard.

''It's Paul,'' she said, moving forward.

Chandler pulled her back by the arm, restraining her. ''Wait. There are two of them,'' he said. He swung around quickly and extinguished the lamp.

The coach doors opened and two uniformed figures came in.

''Anyone here?'' a voice called.

Chandler peered through the gloom. ''Germans,'' he whispered.

Anne-Marie gripped Chandler's arm. ''Oh, my God. No.''

One of the figures had a powerful flashlight. The beam

searched the factory floor, then moved relentlessly toward the office.

Chandler looked desperately around for a line of escape. There was only the doorway, and the beam of light was already there.

"There's someone in here," the voice called.

The beam settled on Anne-Marie and Chandler, huddled together against the wall.

"Light the lamp," the voice said.

Chandler hesitated, then relit the oil lamp. As he turned up the flame he saw the large German sergeant in the office doorway. Under the army forage cap the broad, snub-nosed face was firmly set. "You the ones for the gasoline?"

"Yes," said Chandler, barely able to get the word out.

"I've got some bad news for you," the sergeant said, looking at Anne-Marie. "The gentleman's been arrested."

"Paul's been arrested?" Anne-Marie said desperately. "Paul Litvinov?"

The sergeant's face broke into a grim smile. "He wasn't likely to tell me his name, was he? The gentleman who agreed to the deal. This *is* the right place?"

"Yes, it's the right place," said Chandler quickly.

The sergeant swung into the room. In one hand he carried a jerrican. Behind him the other German placed two further jerricans of gasoline inside the office.

"Please," said Anne-Marie, "where was he arrested?"

The sergeant pushed the cap to the back of his head. "He asked to be taken to some place near Boulevard St-Michel before we came here. He said he wanted to pick up some money. It wasn't for us," the sergeant said earnestly. "We'd already been paid."

"He went to his apartment?" asked Anne-Marie.

"Could be. We waited at the end of the street. Then a car comes screaming around the corner. We hung around long enough to see them drag the gentleman into the street and bundle him into the car, then we left.''

Tears were building in Anne-Marie's eyes.

"Who were they?'' Chandler asked.

"Plainclothes,'' the sergeant said.

"French?''

The sergeant shook his head. "Gestapo.'' He paused. "Look, it's not difficult to guess what this is for.'' He pointed down to the jerricans. "If I were you, I'd go now. There's no point in hanging around. The gentleman —he's Jewish isn't he?''

Anne-Marie nodded glumly.

The sergeant moved closer to Chandler and lowered his voice. "They'll have this address out of him in no time. You and the lady get moving or you'll both end up in Gestapo headquarters.''

"Please hurry,'' Chandler said, squeezing a last suitcase into the trunk of the old Citroën. "Get into the car. The rest of your bags will have to go inside.''

The first hint of dawn was already lightening the eastern skyline.

The Mendels obeyed, their faces expectant. Golda and Sarah sat in the rear with bedrolls on their laps.

The professor was the last to get in. He held out his hand as he stood by the front passenger door. Chandler shook it; the grip was firm.

"Goodbye,'' said Mendel. "If we do meet again, be assured we will remember you, Mr. Chandler.''

"Good luck,'' said Chandler, as Felix started the engine.

Chandler found himself waving until the car turned a corner and was gone from his sight. As he walked back toward the factory entrance he glanced at the other car, a Renault. He had shared the gasoline equally between the two tanks. Both had been empty, both were now almost full.

Anne-Marie was waiting by the tangle of scrap machinery inside the factory. Chandler could see she had been crying.

"We have to leave," Chandler said simply. "Now."

"I told you, I can't. Not yet."

Chandler took out a cigarette and lit it. "If the Gestapo has Litvinov, he won't hold out for long; nobody can. We can't expect him to."

"You should have gone with the others."

Chandler pulled on the cigarette. "Do you think they'll release him? Is that what you think?" He felt his frustration rising. " 'Thank you very much, Herr Litvinov. We know you are head of the resettlement agency and a Jew yourself, but you are free to go.' "

The tears were streaming down her face again. "I can't leave him," she sobbed. "I must be sure."

"One hour," Chandler said, grinding his cigarette into the oily floor.

"Why are you doing this?" Anne-Marie asked. "Why didn't you go with the rest?"

"We'll wait one hour, no longer," he said firmly. Why *was* he doing it? Chandler wondered ruefully. Could it be he was, at last, taking sides? If so, he was sure it was a lost cause. The Gestapo would be here well within the hour; he felt certain of that.

Alone in the room as the key turned in the lock behind him, Paul Litvinov stood with his back to the wall. Someone had taken his jacket, and his paunch sagged out over the top of his neat, pin-striped trousers. The space was lit by a single naked light bulb, hanging from the ceiling, and was empty of furniture except for a table and wooden chair. Perhaps it was the simplicity of the room that made the horror of the smears of blood across the walls and the full hanks of bloodied hair on the linoleum-covered floor seem remote, unreal.

He crossed quickly to the single window and pulled the curtains aside. Four iron bars had been screwed into the window frame. To lever one off, even if he were able to do it with a chair leg, would be impossible with a guard outside. He drew the curtains neatly together and sat on the edge of the table. Whatever happened to him, he knew Anne-Marie and the others needed time.

The key turned in the lock. The door opened and Inspector Krebs walked in. He wore a neat suit and what seemed to Litvinov, even in his present plight, a ridiculous bowler hat. Litvinov stood. Ignoring his prisoner, Krebs removed his hat and, carefully choosing a place free of bloodstains, laid it on the table.

"I had your friend Bilescu in here earlier tonight," Krebs said in an almost conversational tone. He pulled the chair away from the table and sat down.

"Bilescu is no friend of mine," said Litvinov.

"Nevertheless, you may be interested to know that a relatively young man like Bilescu didn't last ten minutes," Krebs said.

"I assume he told you everything. Whatever everything was," said Litvinov, surprising himself with the calmness of his voice.

Krebs scowled. "Kneel there," he said. "Just in front of the table."

Litvinov lowered himself onto his knees. The hank of hair on the floor in front of him was blond, once brightly dyed and now matted with blood. He raised his eyes barely above the level of the table. The round, almost childlike face of Krebs stared down at him.

"When you were arrested at your apartment you denied you were Paul Isaak Litvinov," Krebs said. "Why was that?"

Litvinov shrugged.

Almost as he did so, Krebs propelled himself forward from the chair, his boot slamming into the small of Litvinov's back, hurling him forward onto the floor. Bawling, stamping, kicking, inspired by some professional fury, the Gestapo officer as suddenly turned away and resumed his seat.

Litvinov raised his hand to the open split in his nose. He was lying flat on the floor, his face turned so that the wet linoleum touched his cheek.

Somewhere above, he heard Krebs's voice commanding him to kneel. He felt little pain, but his body

responded slowly. He rolled over and pushed himself up
on his hands. He had heard from someone—he could no
longer remember from whom-—that these frenzied as-
saults by the interrogator were a favored Gestapo technique, designed to induce in the prisoner a sense that he
was now beyond all canons of human behavior.

"Where is she?" Krebs said, looking down at him over
the edge of the table. "Where is Anne-Marie Claudel?"

Litvinov's mouth was full of blood. The palms of his
hands squeaked on the bloodied linoleum. He brought his
head up. Now the pain was hammering inside his skull.

"Where is she?"

"You're too late." Blood dribbled from his mouth.
Since the day the Germans had arrived in Paris he had
wondered how he would withstand capture and torture.
What he had not anticipated was the strength that came
from knowing that, minute by minute, he was thwarting
them. "She left Paris days ago."

"With the American, Chandler?"

Paul Litvinov climbed to his knees. His head was
spinning. He made a massive effort to think clearly. What
harm was there in saying she was with the American? He
had no idea where the American was, probably on his way
back to America. But for the Gestapo, it could only
confuse the issue.

"With the American?" Krebs repeated.

"Yes," Litvinov nodded. "With the American."

They had waited the full hour.

In the passenger seat of the old Renault Anne-Marie
slept fitfully. Next to her, at the wheel, Chandler was
hunched forward, his face drawn with tension and lack of
sleep. For several moments, as her eyes opened once
again, Anne-Marie struggled to make sense of the sounds
outside: it was as if they were surrounded by a huge flock
of chattering birds.

She rubbed her cheeks, aware now that the sounds on
the road outside were human voices. Drawing herself
upright in her seat, she found herself looking out on a sea

of humanity, moving past the front of the car, back in the direction of Paris. As Chandler edged the car forward into the mass of people, she became fully awake. In the wide fields on either side of the road thousands of peasant families sat despondently, or drifted aimlessly, as if at some massive, nightmarish picnic. Abandoned cars leaned drunkenly in the ditches. Groups of unarmed French soldiers were sprinkled along the line of approaching people or lay sleeping under the hedgerows. On a distant hill smoke rose from a burning farmhouse; somewhere to the south, in the direction they were heading, she could hear what she thought was gunfire.

The fate of Paul Litvinov flooded back, making her gasp out loud.

"It's been like this ever since we left Paris," Chandler said, glancing across at her. He gestured to the press of bodies—women and men, children, young and old—as they flowed past the car.

For a few moments Anne-Marie watched, appalled. "Do they know where they're going?" she said.

"They did. They were running from the Germans. Now the German Army has overtaken them, I guess they're going home."

She stared ahead through the dusty windshield at the glowering faces. An old woman shook her fist as she was forced to squeeze around the car. Anne-Marie didn't seem to notice. Chandler knew she was thinking of Litvinov but he could find no words of comfort.

"Perhaps he is dead already," she said. "What else is there to wish for?"

Litvinov lay unconscious on the linoleum floor. The curtains were still drawn over the window, although daylight was clearly visible through the thin material. A small, blackened kettle stood on the table above his head, a wisp of steam floating from the spout.

The morning sounds of Paris filtered into the room. In his vomit, blood, urine, and the boiling water that had been poured over his head, Paul Isaak Litvinov stirred.

The surge of pain from his scalded face brought him quickly to consciousness. Slowly he became aware that he was alone in the room. His tormentor had left.

He dragged himself onto his knees. The pain was lessening now. He reached out for the edge of the table with his left hand; the right was blue and twisted, the fingers splayed out, swollen to twice their normal size. He found he had no memory of how this had happened. Grunting with effort, he hauled himself upright.

Standing, he experienced a wave of exhilaration. The pain had faded. His eyes saw nothing. His brutalized body felt apart, separated from the untouched clarity of his mind. Krebs had done his worst and Litvinov had told him nothing. He had won. He was free.

Paul Litvinov crashed to the floor. Life had left him.

Chapter
Fourteen

FOR TWO DAYS the leafy silence of a clearing in the
Forest of Compiègne, north of Paris, had been broken by
the roar of pneumatic drills as a company of German
Army engineers demolished the wall of a museum that
housed the most famous *wagon-lit* in the world. In this
same sleeping car, at 5 A.M. on November 11, 1918, the
vanquished German generals of the Kaiser's army had
signed the armistice that had ended the Great War. Now
the *wagon-lit* was to be removed from its museum and
replaced on the rusting railway tracks where it had once
stood, and in front of which was a granite block whose
inscription read: HERE ON THE ELEVENTH OF NOVEMBER,
1918 SUCCUMBED THE CRIMINAL PRIDE OF THE GERMAN
EMPIRE —VANQUISHED BY THE FREE PEOPLES WHICH IT
TRIED TO ENSLAVE.

It was Adolf Hitler's chosen setting for the harsh terms
he was about to impose on France to be delivered. He
stood now, flanked by his generals, and by Raeder,
Goering, Ribbentrop and Rudolf Hess, in the midafternoon of June 21, before the great granite block, reading
the engraved French words.

Nobody moved as the Führer stood, savoring the moment of his greatest triumph. Then he turned and, with a peremptory movement of his hand, he gestured his officers to follow him into the *wagon-lit*.

In the twenty-four articles handed to the French delegation by General Keitel, the German terms were made known. The French Army was to be disarmed and the million prisoners already taken by the Germans were to remain in captivity. More than half the area of France was to be occupied and under the administration of the German forces. The remaining lands, south of the demarcation line, were to be under the administration of Marshal Pétain's government. But the slender hope that even this remaining area would be free from German interference was destroyed by a later clause of the document. The Pétain government would be required to deliver to the Gestapo all anti-Nazi German refugees who had left Germany for France since Hitler came to power—and all French citizens who were designated as offenders against the German Reich.

The terms of the armistice were declared by Keitel to be "unalterable." Throughout that night and through most of the following day Pétain and his government in Bordeaux debated the document. Then came a further message from the French delegation at Compiègne: Keitel had given the government in Bordeaux just one hour in which to sign. Within the hour, the terms were formally accepted.

In London, General de Gaulle used the BBC to speak to France. He detailed the terms of the armistice, then scornfully addressed himself to Marshal Pétain: "The country, the government, you yourself are reduced to servitude. Ah, to obtain, and accept such an enslavement we did not need the conqueror of Verdun. Anyone else would have sufficed!"

News of the armistice spread like fire through dry grass. Refugee peasants shouted the terms to cars plowing south. German soldiers in heavy trucks called down to the columns of people on the road, and with them shared a pleasure that the war was over. At crossroads cafés and in small villages it was sometimes possible to see local people and German soldiers celebrating together as this strangest of wars dwindled. By early evening, roughly printed ten-franc broadsheets that listed the details of the armistice were being hawked along the side of the road.

As night began to fall, small groups of refugees lit fires on the hillside and unpacked cooking pots. Cows were milked and young children bedded down for the night. From the side of a wood the strains of a harmonica floated across the night.

Darkness, blurring the events of the day, the fatigue and anguish on the faces of the refugees, extinguished reality. Chandler had turned the Renault off the road and parked it under a clump of trees at the foot of a rolling hill. Wearily he and Anne-Marie climbed out.

Leaving the car, they walked along the groups of peasants around their cooking fires. Catching the warm smell of soup and drifting wood smoke, it was easy to imagine they were passing through some vast gypsy encampment. Some groups were singing to the strains of an accordion; children skipped in and out of the firelight, collecting wood from the copse. Nobody any longer paid attention to the sound of aircraft passing high overhead or to the flashes of gunfire still to be seen on the hills around them.

"Have you heard?" A man stumbled toward them, a liter bottle of wine in his hand. "The Germans want us all back on our farms. They say they're willing to pay five hundred francs per person to help us back north."

"And are you going?" Chandler asked as the man stumbled along beside them.

"I sold my stock on the road," the man said. "What use am I to the Germans now?"

"In any case," said another farmer, who joined them, "it's the young ones they are interested in, not us. Watch yourself, monsieur." He nudged Chandler. "They've set up roadblocks. Any man of military age can find himself arrested. They want workers to clear up the mess. In this war you don't have to be in uniform to be a prisoner.''

Chandler and Anne-Marie moved on, leaving the farmers behind. Ahead of them kerosene lights glowed, and as they approached they saw a makeshift market had been set up in a glade of oak trees. Lamps hung from the branches overhead, and from the back of farm carts and trestle tables peasants sold eggs and milk, vegetables and meat. A German patrol, rifles slung on their shoulders, passed through the lamp-lit glade, the leading soldier munching on a piece of sausage.

They stood back in the darkness while the patrol passed. Chandler watched, as the Germans, without unslinging their rifles, passed a group of French soldiers drinking around a makeshift bar.

''When it's all over,'' Anne-Marie said, ''will anybody understand what happened here in France in these days?''

They bought hard-boiled eggs, bread and a liter of wine and carried them back to the car.

From a small boy, singing like a Paris news vendor, Anne-Marie bought a copy of an armistice broadsheet. While Chandler collected sticks for the fire she stood in the light of the Renault's headlamps, reading.

He arranged thin twigs in an inverted cone over a few sheets of rolled-up newspaper.

''Officially,'' she said, looking up from the broadsheet, ''the armistice comes into force tomorrow. In fact, France is already out of the battle.''

He put a match to the newspaper under the sticks. ''Does it give details of the terms?''

''There's to be a line drawn across the country,'' she said. ''Somewhere south of here, in the Loire. North of the line will be the occupied zone.''

''And the French government will still rule in the south?''

''The French government will rule nothing without German permission,'' Anne-Marie said bitterly. ''Marshal Pétain has agreed to return people on the Gestapo's wanted list to Paris.''

She screwed the broadsheet into a ball and threw it on the now blazing fire. "Where did you learn to light a fire like that?" she said. "In the Boy Scouts of America?"

He could see how moved she had been by what she had just read.

"I learned to light a fire like that," he said deliberately, "in the Hitler Youth."

He watched the words send a perceptible shock through her. "The Hitler Youth!"

"Sit down." He drew her down beside him in front of the fire.

"You were in the Hitler Youth?"

"When I was a boy," Chandler said, "shortly after my mother died, my father decided to make a visit to Germany. His father had emigrated to the United States as a young man, and the family had kept up some sort of correspondence with various German cousins in Bavaria. I remember my father even then as a strange man, a solitary, anxious to impress his Bavarian relatives with the quality of his very poor German."

Chandler held out his glass, and Anne-Marie filled it with red wine from the bottle. "I guess this is as good a time as any to get the story off my chest," he said.

"I think you're saying," she said, "that your father was more at home in Germany than in America."

"Without a doubt. From a fairly average American, something of a failure in the business world perhaps, he became a German patriot pretty well overnight. More than a patriot, he became a nationalist. We were staying in Munich at the time, and the name of Adolf Hitler was already on everybody's lips."

Anne-Marie shivered involuntarily. "Your father became a Nazi?" she said.

"He joined the Nazi Party. And I joined the new Hitler Youth organization," Chandler said ruefully.

Anne-Marie sipped her wine. "What happened to him? Your father?"

"For a few months he worked as a translator on the Party newspaper, the *Völkischer Beobachter*, but I knew he was really looking for glory.'' Chandler paused, remembering those days. "I was sent back to America, to my grandfather's very anti-Nazi care.''

Chandler drank some wine. Anne-Marie waited patiently for him to go on.

"I pieced the rest of it together later,'' Chandler said. "It seems he joined the local Bavarian unit of the Storm Troopers, the SA, and found his life's fulfillment in breaking up the opposition's political meetings. Odd for such a retiring, shy man. But that's how it was. Then, at one of the meetings, he was hit by a flying beer bottle. He fell in the middle of a milling crowd in the Hofbräuhaus. He was trampled to death. July 1929.''

Chandler was aware that Anne-Marie's eyes were unwaveringly on him.

"They sent his uniform back to my grandfather. He burned it.'' Chandler drained his glass.

"What made you tell me this?'' she asked.

"I'm not sure,'' Chandler said. "Sometimes confidences encourage confidences.''

For a moment their eyes met. Then Anne-Marie turned her head away.

When they had finished eating they unrolled their blankets beneath a heavy-leafed oak tree. All around them on the hillside they could hear the bargaining and gossip of what seemed to be a village fair, the cries of small children and the barking of dogs. Beyond the branches of the oak tree an almost full moon stood motionless in the clear night sky.

Anne-Marie lay on her back, her hands behind her head. "I thought you were a simple man; by simple I mean uncomplicated. Simple needs, simple lusts, simple hates, simple loves. Now I'm not so sure.''

"I'll have to think about that,'' Chandler said.

"Are you frightened about tomorrow?'' she asked.

"Of course,'' said Chandler. "All this is only tolerable in the dark.''

*   *   *

Shortly after noon, along the straight-ribbon of road that led north from Paris, the five black Mercedeses made good speed. Leading the way, the Leutnant commanding the motorcycle escort detachment urged his men on as he saw, in his rearview mirrors, the leading limousine begin to close. Bringing up the rear, the half-track platoon was forced to push its heavily armored vehicles at maximum speed.

After his whirlwind tour of the French capital Adolph Hitler was in an irrepressible mood.

"As a young man in Vienna," he said to his architect, Albert Speer, seated beside him in the backseat of the leading, open-topped Mercedes, "I dreamed constantly of seeing Paris. Naturally I am not referring to the tourist Paris, to the decadence which, even at that time, was beginning to eat out the heart of the French nation. No, I had one object only: I wished to see, to bathe in the splendor of the Opéra, the finest building constructed by man. Now my wish has been granted."

Speer nodded silent agreement.

"When we rebuild Berlin, Speer, the Paris Opéra house will be our model, our guide to the canons of good taste and great architecture. You agree?"

Without waiting for an answer Hitler leaned forward and tapped the driver on the shoulder. "Erich, where are we now?"

"We're only a hundred kilometers from Paris. Shall I put my foot down?"

Hitler laughed into the slipstream. "You will have to face the commander of the escort if you do."

The convoy sped on across the flatlands of northern France, through hamlets and villages straddling the poplar-lined *route nationale,* or nestled on the side roads leading off into the countryside. The gleaming vehicles raced north through Foy-la-Paix, Helran, Bocusse.

"Stop," bawled the Führer, above the wind.

The chauffeur slammed his foot down. The big Mercedes, its brakes screeching in protest, came to an even halt. Behind, the other limousines skidded and slithered to shuddering stops, hurling their occupants forward. Out in front the Leutnant glanced again in his mirrors and signaled frantically to the *Zundapp* detachment to turn around. Heinrich Himmler led the group running forward, scrabbling to try and free his pistol from the holster at his waist, his face white with alarm.

"What's wrong, mein Führer?" Himmler asked, fluttering the pistol about his head.

"Put that thing away before you do yourself some damage." Hitler stood in the open car, resting his arms on the raised side window.

The *Zundapp* riders screamed their machines to a stop, and the Leutnant sat back in his saddle in relief. Hitler was smiling.

Martin Bormann came to a slow halt, dabbing a handkerchief at a graze on his forehead. The sudden braking had sent his head crashing into the seat in front. The entourage gathered around; all eyes were on their leader.

"There, gentlemen. I knew it couldn't be far from here." Adolf Hitler pointed to a battered signpost. "Jean-le-Blanc. In the last war, gentlemen, I spent eight months in this area as a front-line soldier."

Himmler fumbled to replace his pistol in its holster. Bormann sniffed. Hitler didn't seem to notice, he was staring out across the countryside.

"We were up against the Scots," he said. " 'The devils in skirts,' we called them. For eight months we tore at each other's throats." Hitler scanned the landscape again, in quick darting glances from landmark to landmark, as if trying to gain his bearings. Now he looked down at the *Zundapp* riders, staring up at him from under their helmets. "You lads are too young," he said, "to know what an old soldier feels. Attachment to dead comrades; the burning determination to continue the struggle. For them."

Hatless, his dark straight hair ruffled by the breeze, he

clasped his hands together in front of his pale trenchcoat in the familiar pose. "The ghosts of thousands of good Germans inhabit these woods," he said. "Let's visit the village and call on their memory."

Himmler suddenly felt his pulse thundering throughout his body.

"*Putain!*" the hotel café owner shouted. "This is my hotel."

"Back against the wall, old man," the young Leutnant said, pressing the flat of his hand on the Frenchman's chest.

The owner stood against the wall with five or six others. "Who is out there?" he asked. "Who is so important that we have to be lined up like cattle?"

The Leutnant stepped forward. "Be patient," he said. "Stay back against the wall. You'll soon be able to finish your drinks."

Outside, the village square had been cleared. In one corner an armored half-track stood as a silent sentinel.

The disused pump creaked rustily as Hitler tried the handle. He turned slowly on his heels and gazed around at the church, the *boucherie*, a couple of ancient bicycles leaning against a wall, the shuttered windows of the drab, anonymous houses.

"The same," Hitler murmured almost inaudibly; then he strode off to the café-hotel, Himmler, Bormann and the rest in his wake.

A trooper with a Schmeisser pointing at the floor stood in each corner of the room. The café's owner could hear the approach of German voices.

The door opened.

Neither the owner nor the others pressed against the wall could believe their eyes. Standing in the doorway, his weight on one leg, his head slightly bowed, taking in the room with penetrating eyes under dark eyebrows, Adolf Hitler pervaded all with his presence.

He stepped forward. Jostling behind him in their anxiety to examine the café-hotel, Himmler and the young architect, Speer, pressed forward among the other officers.

"Unchanged," Hitler announced. "The tables, the chairs; all the cafés in all the villages are the same. On some nights the British counterbatteries would knock your glass against your teeth."

For a moment his pale eyes raked the faces of the men against the wall, then he smacked his hand down flat on the table beside him. "This was our *Stammtisch*," he said. "Breitmann, Schpentzer, Kroll, Rumminger. Simple soldiers. They gave their lives for today."

The Führer stood for a moment and then turned. As his entourage pressed back to clear a path to the door, the Austrian-born leader walked slowly out into the square.

Back at the line of waiting Mercedeses on the narrow road just outside the village, Himmler found himself alone at Hitler's side. Could he speak? Was this the moment, he wondered? Then he noticed the Führer was staring at him, the eyes penetrating, the head a little on one side. The Reichsführer-SS almost froze with panic as he suddenly thought, by some mysterious means, those eyes might bore into his head and read what was in his mind.

Himmler's lips moved soundlessly, the words unformed. But Hitler was already turning away to climb into his Mercedes.

As the Reichsführer stumbled back to his own car, the photograph in his wallet seemed to burn like a hot coal in the breast pocket of his shirt.

Rejoining the main road, the convoy headed north. As it gathered speed, nobody noticed the small road sign pointing off to the right; it read: ST-ELOI 2 KILOMÈTRES.

At the newly established Gestapo 1 headquarters on the Rue des Saussaies, Emil Krebs was hunched over a large-scale map of France. Around him the activity among the dozen Gestapo clerks in the long, third-story room was intense. Details of an American wanted for murder had been circulated to every French gendarmerie between Paris and the demarcation line now being established from the Spanish border near the coast diagonally up to Tours and across France between Tours and the Swiss border.

The description of Theo Chandler was accurate: a man in his early thirties, 1.90 meters tall, fair-haired. Almost totally fluent German, accentless. Fluent French, but with a marked American accent. Most importantly, a photograph had been issued, a rough blowup from the catalogue of an exhibition of paintings Chandler had held at a small gallery in Paris.

The description of an accomplice, Anne-Marie Delpech, formerly Claudel, was less helpful. A woman in her twenties, dark haired, above average height at 1.75 meters. Krebs, of course, knew the exact date of birth but had avoided using it.

It was on the demarcation line itself that the Gestapo inspector concentrated. Every principal road to the south was already sealed off, according to the latest Wehrmacht reports. A detain and arrest order with an "urgent action" classification had gone out to each of the crossing points, and Gestapo officers were already supervising the processing of refugees.

Yet Krebs knew it was not enough. There were eight million people on the roads of France. The chances of his quarry slipping through the net were far higher than he dared risk.

In the middle of the bustling activity of his clerks, Krebs examined the problem. Litvinov was dead, although before he died he had given the information that Anne-Marie and Chandler had left Paris and were together. Bilescu was in a room immediately above. Perhaps he might yet prove useful. But at present Krebs was sure the Rumanian knew nothing of the destination of the American and the girl. One savage beating had produced every confession one could wish, except the one Krebs wanted most.

Again Krebs ran his finger up and down the main roads

leading from Paris to the south. Where would they stop at night? Where would they buy food? The girl came from the north, St-Eloi, but it was possible, of course, that she had relatives in south or central France. Krebs's finger stopped on the map. Short of food and gasoline, might they not be heading for a village somewhere where they could rest for a day or so? Even if they had already succeeded in crossing the demarcation line, might they not be heading for help from a cousin or aunt?

Krebs picked up the telephone on the desk in front of him. From the map, he saw that Amiens was the nearest town of any size to St-Eloi.

"Give me the Gestapo unit in Amiens," he snapped into the phone. He knew it was a slender chance, but as he waited for the connection his confidence began to grow.

"I want a section sent to the village of St-Eloi," he said to the Gestapo duty officer. "Find anybody who knows the Claudel family. I want a list of every relative or friend of the family living south of Paris. A complete list. Don't be gentle." He frowned as he listened to the reply. "Inspector Emil Krebs," he snapped, "and you may be certain I have the highest authority."

The attic room was completely devoid of furnishings. Bilescu crouched on the dusty floorboards, finishing off the list. His fingers holding the pencil were trembling. He was naked except for underpants and socks. Krebs had had the rest of his clothing removed as a precaution against the prisoner taking his own life. Suicide, of course, was the last possible idea that would have entered the Rumanian's mind. Above all else, he was a survivor.

After the first incredible, shattering assault, during which Krebs had literally yanked a great handful of golden hair from his scalp and tossed it on the floor, there had been no violence. Bilescu had answered every question, cooperated in every way, confessed to anything.

He felt gingerly between his swollen lips, checking the

line of his perfect teeth by touch. One was loose, but by
some miracle all were still in his head.

An hour ago Krebs had appeared with paper and
pencil, demanding a list. All names, all addresses, all
contacts no matter how tenuous, the Rumanian had ever
had with Chandler, Anne-Marie Claudel, Jacqueline
Claudel, or Litvinov and the Jewish Resettlement Agency.
That was simple enough; he had complied.

Krebs was a sadistic bastard; he recognized that fact.
But Bilescu's agile, devious mind was already scheming
ways in which he might ingratiate himself with the brute.
The Gestapo was the power in France now; he saw that
clearly. And the Rumanian had always found it expedient,
and true to his own instincts, to align himself with those
in power. It was the obvious, logical thing to do.

A last name occurred to him. Bilescu added it to the
bottom of the list. Beckerman.

In a full day's traveling Chandler and Anne-Marie
found they were lucky to cover more than thirty or forty
kilometers. Sometimes they would find a relatively clear
stretch of road, not blocked by peasant carts. But at other
times the holdup could stretch through the whole, blaz-
ingly hot, afternoon.

They had decided not to travel at night. The massive
congestion during the day at least provided anonymity,
and at night long convoys of German supply trucks swept
along the road. The encampments in the woods were full
of stories of arrests by the German Field Security Police,
on suspicion of sabotage. For the most part Chandler and
Anne-Marie discounted the rumors; the Germans were
still too busy supplying a vast army, rounding up the
scattered units of French military personnel and establish-
ing their demarcation line to concern themselves with
suspected saboteurs. But it was becoming increasingly
clear that men of military age were being detained and
assembled in roadside camps. Although nobody knew it
yet, they were destined to be part of the huge, million-

strong labor force that France would be required to send
to Germany as a price of her defeat.

That night they stopped in a small wood beside the
road. They were too weary to light a fire and, instead,
rolled themselves in their blankets and lay talking of the
dangers of the demarcation-line crossing that they knew
they would have to make sometime the next day.

Lying on his back, listening to the even breathing of the
sleeping girl next to him, it seemed to Chandler as if this
strange peripatetic existence had always been his life.
Certainly there was no reality in the idea that it had lasted
just five days; or that he had known the girl asleep beside
him so short a time. And yet he was aware that he knew
little more about her now than when they had left Paris.
He realized how devastated she had been by the arrest of
Paul Litvinov, but she had never spoken of him since that
first morning on the road. She had said she was not his
mistress and that was probably true. But the intensity of
her feeling for him was clear. A surrogate father maybe?
Chandler was surprised to find himself hoping so.

It was too hot, or perhaps he was too tired to sleep.
Quietly, he rolled back the blanket and got up. Walking
into the woods beyond the parked Renault, he stopped
and lit a cigarette. He was surrendering to the cool breezes
that came across the valley when he heard a footstep
behind him and turned to see Anne-Marie.

"I couldn't sleep either," she said. She reached him
and, to his intense surprise, slipped her hand into his. He
felt it as one of the most erotic gestures he had ever
experienced.

"There," she smiled at him, "I've said it. Said I'm
sorry for all that's happened. Without you, I think I
would have been wherever Paul is now."

Chandler stood beside her without speaking, feeling
the warmth of her hand in his. "Paul Litvinov," he said
after some few moments, "came to mean a lot in your
life."

"Yes," she said slowly, "yes, he did."

He waited, looking down at her as she stared out across the lights of the camp fires on the other side of the valley.

"I came to Paris full of hope," she said. "I was nineteen and had never been to a big city in my life. Perhaps I'd heard one or two stories, or read in the *Écho du Nord* about local girls who had become dancers or café owners in Paris. To me it just meant they were famous —they had their names in the newspaper."

"Is that what you wanted to be?" said Chandler. "Famous?"

"I suppose so," she smiled, almost for the first time he could remember. "Isn't that what you wanted to be when you were nineteen?"

"It's what I wanted until a couple of weeks ago," Chandler said wryly. He tried to make out the line of her profile in the gloom. "How did you meet Litvinov?"

"I accosted him."

Chandler watched her face turn to him.

"It's true," she said. "I tried to get work. But it wasn't easy to find a job in Paris before the war. My money ran out, the little I had. I slept out like a *clochard,* under the bridges, anywhere. It was April and cold. Then one night a young man, a foreigner, offered me twenty-five francs to give him gratification. And I did. And when I'd spent the money, I did the same for another man, older this time. I soon found I could live in a cheap hotel, eat twice a day. I'd stopped trying to find work. Then, one night along the Seine, I accosted Paul Litvinov."

"And?"

"He burst out laughing. He said he was much too old for that and offered to take me to a restaurant. He gave me a job as a maid. Within two months I was working for the Jewish Resettlement Agency. I have a lot to be grateful for, to Paul Litvinov."

They stood facing each other, still holding hands.

"And I thought you were a simple girl," said Chandler, smiling.

* * *

At dawn a *Zundapp* motorcycle combination pulled into the courtyard of the gendarmerie in Amiens, in northern France. The two young men who dismounted wore leather flying helmets and long, brown leather coats. Beneath the coats, as the French police sergeant who greeted them noticed, they wore neat dark suits that seemed to fit a shade too tightly.

In one of the cells below the late nineteenth-century building, the railway station master, Jacques Murville, sat nursing the ache in his missing arm. The weather could do it, or any sort of worry at home or in his station master's job. After all these years since the German surgeon had carried out the field amputation, he still experienced the sensation of an aching arm.

Murville stood up as the two young Gestapo men came into the cell. There was no sign of the friendly French gendarme sergeant who had brought him from St-Eloi. He was baffled, and he told them so, by the interest shown in his niece Anne-Marie, first by the American at St-Eloi, and now by them.

The two men took careful notes on the American's visit and then began questioning him about any family connections Anne-Marie might have in central or southern France. Murville saw no reason to dissemble. There was an uncle of Anne-Marie's, her father's brother Georges, who had settled in the Cher.

"We need details," one of the young Germans said politely.

"He owns a café, at Passy," Murville said.

"Any other relations south of Paris, monsieur?" The station master shrugged. "Two or three times removed, I suppose."

"Details please."

"They married war widows, sisters. They're farmers now, in the Poitou. I haven't heard from them in years. But the fields are very rich there. The soil is good around Poitou."

"That's all?" one of the young Germans asked. "You

haven't forgotten anyone?'' There was a sharpness in the voice now.

''The rest of the family is still in the village at St-Eloi. We're not the sort of people who travel a lot,'' Murville assured them. He felt at the empty sleeve; the ache was back.

''So, you are absolutely certain you have missed no one.''

''Let's see now . . .'' Murville frowned. ''My memory isn't what it was.''

It was only when they began beating him with short rubber truncheons that the old station master recalled his conversation with the young American. ''Won't you drink with Germans?'' he had asked.

As the steady fall of blows rained down, Murville remembered his reply: ''So far, why not?''

The Renault was still less than two hundred kilometers south of Paris. Anne-Marie awoke in the cramped passenger seat, suddenly aware that they were traveling faster than before. Across the low hills to their right the setting sun seemed about to roll off the edge of the world. She made an effort to focus her thoughts. There were a few abandoned cars on the roadside, and from time to time a peasant family gathered around a horse and cart. But the trailing, pathetic columns of yesterday had been reduced to a line of cars and trucks moving steadily forward.

She looked at Chandler. Concentrating on the road ahead, he was unaware that she was awake. He was unshaven, the side of his face running with trickles of sweat, his hair whitened with road dust. She experienced a sudden need to stretch out and touch him. Lifting her hand, she hesitated and let it fall back into her lap.

The movement made him glance toward her. ''Are you awake?''

''Yes. What's happened to the people on the road?''

''Light me a cigarette, will you?'' he said. ''It's been like this for the last hour or more. The farm carts started thinning out as we approached Vierzon. It's mostly cars now.''

She lit a cigarette and put it in his mouth.

"I think," he said, drawing on the cigarette, "we're coming up to the demarcation line."

He edged the Renault past a burned-out tank, German or French—it was impossible to tell. Its sides were blackened, its tracks hanging loose. Some charred object that might have been a body lay on the road beside it. Passing the hulk, catching the stench of burned rubber and cordite, he accelerated to the top of the gentle slope.

"Look down there," he said, pulling the Renault to a halt. In the fading light, her eyes followed the ribbon of almost empty road. Five hundred yards ahead, a bridge crossed the sun-reddened surface of the river Cher. Half a dozen German vehicles were parked among the trees on the riverbank, and the dark figures of German soldiers could be clearly seen setting up a field kitchen. The bridge itself was patrolled by helmeted men, their rifles slung on their shoulders. A red light flashed on a tripod where the road sloped up toward it.

They sat in silence watching the movement of the distant figures. A line of cars with mattresses and boxes roped to the roofs had stopped before the red light.

"I know the bridge well," she said after a few moments. "My uncle's village is a few kilometers on the other side. When I was a child I was often sent down here for the summer. My Uncle Georges used to take me fishing along the river."

"Have you seen him since?"

"Once only," she said. "Just before the war. He's a good man. I wouldn't have sent the Mendels to him if I'd had any doubts about him."

Behind them a driver was blasting his horn. They drove on down the slope and joined the line of vehicles. Within a few minutes other cars had closed up in back of them.

They got out of the Renault and walked down the line of vehicles toward the bridge. Stopping a few dozen yards from the checkpoint, in the shadow of a farm cart, they listened to the German soldiers struggling to understand peasants desperate to join families who had already crossed into the unoccupied zone. Or others, coming back from the south, equally desperate to return to their farms in northern France.

An old Frenchman, leading a horse and cart on which his wife sat slumped on the pile of household goods, came from the direction of the bridge.

Chandler emerged from the shadow. "What's the holdup?" he asked.

The old man stopped, his gnarled hand high on the horse's bridle. "There's no holdup coming this way," he said. "Your way they're checking everybody. They've got German police there, plainclothes men. They're showing pictures, asking people if they recognize someone they've seen on the road. A man and a woman. Committed a murder in Paris, the Germans say." He lifted his shoulders. "What's one murder more." He raised his hand in salute and plodded on.

They moved quickly back to the car. Anne-Marie packed some bread and cheese and the remains of the liter of wine in a bag.

"I hope you can swim," Chandler said, shoving a last pack of cigarettes into his pocket.

She looked up. "Well enough," she said grimly.

Crossing the field, Chandler was surprised to see that the grass, parched by the day's sun, was already wet. The moon, rising above the line of trees before them, was almost full, and they knew that it would be a danger when the moment came to cross the river.

The line of trees, they saw as they approached, was one side of a deep country lane. Scrambling down the bank, they moved forward cautiously. So far there were no menacing signs that the north side of the riverbank was patrolled—no German voices, no coughing engines of reconnaissance half-tracks.

Suddenly Chandler stopped dead.

She stood beside him, rigid. "What is it?"

"Listen."

Somewhere before them she could hear the distant yelp of dogs.

"A farm, perhaps," she said. But already her imagination invested the high-pitched barking with the chilling shapes of German guard dogs. Deep in the shadow of the lane they listened for long minutes, but they were unable to guess how far away the dogs were. Even whether or not they were moving. Then suddenly the yelps and barking stopped.

There were signs of last week's fighting. Trees stripped by shellfire. The barrel of a French antitank gun poked out of the bushes. Beside it, gleaming in the light of the rising moon, they saw a stack of slender brass shells. Farther on, a second gun, blasted from its emplacement beside the lane, lay shattered across the road. Leading Anne-Marie through the wreckage of twisted metal, anxious to avoid the jagged shards, Chandler brushed against a pile of empty ammunition boxes. The clangor of falling metal boxes seemed to echo across the fields almost to the distant bridge. Again they stopped and listened. There was no sound but the wind rustling in the tops of the trees. From somewhere close by they caught the sour smell of dew-damp ashes. From the direction of the river came the unreal mellifluence of the nightingale, weaving its song with careless skill. Then the sound of voices, male, German, interspersed with the short barks of dogs. In silence they quickly moved beyond the tumble of ammunition boxes. A shaft of moonlight through the trees illuminated the corner of a farmhouse built to overhang the deeply gouged lane. Through the holes in the stonework where windows had once been they could see charred beams. Chandler scrambled quickly up the bank and reached down to help her. Beyond the farmhouse doorway was a single, roofless room. The smell of the recently burned woodwork was strong in their nostrils as they stepped carefully among the collapsed beams and took up a position in deep shadow from where they could watch the lane.

The German voices were no more than twenty yards away. There were at least three men and perhaps two dogs. Standing in the dark interior of the ruined farmhouse, they could see the beam of a handheld flashlight stabbing erratically through the bushes.

"The best posting," one of the soldiers was saying, "would be Paris, of course. But I still like the idea of one of the smaller towns. Ten, fifteen thousand people . . ." They were directly opposite the farmhouse now, four men, one of them with two Dobermans on a double leash, another carrying a bucket in one hand.

They stopped below the farmhouse wall, not ten yards from where Chandler stood.

"The French prisoners," the German continued, "are to remain in custody, did you hear that?"

Another German grunted. "I'll put one up here," he said, fiddling with the bucket.

"They say we've taken over a million men," the first German pressed on. "Perhaps two million. Think of what that's going to mean in these little country places. For every absent man there's a woman alone. After a month or two they'll be chasing everything in a German uniform. Even you, Hans."

The man with the bucket laughed. Taking a brush, he began to swab paste on the stone wall. Another soldier came forward and peeled off a poster from a roll he carried. Holding it against the wall, he waited while the other man daubed more paste across it. In the bright moonlight the black lettering under the Nazi eagle stood out clearly from the white background. It read, in French: Limit of the German Occupied Zone. It is forbidden on pain of death, to attempt to cross into the Unoccupied Zone without permission from the Military Authority.

"If we follow that line of trees," the man with the dogs said, "we can paste up notices all the way to the road."

The tension in Chandler's leg muscles was rapidly

becoming intolerable. After the days of driving, much of it at only a few miles an hour, braking, changing gears, he could no longer maintain the total immobility of his present stance.

"My father was in the last war," the first German said, lighting a cigarette. "He told me a thing or two about French women. They'll do anything for a half-kilo of coffee. But they like to do it in private. As long as the neighbors never know."

Involuntarily Chandler's foot moved. Both dogs turned their heads upward toward the shattered hole in the stonework. The first German unslung his rifle. "There's someone up there. Listen."

A second German took his rifle from his shoulder and drove a cartridge into the breech. "Send the dogs up," he said nervously.

"It's probably a rat," the man with the dogs said. "I'll never get them back if I let them go."

"I swear to you," the first soldier said, "I heard something up there and it wasn't a rat." He was moving past the edge of the stone wall toward the bank. "Let's have some light up there."

The beam hit Chandler full in the face. From below, he heard a confusion of shouts and barking dogs. Anne-Marie was already backing away from the light.

"The window," Chandler said urgently. "Jump."

He saw her scramble up onto the sill. As she jumped, a rifle shot cracked by his head and sang away into the darkness. Seconds later he hurled himself through the windowless opening and landed, rolling, in the bushes outside.

He reached out for Anne-Marie in the wet grass beside him. "Run!" he said. "Get into the water. Run, for God's sake!"

Three of the Germans were now firing into the darkness. The fourth, still in the lane below, struggled against the dogs' wild excitement to unleash them. As the catch loosened they leaped forward, still joined together by a yard-long chain, and raced down the lane.

His breath burning his throat, Chandler saw the chained dogs even with him in the lane below the copse. When the nearest turned, dragging the head of the other dog with it, and scrambled up the bank, it was no more than yards away. He swung around to kick out at it with his last strength and saw the dog's head jerk backward, hauled by the chain as the other dog tried to attack from the other side of a bush. In savage fury the two dogs leaped and struggled and doubled back on themselves in an attempt to drag free. Through the confusion of barking and snapping branches he heard distantly the voices of the Germans. Then, with the trapped dogs barking madly, he turned and ran on toward the river.

It opened before him as a wide, placid stream, the moonlight catching metallic ripples along the reeded banks. He was still yards from the water's edge when the dogs reached him again. Trailing the uprooted bush the chain had dragged from the ground, they hurled themselves into the reeds, snapping and tearing at Chandler, who flailed out wildly at them. A branch, snatched from the surface of the water, kept one dog at bay while the other bucked and leaped through the shallows. Striking out, he caught the bigger dog a blow across the muzzle, causing it to fall back into the water. As it regained its balance and charged again, the chain pulled the second dog off balance, dragging its head below the surface. For seconds the smooth, wet back of its neck was exposed. With the first dog tearing at his legs, Chandler brought the stick down on the exposed neck and fell backward, rolling in the reeds, scrambling for the clear water.

Snarling and thrashing through the shallow water, the first dog struggled to drag its drowning companion on the end of the chain. At the edge of the reeded bank Chandler fell forward into the water, then felt it take him up as he kicked out toward midstream.

For some while he floated with the current, too exhausted to swim. He reached the far bank at last, eighty yards downstream from where he had started. He could still hear the barking and wild thrashing of the chained dog, now joined by the voices of the soldiers.

He lay in deep shadow, half in and half out of the water. From the other bank the thin beam of the Germans' flashlight played on the bushes around him, then passed on. Once or twice, shots were fired randomly into clumps of reeds palely illuminated by the light. Then, from the direction of the bridge, he caught the sound of an outboard motor.

From a position almost a hundred yards along the riverbank, Anne-Marie saw the shadowy figures of German soldiers standing upright in the flat-bottomed river boat. Then a powerful light sliced through the darkness and began to sweep back and forth along the bank.

It caught her as she stood among the bushes. Paralyzed for a second, she heard the shouts of the German soldiers from beyond the blinding light, and the bolt action of their rifles. Hurling herself sideways, she rolled down a grassy slope. The boat had turned sharply and was already crunching through the reeds as she rose to her feet and began to run.

She had never heard the crack and whine of rifle shots before, and when a bullet stripped a handful of bark from a tree a foot above her head, she veered wildly and plunged into the thickets beside the path. Scrambling like an animal through the bushes, she came to a deep ditch. To her surprise she found she was only a few hundred yards from the road. There were no longer any sounds of pursuit. For a long time she lay in the ditch, until the hammering of her heart subsided. She was trembling violently, but ordinary thought processes slowly returned. She knew she could not go back to the riverbank to look for Chandler. She was not even sure that he had survived the crossing. But that thought she dismissed.

She looked out from above the lip of the ditch across the serene moonlit fields and woods. At first light she could come back and walk the riverbank posing as a girl from one of the local villages. But not now, with her matted hair and dripping clothes.

She had never felt such misery, such a sense of defeat, as she regained the road and began to push past the returning refugees, on her way to her uncle's village.

Chapter
Fifteen

THE CAFÉ-HOTEL AT Passy stood on the moonlit bank of the canal, its pale facade peeling, the closed blue shutters loose on their hinges. The old Citroën in which the Mendels had left Paris was parked beside rusting scraps of machinery littering the forecourt of the collapsing barn. On the wall a mobilization plaque from some other war was stamped in the soft lead. It read: Two horses, three mules, one man.

On the towpath side of the building a sheet draped from the upper windows carried, in crude, hand-painted, red letters, the single word FERMÉ. A rough barricade of farm carts and barbed wire blocked the entrance to the hotel courtyard.

A man with a shotgun came from the hotel and stopped at the barbedwire barricade. "We've no food," he shouted. "No wine. Nothing." There was a note of desperation in the voice. "You've got to go on," he called. "We've nothing for sale. Nothing."

Anne-Marie stood in the rutted lane, shivering wet. "It's Anne-Marie," she called. "Your niece, Anne-Marie."

Georges lowered his shotgun. "Anne-Marie," he barked. "It's you. I thought it was more Paris refugees."

"No, it's me, Uncle Georges," she said, approaching the wire barrier as the man struggled to open it.

"You're welcome," he said, "you know that." Claudel dragged the makeshift gate open and came forward. "It's sad it takes a war to bring you down here." He stopped, looking at her sodden clothing.

"There was a checkpoint on the bridge," said Anne-Marie. "I had to swim across the river."

They stood together in the moonlight, the short, broad-shouldered man and the tall girl. Then they embraced, kissing each other's cheeks, four times as they had done when she was a young girl.

"It is true you have no food?" she asked.

"Very little." He shrugged. "The last two weeks have been a nightmare. Even worse for the people on the roads. At first we gave them what we could. Then only to the children. Now I need to have the shotgun ready to stop the cow being dragged away. What have we come to, my niece?"

Georges led the way to the house. "Your friends," he said, "are already here."

Anne-Marie hesitated. "You know they are Jews, German Jews? I have to tell you that."

Georges nodded. "Can you imagine that a gentleman like monsieur Mendel had not made that clear already?"

Every night breeze cut through Chandler's wet clothes like knives. The right arm of his shirt hung shredded by the dogs' teeth, and he could see the deep gouged marks in his flesh. His right leg, too, had been badly savaged just above the knee but, as far as he could tell under the torn, wet cloth of his trousers, it was no longer bleeding.

He had dragged himself up with difficulty into a thick mass of hawthorn bushes on the bank. Six or eight times the searchlight from the river had passed over him and then moved on. He felt strangely dangerous, content. From the exchanges of the German soldiers shouting from the boat to the far bank, he concluded that Anne-Marie had escaped.

All was now quiet except for the gentle, lapping flow of the river and the occasional splash of a fish out beyond the reeds. The moon had disappeared, leaving a misty blackness. Chandler scrambled clear of the clawing thorns of the bushes and stumbled off through the long, wet grass, brushing past saplings and low clumps of gorse.

The ground was more open now, but as Chandler limped through the darkness, he realized it was useless; he had no real purpose and had lost all sense of direction. Perhaps he had lost too much blood to even try to think what he should do.

Some way ahead in the gloom he could just make out a long ribbon of water. Had he walked in a circle back to the river? As he drew closer he saw it was a canal. Exhausted, he crawled into a patch of undergrowth at the edge of some trees. Most of all, he wanted desperately to sleep.

A few miles south, at Georges Claudel's café, Anne-Marie came awake with a start. She had refused a bed and, instead, had dozed for an hour or two in front of the kitchen stove, wrapped in a lined, woolen shawl, her outer clothes drying on a rail. It was there that Georges Claudel joined her.

"You should be asleep," he said. "You have a long drive ahead of you today."

She shook her head slowly. "I'm not going with the Mendels," she said. "I have to go back, Georges. I have to look for somebody."

"Monsieur Mendel talked of an American. Is it him you have to find?"

"Yes."

Claudel put coffee on the stove. "Is he your man?" he asked in his straightforward way.

She smiled. "No."

He was silent, nodding to himself.

"I've only known him a few days."

"And yet you do not sleep," said Georges, still nodding gravely.

She smiled again, lowering her eyes.

"In wartime a few days can measure as long as months," he said quietly. "I'm not an educated man, Anne-Marie, but I know that in war you can pack a lifetime's experience into a week. I learned more about myself in ten days as a soldier on the Marne front than I had in the whole thirty years of my life up to then. I learned more about other people too." He stretched his hands toward the stove and was silent for a moment.

Anne-Marie felt warm and comfortable, almost safe, listening to the gruff peasant's voice.

"The same in these last weeks," Georges continued. "When a man is hungry for soup, he's a thief. When his children are desperate for soup, he's a beast. On the roads people have been killed for a few liters of gasoline, a loaf of bread, a bandage. Here at home," he rubbed his stubbled cheek, "I've learned things about my own wife."

Georges fell silent again. The pot was beginning to bubble on the stove.

"So,"—Georges smiled his brown-toothed smile—"you've met a young man. Just a few days ago."

Anne-Marie watched as he took down two coffee cups from a shelf above the stove and set them on the table.

"What do you think of this armistice," said Anne-Marie. "Is it the right thing for France?"

He turned from the table. "In the last war," he said, "I was a prisoner in Germany for nearly two years. I worked on a farm, as I did in France as a young man. There was no difference. They were good people. Serious, kind. Who can tell what madness has overtaken them. Look at the roads of France these last two weeks. Will any of us ever be the same again? It's not the armistice, rules and regulations. It's people."

Anne-Marie looked at him, a little older, a little thicker at the waist, and thought how much wisdom he had culled from his experiences.

"I've never met an American," he said. "I met some English Tommies. They told me Americans speak the same language. I don't know if it is true."

She laughed. "Yes, it's true."

He pulled up a kitchen chair and sat beside her. "You're not a peasant," he said. "You know about these things. Will the Americans come to the help of their English friends?"

She knew how much he wanted her to say yes. "I think they must," she said. "As soon as they find out what is happening in Germany to people like the Mendels."

Georges nodded, satisfied. "Your friends will go south alone?"

"I think it's safe now in all the confusion, and they crossed the demarcation line without trouble. In the south there is a château; there are people there who will guide them across the Pyrenees."

Georges got up and poured coffee for them both. "The young American—" he said thoughtfully. "He swam the river too?"

"We lost each other at the river, but I think he got across. The Germans were shooting."

"And when it gets light you're going to look for him?"

"Yes."

"Take the bicycle," he said. "Say you're the daughter of Monsieur Bellac, the lock-keeper. He's got land down there on the riverbank."

She enclosed his rough hand in hers as he passed her the cup of coffee.

"And when you find your American, what then?" he said. "The Mendels will leave at dawn. You have no transport to take you south."

"No."

He thought for a moment. "In the barn there's a Peugeot pickup, an old *camionnette,* and a little gasoline. Enough to reach the Pyrenees. Take it. You and your American who is not your man," he said with a knowing grin.

She stood and hugged his grizzled head to her. His

cheek was rough with stubble; tobacco and garlic fumes mixed with the sweat of his shirt. To her surprise she found she was crying.

The same dawn that was about to touch the café-hotel at Passy waited somewhere outside the window of the bedroom where Leo Beckerman lay with his eyes open, uncertain as to whether the dull crash that seemed to have awakened him was real or imaginary. Frau Beckerman, curled in the bed at his side, was snoring gently. There was no one else in the house. The concierge had gone to Nanterre to visit her sister; she wouldn't return until this afternoon. The rest of the house was empty; perhaps that was the reason Beckerman had turned the key in the bedroom door as he and his wife had retired. He listened for a few moments but heard nothing, except the steady tick of the alarm clock with its two brass bells and the rhythmic exhalation of the woman he still loved deeply after almost thirty years.

Allowing his eyes to close, Beckerman dozed and mused about the future. They had tried to drive south, but Magda had become nauseated and weak, unable to eat or sleep, coughing incessantly from the dust on the road. After two days they had turned back, deciding they were too tired, too old to run anymore.

Since their return, Paris seemed to have assuaged itself after the traumas of the threat and then the fact of the German Occupation. The city was slowly returning to a cautious normality.

Yesterday Beckerman had ventured out for a walk; nobody appeared to pay any particular attention to him, or stared, or pointed, or huddled to talk in whispers as he passed. A policeman had even held up the traffic on the Rue St-Clare to allow him to cross the road. He had strolled down to the Seine and watched the barges. A couple of small pleasure boats, with girls in summer dresses and young men with earnest, smiling faces, had paddled by, their laughter echoing off the span of a bridge. He recalled the scent of a flowering shrub growing wild along a wall.

The handle turned silently as someone outside tried to open the locked door.

Perhaps he could persuade Magda to take the train to Versailles. The gardens would be near perfection at this time of the year. A sudden rap on the door snapped him out of his reverie. Could it be the concierge back from her sister's in Nanterre? Not at this hour.

"Who is it?" Beckerman called in a thin voice.

"Open up."

The cold, impersonal command sent a shock of dismay through his body. Now an insistent fist was pounding continuously on the door.

Beckerman stumbled from the bed. As he turned the key, the door was immediately flung open, hurling him back.

Krebs stood framed on the threshold, flanked by the two young Gestapo agents. "Out," he hissed.

Beckerman stood transfixed; the horrific vision of discovery and capture he had played over in his mind a hundred times was suddenly stark reality.

"Get him out," ordered Krebs.

The two young men seized Beckerman by the arms and hurled him from the room. Before he could stop, Krebs was at his back, forcing him to the top of the stairs. The dim electric light was on in the hallway below. Krebs clamped a huge hand on the back of Beckerman's neck and angled his face down the flight of stairs.

"Well?" said Krebs.

Beckerman could see a face looking up at him from the hall. The features were indistinct, but he saw the man's golden-blond hair.

"Yes, it's him," said Bilescu.

In the brightly lit kitchen, the tiles struck cold under the soles of Beckerman's bare feet as he waited, his long frame hunched with despair. A kettle was coming to a boil on the gas burner in the corner. He moaned as Magda was brought in, her face startled, her hair in disarray.

"Magda," Beckerman whispered.

She didn't seem to hear.

"What time is it?" she asked, with a confused glance around at the unfamiliar faces.

"Bring her here," said Krebs.

As one of the young Germans went to take her arm, Beckerman yelled out with a potency he didn't know he possessed: "Leave her."

Even Krebs hesitated for a moment.

Beckerman lowered his eyes. "What do you want to know?" he whispered with infinite sadness.

The grandfather clock against the wall struck six. The morning sun streaming in through the window prophesied another cloudless day. Georges Claudel's wife, Suzanne, served the big mugs of coffee in grim silence.

"We are grateful to you, madame," Professor Mendel said in his soft, cultured voice, "for your hospitality and for your assistance. It means more to us than you can imagine."

Madame Claudel stared out of the window. In the courtyard she could see her husband working on the old pickup truck and Felix Mendel and his young wife, Sarah, loading luggage into the Citroën. She sucked air in through her teeth, snapping her head back. "Marshal Pétain, in his broadcast, said it was illegal to help refugees. German refugees." She seemed to be speaking directly to the black stovepipe before her eyes.

"You mean Jews," Frau Mendel said.

"Yes."

"Do you believe it's a wrong thing to do?" Frau Mendel asked.

"The marshal says we must think of ourselves now. For too long we have been thinking of others. The British betrayed us. It's time to think of ourselves alone."

Anne-Marie remained silent. Georges Claudel had already told her his wife's views.

"Your husband has agreed to let Anne-Marie take the old farm vehicle. I can pay you well for it," said Professor Mendel.

"I'm not letting him give it away, you can be sure of that," said Madame Claudel, drawing her thin mouth even tighter.

"We wouldn't expect you to."

Madame Claudel turned from the stove. "I dare say you can afford it," she said. "But what use is paper money these days?"

"I have gold sovereigns," Mendel assured her, "English sovereigns."

He reached down and removed his right shoe. Madame Claudel stared at the hand-tooled leather. Placing the shoe on the table, Mendel gave a twist to the heel. It moved aside, revealing a hollowed-out section in which nestled a double layer of gold sovereigns.

"Ten sovereigns," Mendel said. "To include thirty liters of gasoline."

He laid the sovereigns on the table.

Madame Claudel bent and picked up the small coins. "If my husband knows you paid me, he'll make me give it back. But it's our *camionnette*," she said. "He can't just give it away."

"He will know nothing," Anne-Marie said, looking at her aunt with flaring contempt. She waited while Mendel rearranged the remaining gold coins and pressed the heel section back in place.

When he was ready, they stood around the table, ignoring Madame Claudel, who had regained her position beside the stove.

Felix appeared in the doorway. "We are ready to leave, father," he said.

Professor Mendel shook hands solemnly with Anne-Marie. "We may yet meet in Spain, or perhaps New York," he said. "Good luck."

Frau Mendel embraced her. "I know you'll find Herr Chandler," she said. "Pray that we all meet again."

Madame Claudel stood with ten sovereigns in the palm of her hand. When she closed her fingers they clinked dully together.

Just after midday, from the courtyard of the café-hotel, Georges Claudel watched the two green armored cars draw up beside the canal. He was not familiar with the black runic markings on their steel doors and assumed these to be German soldiers like any others.

The powerfully built man with close-cropped hair, crossing the towpath toward the hotel, was escorted by four troopers, and again Georges noted the silver runes on their collars, corresponding in shape to those on the armored vehicles. But at this time few Frenchmen attached any special significance to the twin lightning flashes like oddly shaped letters, *SS*.

The Germans waited while Claudel pulled aside his improvised barricade. In the doorway behind stood his wife, slowly wiping her hands on her apron.

"I thought there were no German soldiers allowed south of the demarcation line," Georges Claudel said.

"Except in special circumstances," Gestapo Inspector Krebs replied pleasantly. He turned toward the troopers. "Search the place," he said. "One of you stay with me."

Silently Claudel watched Krebs as he walked forward, beckoning with his finger for the Frenchman to follow. In the doorway Madame Claudel stood aside as they walked into the kitchen. Krebs took a chair at the long table.

"You are related to Mademoiselle Claudel?" Krebs said. "Anne-Marie Claudel? This is the information I have been given."

"She's my niece, monsieur," Claudel said.

"Inspector," Krebs corrected him. He drummed his fingers on the tabletop, glancing up at the sound of heavy boots stomping around above.

"Can I offer you some wine?" Claudel asked.

"A bottle of wine, yes," said Krebs.

Madame Claudel took a bottle from the rack and opened it. Placing a glass before the German, she half filled it, then stood the bottle on the table.

"Your niece," Krebs said, "is she here? If she is, we will find her."

Claudel shook his head.

"When did you last see her?"

"Almost a year ago now," Claudel said. "Just before the war began she spent a few days here. Last June, was it?" He turned to his wife, giving her a quick, stern stare.

She stood with her back to the stove, slowly unscrewing the cork from the corkscrew. It did not escape Krebs's attention that she did not answer. His quarry was near; he could feel it. Throughout the flight from Paris to Limoges in Heinkel-111, he had felt a mounting sense of anticipation. The Frenchman was lying; Anne-Marie Claudel was here in the house, cringing in some corner.

"A trafficker in Jews," Krebs mused. "A Jew herself, but a trafficker in Jews."

"I don't understand, monsieur," Claudel said.

"Inspector," Krebs said evenly. "You will address me as Inspector." He lifted the glass and sipped the wine. "Not bad, not bad at all."

An urgent, muffled shout came from one of the rooms upstairs. Krebs stiffened. Heavy running footsteps. The boots of an SS trooper clumping down the stairs.

"There's no else in the house," the trooper said. "I found these in a piss pot under the bed." He rolled a handful of gold sovereigns onto the table.

Krebs stared down at the coins. "Find the Jew girl," he hissed.

"There's nobody here, Inspector," the trooper said. "The place is empty."

With a roar of rage, Krebs stood and ran upstairs.

For a full ten minutes the Claudels and the trooper stood waiting and listening to the sounds above—the crash of heavy objects, the splintering of wood, Krebs's bellowed orders. At last a silence.

Krebs walked to the table, his anger and frustration now turned to an icy malevolence. With his index finger he slowly arranged the sovereigns in two rows. "These have the English king on the front,'' he said. ''Where did you acquire English sovereigns?'' He stared at Claudel.

The Frenchman shook his head and shrugged.

''I'm told that gold is the currency the Jewish internationalists love beyond all others,'' Krebs said, his face as stone.

''I've never seen them before in my life,'' Claudel said.

Krebs nodded understandingly. ''Take him out,'' he said, ''and shoot him.''

Madame Claudel threw herself across the table. ''They left early this morning,'' she said. ''The Jews were going to Spain.''

''Spain?'' said Krebs.

''I heard them talking,'' Madame Claudel said desperately. ''First to a village in the Pyrenees and then to Spain.''

''And the girl, your niece?''

''She was with an American. She left him at the river last night.''

''Anne-Marie,'' Krebs hissed, ''where is she? Did she leave with the Jews?''

At the doorway, Georges twisted his head as the trooper pushed him forward. From the corner of her eye, his wife saw his pleading look. ''Yes,'' she said. ''Anne-Marie left with the Jews. She left this morning with the Jews.'' Collapsing onto the table, she watched her husband taken out into the courtyard. ''Please,'' she said. ''Please. No.''

Krebs looked at her thin, dry body and the tight, weasel face. She was not worth his attention. He drained the glass of wine and walked away.

Outside, the rifle shots cracked in a sudden staccato report. After a few moments, the troopers came back into the room. Madame Claudel still slumped across the table.

''Inspector Krebs tends to favor a fire,'' one of the troopers said, taking a swig from the open wine bottle.

Madame Claudel looked up from the table, her tongue working in a mouth devoid of saliva.

"No survivors," the trooper said, scooping up the sovereigns. "The inspector has specified no survivors."

Anne-Marie had spent the whole day searching the direct road from Passy, then every lane and cart track for a mile on either side. The stream of homeless refugees had almost dried up. A few horse-drawn carts returning to the north, a convoy of German soldiers pulling back to the demarcation line—she had seen little more all day. It was as if the great tragedy had been suspended for a few hours to be renewed tomorrow or the next day as those who had made the pointless flight south trudged back to their abandoned farms and villages.

In the afternoon she had hidden the bicycle in the woods and walked along the riverbank. On the other side, she saw, from time to time, sections of German soldiers patrolling the thick copse that ran down to the river. She knew what she was doing made no sense. She understood the grisly futility of the fear she suffered at the sight of every floating log. But she was also aware that she was trapped, driven to keep searching until darkness began to fall and the utter impossibility of finding Chandler again had to be recognized.

She knew she was in love. She knew it, more than anything else, from her reaction to her uncle's question: "Is he your man?" Perhaps that had been the first moment she had realized it. She sat, despairing, beside the road as a thin, straggling line of refugees flowed toward the bridge. Pointless as it was, she raised her head to scan each male face as it passed. Equally pointless, her last walk along the riverbank as the sky, striped gray and violet, darkened in the west.

It was dark as she rode the bicycle down the canal path toward the café-hotel. In front of the lock-keeper's house, a small knot of people stood together in the spill of light from an open doorway. She had almost passed when a man's voice called out to her. Stopping the bicycle, she turned toward them.

"*S'il vous plaît,* mademoiselle," the man said again.

She dismounted and walked the bicycle toward the huddle of figures in the patch of light. The man approached and stopped at the wooden gate between them. The women behind him moved forward tentatively.

"Perhaps you are going to the Claudels', to the café, mademoiselle?" the lock-keeper said.

Anne-Marie leaned heavily on the bicycle. "Is there some reason I should not, monsieur?"

"You know the Germans were here today?"

"Germans? But we are south of the line."

"Nevertheless," the lock-keeper said, "they were German soldiers in armored cars."

She stood before him, inexpressibly weary. "They went to the café?" she asked.

"They set fire to it," the lock-keeper said quietly. "The Claudels perished, mademoiselle. Both of them."

Anne-Marie had no memory afterward of getting onto the bicycle and cycling down the track. The sight of the gutted remains of the café-hotel obliterated everything else. A few half-collapsed walls remained, and the blackened chimney stacks stood starkly out against the moonlit sky. Smoke rose in slow wisps from the ruins of the barn and curled up from the pile of embers at the very center of the debris.

When she returned to the lock-keeper's house, she had managed to achieve some surface control of her horror and guilt. Uncle Georges and his wife were dead, murdered, and she knew, beyond doubt, why it had been done.

"The house was mostly timber," the lock-keeper said. "It was all over in an hour. The Germans stayed until there was no chance of bringing it under control. Then they left. Why should they do such a terrible thing, mademoiselle?"

Anne-Marie shook her head dumbly.

"They came especially for them," one of the women said, pressing forward to the gate. "Georges Claudel didn't die in the fire," the woman went on. "He was shot and his body thrown into the flames. I saw it all from the top window here."

"You knew the Claudels?" the lock-keeper asked.

Anne-Marie stood in silence.

"You are a relative, perhaps?"

"A friend," Anne-Marie told him cautiously. "A good friend. The Germans asked no questions here?"

"They drove off when they had done their dirty work," the lock-keeper said, pulling open the gate. "Can I offer you something, mademoiselle? For the shock?"

She shook her head. "No, thank you."

"They came especially to kill them," the woman said again, shaking her head.

"I must go," said Anne-Marie, turning the bicycle back toward the track.

"Mademoiselle," the lock-keeper said, "you're not, perhaps, Georges Claudel's niece, Anne-Marie?"

She stopped. There seemed little point in denying it to him now. "Yes, I'm his niece. Why do you ask, monsieur?"

The lock-keeper shrugged. "A man was here just after it happened. A foreigner."

Anne-Marie struggled wildly to form the questions. "A foreigner? Who was he?"

"An American," the lock-keeper said. "His leg was in a bad way." He jerked his thumb over his shoulder. "He's in the house now."

Some curtain fell between her and the tragedy that had overtaken her family. For these moments, at least, she could only think that he had survived the river crossing, that he was alive.

She followed the woman into the house.

"He's upstairs," the woman said, standing aside.

Anne-Marie thanked her and ran up the uncarpeted wooden staircase. There was only one door at the top, and she pushed it open.

Chandler was lying on a brass bed. She took a step

inside the room and was suddenly afflicted by a stunning shyness.

Chandler smiled, lifted himself on one elbow and held out his hand to her. She came forward and sat on the side of the bed, sliding her arms around him. When he kissed her on the neck, she pulled back slightly and, holding his head in both hands, she pressed her open lips to his.

Chapter

Sixteen

ON THE LONG, downhill slope the engine of the old Citroën finally coughed into silence. For the last five kilometers the fuel gauge had registered zero. Golda Mendel looked anxiously at her husband.

"We're fortunate to get this far," Professor Mendel said. "After riding all this way, we can walk the last few miles."

"It'll be dark when we arrive," said Felix Mendel from behind the steering wheel.

"So much the better," Mendel replied.

The Citroën coasted on down the narrow road. The setting sun tinged the distant Pyrenees a gaudy pink and mauve. Each new curve, silently negotiated, seemed to bring another mountain into sight, rising mysteriously from the vast ridge of peaks before them.

On a level stretch of road, the car finally rolled to a stop. The family got out, dragging their suitcases with them. For a moment they stood among the darkening pine trees, overwhelmed, all four of them, by the majestic loneliness of the mountains.

"Courage," Mendel said, "although after all that's

happened to us this last year I've no need to say that to any of you.''

They began to walk, the younger couple stepping out ahead. Felix carried the map with the route all the way down from Paris marked in red.

''What do people here think about us?'' asked Frau Mendel, taking her husband's arm. ''What do they think about Jews?''

''I know so little about this part of France,'' said Mendel, his voice echoing off the rock face that rose steeply on one side of the road. ''For the most part, people who live in small mountain villages are very alike. Not too different perhaps from our Bavarians or Austrians. They're inbred; the men travel only when they are called to war. What do they think of Jews?'' He shrugged. ''I don't suppose anyone here has addressed himself to the question for five centuries.''

The road ahead turned and climbed. The darkness, when it came, fell rapidly, changing the configuration of the landscape. The distant mountains faded in an order of their own design, until the last peak disappeared. It was cold now, the earth losing its heat with the suddenness with which the light had left the sky. The song of day birds changed to the guttural shrieks of night predators.

There were no villages along the road, but from time to time the travelers saw faint lights from a hamlet or cluster of farm buildings on a hillside. At a stone bridge over a fast-flowing stream they stopped to eat the last of their bread and sausage.

Sitting on the low stone parapet, Golda Mendel munched her bread and smiled.

''What is it?'' her husband asked. ''Some thoughts of the past to put against the ironies of the present?''

Frau Mendel nodded. ''I was thinking of Professor Mendel and his overproud wife, holding court at a dinner party at home in Heidelberg. I was thinking how your young students scrambled for an invitation to the great Professor's house.''

Mendel nodded in agreement.

"The same young men," she said, "joined the Nazi Party a year later." The smile was gone.

"Not all joined the Nazis," said Mendel. "Think of those who were prepared to help, despite the danger to themselves and their families. When we are safe in New York, we must take care to remember all those people. They're Germans too."

When they had finished eating, they rearranged the contents of their suitcases, emptying one and throwing it into the bushes by the roadside. Then they set off again.

"How much farther, Felix?" Mendel asked his son.

"It's not far now, father. A few kilometers and we'll be safe."

In his office at Wewelsburg Heinrich Himmler was fretting. He looked at the column of figures on the sheet of paper before him and shook his head, baffled. He had just completed the list of his personal expenses for May and was unable to account for 123 marks 17 pfennigs. His secretary had suggested inventing an item to make up the balance. But personal dishonesty was anathema to the Reichsführer-SS. He had sent the girl off with a strong rebuke. No, the 123 marks 17 pfennigs had to be accounted for. Was it possible he had paid his wife's coal bill out of the office petty cash? He had been at home one day in early May, and his wife had been complaining about her inability to manage on her allowance. Perhaps that was the answer. They had so many squabbles about money these days one seemed to run into the other. She appeared to think the Reichsführer-SS was a law unto himself in the Third Reich.

Himmler sat back in his chair. There was something else that was troubling him. He felt he should talk to Kaltenbrunner again. He got up and left the room. It was not yet midnight; Kaltenbrunner should still be in his office. He padded down the flight of stone steps in his carpet slippers and knocked on Kaltenbrunner's door.

Sitting at his desk, Ernst Kaltenbrunner lifted his huge head. The Reichsführer-SS was standing in the doorway.

Between the carpet slippers and his full-cut uniform breeches, six inches of pale, thin leg showed.

"I'm deeply worried, Ernst—" the Reichsführer announced, "this question of the girl."

Kaltenbrunner stood as Himmler came into the room. "Colonel Reichenau lacks imagination," Kaltenbrunner said, "but Krebs is a good man. He'll resolve the problem."

Himmler stood in the middle of the stone-walled room. "It's not that," he said. "I'm seeing the Führer sometime in the next few days. I think he should be consulted on this question."

Kaltenbrunner walked around his desk, careful not to get too close to the Reichsführer. The disparity in their heights became embarrassing if they stood together. "I'm sure the RSHA can handle this," he said. "The Führer has enough problems as it is."

"Perhaps you're right, Ernst." Himmler moved toward the door.

Kaltenbrunner waited.

"Nevertheless, perhaps I should confide in him."

Kaltenbrunner sat back on the edge of his desk. "The leadership principle of the Third Reich, the *Führerprinzip*," he said carefully, "applies to all levels of leadership, as I understand it."

"Of course," said Himmler.

"Again, as I understand it, perhaps wrongly, it is essentially a testing of the man by his responsibility."

"Exactly," Himmler agreed. He thought for a moment and then reached forward and opened the door. "I enjoy a little talk with you, Ernst. The leadership principle, yes. Personal responsibility. I had occasion to rebuke one of my secretaries tonight, this very evening. A leader, I told her, must take a vigorous view of his responsibilities. Let me know," he said, "the moment Krebs finds the girl. You understand me, Ernst?"

"Yes, Reichsführer."

As the door closed behind Himmler, Kaltenbrunner's face dropped into a scowl. He lifted the telephone receiver and asked to be connected to Colonel Reichenau or Inspector Krebs at Gestapo 1 in Paris. "I want to talk to one of them immediately," he snapped.

The phrase "You understand me, Ernst," said in the Reichsführer's mild, inoffensive way, had a special meaning for Kaltenbrunner. He had learned to recognize its underplayed significance. Any request coupled with that phrase, should be taken as a direct order and acted upon at once.

The telephone rang and Kaltenbrunner snatched up the receiver; it was Gestapo 1 in Paris. As the voice on the other end of the line politely informed him that Inspector Krebs had flown to Limoges and his exact whereabouts were now unknown, and that Colonel Reichenau had unfortunately retired for the night, Kaltenbrunner's anger rose. "Then wake him up. I said I wanted to talk to one of them immediately. That means now," he roared.

The Mendels had taken a small flashlight from the abandoned suitcase, and now, as they struggled the last few hundred yards, Felix Mendel occasionally flashed it to illuminate the road ahead. Emerging from the great arching trees, they could see against the night sky the shape of the nearest hills, which showed as a dark line toward which the road windingly led. The Château d'Arblay, an old stone *manoir*, lay in a cleft in the hills, the separate buildings and surrounding walls of the village set out flat and one-dimensional on the hillside like a medieval painting.

They had no doubt it was the house they were seeking. Even from this distance they could see a thin skein of smoke drifting from a chimney and the faint glimmer of light from the cracks around shuttered windows. The beam of the flashlight touched the twisted branches of a dead tree. A panic-stricken, fluttering black shape made them all recoil.

"What was that?" Frau Mendel clung to her husband's arm.

Felix laughed at his own alarm. "An owl," he said.

"Just an owl, mother."

"It made no sound," said Sarah.

"Their flight is silent," said Felix. "Owls have special feathers that make no sound so that their prey will not be warned as they swoop."

They walked on, now in single file, Felix leading, then Sarah and Frau Mendel, and the professor at the rear. At the crossroads before them, Felix shone the flashlight at a signpost set into the hedge.

"What in God's name is that?" said Frau Mendel.

From the gibbet arm of the sign reading Château d'Arblay, a shapeless mass hung, turning slowly.

Mendel came quickly forward, pushing the flashlight in his son's hand down, away from the sign. "We're nearly there," he said.

Mendel hurried past, leading the way, urging them on. A long, narrow bridge spanned a mountain stream. They crossed and continued toward a timber gate set in a high stone wall.

"Something was hanging there. What was that thing?" Frau Mendel insisted. "I want to know."

"In country districts," Mendel said, "in some of the more remote parts of Europe, they hang out the afterbirth of a cow at certain crossroads."

"Why, for God's sake?" Felix asked.

They reached the gate. The wind was rising, blowing down from the mountains. The first spots of impending rain touched their faces. Mendel looked toward the château, reassured by the scent of wood smoke and the cracks of welcoming light they could see at the upper windows. He let the suitcase in his hand swing to the ground. "Perhaps it is appropriate that we should put Europe's ugly past behind us, here at this gate." He glanced at the faces of his family; at last their ordeal was over. They were safe. Soon they would be in neutral Spain.

"In medieval times," Mendel said, "the crossroads were the danger point for travelers. It was where the thieves, the footpads lay in wait, for the simple reason that at the crossroads there was twice the chance of a traveler passing. But that simple reason was not good enough for medieval man. He preferred to believe that the traveler, robbed and probably dead when he was found next day, was the victim of something far more sinister.''

"A form of horned devil.'' Frau Mendel smiled, relaxed now.

"Yes. Mounted on a great black horse,'' Mendel said. "A frightening figure for medieval man. A figure to be placated. Thus the offer of a hanging afterbirth, with all the symbolism that goes with it.''

Beside the timber gate hung a chain. Mendel pulled it down, and somewhere inside the walled courtyard a bell jangled. The rain was increasing, falling in huge, splattering droplets. They heard a door open and close again; then a shaft of light touched the top of the wall. Footsteps sounded in the courtyard, approaching the gate.

Golda Mendel reached up and kissed her husband on the cheek. Felix and Sarah huddled close together, their faces shining wet.

"We've come a very long way from Heidelberg,'' Frau Mendel said.

"Yes, my dear,'' Mendel said. "We've negotiated a lot of devils at a lot of crossroads.''

The timber gate swung open. From the shadow a tall, slender man stepped out.

"Welcome to the Château d'Arblay, darlings,'' Peter Bilescu said. His face was bruised, but he still flashed his brilliant smile.

The Paris-Toulouse express sped south, now cutting through the rocky escarpments and rolling landscape of the Central Massif.

The rain on the coach window, flattened by the slipstream, formed ever-changing patterns on the glass. Colonel Reichenau idly watched the films of water spreading across the pane, one booted foot resting on the opposite seat.

The telephone call from Kaltenbrunner had left no

possible room for doubt. Inspector Krebs must be located as quickly as possible. Reichenau had reserved two first-class compartments on the first train leaving the Gare Montparnasse this morning.

The early weather had been fine, but once the flat fields of wheat and vegetables of the Paris basin had been left behind, the skies had slowly clouded over. Now the train had entered the belt of rain spreading north across the whole of the country from the Pyrenees.

The colonel lit a slim cheroot. In these last few days, Krebs had become impossible. Armed with his carte blanche authorization from Reichsführer-SS Himmler himself, the inspector had pursued the investigation with single-minded ruthlessness, leaving Reichenau to pick up the pieces.

The savage murder of the American columnist, Beth Kately, had come close to sparking off a major international incident. Diplomatic exchanges had taken place between the German Foreign Office and the U.S. State Department. Reichenau had been able to cobble together a report which concluded that the unfortunate Martin Upton, having suffered Beth Kately's insults and humiliations over many years, had finally snapped and killed his hated employer before taking his own life. But the affair might reach into higher circles yet. President Roosevelt had apparently asked that he be ''kept abreast'' of any developments.

The train was suddenly braking violently. Reichenau braced himself as his back was forced into the seat. From other compartments he could hear the muffled cries as people were flung forward. Under his feet steel screamed on steel as wheels locked.

Two hundred meters past the grade crossing, the locomotive finally came to a grinding halt. The grisly remains of a horse and cart, twisted into an unrecognizable tangle of bloody flesh and wood, were splattered across the front of the engine and wedged under the front wheels.

Unaware of what had occurred, Reichenau cursed at the

delay. Kaltenbrunner had also made it abundantly clear that time was of the essence and that he, Reichenau, as of midnight, was to assume overall responsibility for all further action taken by agents in the field. By that, the colonel knew full well, he meant Krebs.

Men were running through the downpour to the front of the train. The locomotive hissed rhythmic jets of steam, as if as impatient as Reichenau to go on.

In the Pyrenees it had been raining since morning, with a southern violence Anne-Marie had never met before. The Peugeot *camionnette* had died in the surging ford of a mountain stream, and they had been forced to wade, thigh deep, through the freezing torrent. Once, Chandler had almost lost his footing, and she had clung desperately to him until he regained his balance.

All around them streams of water seemed to leap down the rock faces to swirl in mud pools or pour in rivulets down tracks toward the stream where they had abandoned the pickup. The force of the pelting rain was exhausting, and the thunder exploding and echoing around the surrounding mountain peaks unnerved them both.

She was desperate to stop under one of the overhangs of rock to let him rest his leg but she knew darkness could not be more than an hour or two away now, and she had no relish for the thought of a night spent in this grim wilderness. Worse, their small-scale map was of little help in identifying the tracks and paths that crisscrossed the rocky sides of the valley.

For Chandler, every hundred yards was a nightmare. He knew that his leg was now infected, and every step sent a new throbbing pain to his head. The torrential rain had converted every path to a shallow, mud-colored stream, disguising stones and cavities so that he slipped and stumbled, only prevented from falling headlong by the unceasing attention of the girl.

She had no watch, and with the rain and heavy cloud it was difficult to know, but she guessed it was almost nine o'clock in the evening when she saw a horse and cart coming down a hillside path. The man driving it had willingly enough offered them a seat next to him on the plank bench below the sagging canvas covering. Château d'Arblay, he said, was not far. Beside her, Chandler rocked, already half-asleep.

"You come from the village, monsieur?" she asked him. She was sure she recognized him as the big, lumbering figure she had sometimes seen in La Maule-sur-Caveyron. But he showed no signs of recognizing her.

He wrapped the reins around his huge wrists and let the horse plod forward at its own speed. "Yes," he said, after a few moments, "I come from La Maule."

"I can pay you when we get to the château," she said.

He shook his head, still staring forward at the rain pouring down the flanks of the horse.

"Who else is there?" She half turned toward him. "At the château?"

He rubbed the water from his jaw with the back of his sleeve. "They're all in the woods," he said. "In a storm like this, cars can't get through."

"Why are they in the woods? Are they looking for someone?"

He grunted something she took as an assent.

"Are they looking for me? Did four people arrive yesterday and say I was coming?"

He looked down at the mud-covered toe caps of his shoes. "They said mademoiselle would be coming perhaps today," he muttered.

She nodded, too weary to try to draw more from him. But what he had said seemed clear enough. The Mendels, at least, had arrived. Perhaps they were already on their way across the mountains to Spain. Despite all that had happened in the last days, blackened by the arrest of Litvinov and the deaths of her uncle and his wife, she began to feel the stirrings of some half-guilty hope.

The driver spoke no more for the next ten minutes, except to mutter or grunt at the horse as it momentarily lost its footing in the stony mud. Then, as they emerged from the woods, with the reins still wrapped around his wrists: "La Maule, mademoiselle," he said.

She found herself staring through the sheeting rain at the familiar cluster of buildings and the château rising through the trees behind the village. Lights sparkling through the falling rain gave the tiny hamlet a welcoming appearance after the emptiness of the mountain paths.

In the gathering dark, she had not at first appreciated just how swollen the river had become. Only as the old horse drew them on down the slope did she see that the water had risen to cover everything but the topmost stones of the narrow pack bridge. Spilling over its banks, the river had spread across the flatland in front of the village, swirling past trees and over fences, widened from what must have been only a few meters to a broad floodwater.

At the bottom of the slope, the driver climbed down from his seat and stood patiently in the rain, unharnessing the horse. Along the path to the left of the half-submerged bridge stood a small covered stable into which the horse was led.

"Then you know Monsieur Litvinov, who bought the Château d'Arblay last year," Anne-Marie said.

"Yes," he nodded to himself. "Monsieur Litvinov. Yes." But she was aware that he was not really talking to her.

She glanced at him as he leaned forward, his elbows on his knees. He was an unusually big man, perhaps not much more than thirty. His great jaw dripped water as the rain was driven into his face. It was a head that made you think of isolated hamlets and inbred families.

"I've never seen rain like this before," she volunteered, uneasy that he seemed to have no wish to ask what they were doing wandering the hills in the middle of the storm.

"We'll have to get the boat out," he said, nodding to himself.

The village was built into the sharp bend of a mountain stream. She could easily imagine that after today the stream had become a torrent.

Watching his slow footsteps, his apparent indifference

to the rain, Anne-Marie realized that he was performing what must be a practiced routine in this part of the Pyrenees. Such floods were in all probability not unusual during the spring melting of the snow, or summer storms of the ferocity they had seen today.

She helped Chandler down from the cart. He stood with his arm around her, leaning his weight against her as he stared through the downpour. To her astonishment she found first he, and then both of them were laughing, the drops of water flying from their faces as they hugged each other in the pouring rain.

When the driver returned, he was carrying a small kerosene lantern, which he used to locate the end of a rope tied at shoulder height to the branch of a tree. Handing the lamp to Chandler, he turned back to the rope and hauled on it until they saw, being dragged through the racing water, a small rowboat.

It was now almost completely dark. Untying the rope, the man scrambled down the slope toward the water's edge and held the boat steady for them to get in. He had still not spoken more than a few dozen words since he had first stopped to give them a lift.

Sitting in the back of the boat, he worked the one fixed oar with a deftness his size and cumbersome movements belied. Sitting opposite him in the narrow prow, the lantern between them, Chandler and Anne-Marie watched him steer skillfully between the trees of the flooded riverbank.

She felt at first constrained to offer him some sort of compliment on the way he handled the boat, but there seemed little point. They had moved past the main rush of water by now, and the surface, like a great swirling millpond, made the boat easier to handle.

Cold and tired and above all wet, she huddled forward toward the kerosene lamp between them. Her eyes half closed, then opened as she forced herself to stay awake. It was almost unbelievable to her that she might be close to sleep in conditions like this. Yet, as her eyes fixed on the man's sodden legs, her mind again drifted toward sleep.

The yellow light from the lantern gleamed on his shoes. They were foreign shoes, she noted with that infinite attention to detail exhaustion brings. Not French and of very good quality. Every scrap of mud had been washed from them by the rain. She rocked forward, forcing her eyes to focus. Between the heel and sole of the right shoe, the lantern shone on the maker's name: Hochholtz, Heidelberg. The realization was slow, but when it came it shocked her awake. "Those shoes—" she said, "they're Professor Mendel's shoes."

Without thinking, she came forward onto her knees. Reaching out, she grasped the heel of the right shoe and twisted it as Mendel had done in the kitchen at Passy. She watched in horror as a stream of English sovereigns fell from their hiding place.

The man lurched to his feet, pulling the oar free as a weapon. As he raised it to strike, the boat was bathed in light. Turning his head, Chandler saw flashlight beams cutting across the misty surface of the water.

A voice called from behind the lights, "Welcome, darlings."

Chapter
Seventeen

PETER BILESCU WAS the first to enter, holding the door open for the rest.

Two Gestapo men, dressed in dripping oilskins, pushed Chandler into the long kitchen of the château. He stumbled forward on his injured leg and steadied himself against the pine table.

Behind him, Anne-Marie angrily shrugged off the hands of a third Gestapo man.

The room, lit by guttering oil lamps, had until recently served as the working kitchen of the château. One wall was lined with cast-iron bread ovens and a huge, chipped, stoneware sink.

Bilescu removed his coat and cap, revealing a small, bald, red raw patch of scalp at the side of his head. He wiped the rain from his face and smoothed his golden-blond hair down to cover the blemish.

"What the hell are you doing here, Bilescu?" said Chandler, standing near the table and heavily favoring his bad leg.

"Can't you guess, Chandler?" said Bilescu. "The road that brought me here was called expediency." He smiled, but for a moment there was a hint of remorse in the smile.

"How did you find this place?" said Anne-Marie, her eyes alive with contempt.

"Herr Beckerman was kind enough to give us his help." Emil Krebs rose from his seat beside the Pyreneean fireplace. "A map with the Litvinov escape route for Jews clearly marked in red."

The German came forward into the light, unable to disguise his sense of triumph. He clicked his heels to Anne-Marie. "Inspector Krebs," he said formally, "RSHA, Gestapo."

Anne-Marie looked at him with hard, glittering eyes.

"I have been looking forward to this opportunity for some time," Krebs said, in high humor. "I have already met various members of your family, at various times, in various parts of your country." He threw a knowing glance at the Rumanian.

The two Gestapo men struggled to hold Anne-Marie as she fought to hurl herself at Krebs.

Krebs stepped forward and struck Chandler across the side of the head with the edge of his hand, sending the American spinning to the floor.

"Release her," the inspector ordered.

The Gestapo men let her go. Anne-Marie sprang forward, trying to claw at Krebs's face, but he grabbed her wrists and held them in an unbreakable grip. As he slowly increased the pressure, her eyes filled with tears of pain and frustration. Krebs pushed her away to arms' length, still holding her wrists.

The bell in the courtyard jangled above the sound of the rain.

"Who's that?" said Krebs, freeing Anne-Marie from his grasp and pushing her away.

"It'll be the boatman," said Bilescu. "I promised him something for his trouble."

"Pay him and send him away," said Krebs.

As Bilescu put on his coat and cap and went out, Krebs watched Chandler slowly pulling himself to his feet.

"Take him outside," said Krebs, scratching the back of his neck. "Make it look as if he drowned."

The two Gestapo men gripped Chandler by the arms. He was still too dazed to resist.

"No," cried Anne-Marie in anguish. "You can't. He's an American. Please. No."

As Chandler was propelled to the door, it opened. Borel stood on the threshold, an unlit Gauloise dangling from his lips, the shoulders of his raincoat drenched. As he stepped forward, the distinguished figure of Colonel Reichenau appeared behind him.

Reichenau scanned the room and then settled his gaze on Krebs. "Ah, Krebs," he said evenly. "You're a hard man to find. But here I am"—he paused, taking in the bedraggled figures of Chandler and Anne-Marie—"and just in time, it seems."

He strode forward, taking off his SS colonel's cap and topcoat and placing them on the table. "Outside," he said to the Gestapo men.

They hesitated, looking at Krebs. Since he had picked them out from the new arrivals at Gestapo 1 in Paris and flashed his authorization before their startled eyes, they had held Krebs in something close to awe.

"I am Inspector Krebs's immediate superior," Reichenau said calmly. "A fact I'm sure he will confirm. Leave us."

Krebs gave the slightest of nods to the three men and they went out.

"Inspector Borel, if you will excuse us for a few minutes," Reichenau said, ushering the Frenchman toward a door leading to the main part of the château.

Krebs had remained motionless since the moment he saw Reichenau. Now he spoke. "Why are you here, Colonel Reichenau?" His voice was full of carefully controlled contempt; his stare insolent.

"To take charge of your prisoners," Reichenau said.

Krebs glared. "No. I caught them. It ends here. *I* end it here," he hissed with open defiance. "I am authorized."

Reichenau glanced at Anne-Marie, who stood quietly in Chandler's arms in the shadows by the fireplace. He moved closer to Krebs and lowered his voice.

"Listen to me, Inspector. Nothing will be done with the girl until it is cleared with the Reichsführer-SS himself. Is that clear?"

A muscle worked in Krebs's cheek. "What about the American?" he asked sullenly.

"I have made arrangements with the French inspector. The American is to be charged with murder."

"No," said Krebs, stepping away.

"He will be tried and certainly convicted," said Reichenau.

"Tried!" Krebs's face was contorted, his voice rising.

"Control yourself, Krebs."

"No," yelled Krebs. "I finish that one here."

"We cannot have another incident involving an American," hissed Reichenau.

Krebs stood in the middle of the kitchen, his powerful body heaving with rage. "Don't you understand," he bawled. "He knows." He flung an accusing finger at Chandler. "Do you imagine she hasn't told him? Why else would he have gone to St-Eloi? How can he be put on trial? He will talk. What will he have to lose?"

"Silence!"

Krebs did not seem to hear, saliva flecked the corners of his mouth. He snarled at Chandler like some savage beast. "He knows she's the Führer's daughter. He knows her mother was a Jew!"

Chandler felt her slender body stiffen. The full impact of what Krebs had just revealed hit him like a physical blow.

Krebs was staring at him. Slowly, lines of self-doubt began to furrow his face.

Reichenau ran the palm of his hand over the top of his head, smoothing his iron-gray hair. "Whether he knew or not is now irrelevant." He turned to Krebs. "Tell someone to drive over to the telephone exchange in

Matignac. Get them out of bed. I have to make a confidential call to Kaltenbrunner. Make sure no one is listening in.''

In the narrow cot he favored at Wewelsburg, the Reichsführer-SS sat up, his pajamas buttoned tightly to the neck as proof against drafts. "Reichenau telephoned, you say. At this time of night?" These interruptions to his rest were becoming intolerable.

Kaltenbrunner sat beside the cot. "Krebs has found the girl, Reichsführer; you insisted on knowing at once."

"Yes, yes." Himmler fluttered his hand in a dismissive gesture.

"They are holding her in the south of France," Kaltenbrunner said. "Together with an American."

"Another American? Not a journalist, I sincerely hope." Himmler reached out for his rimless spectacles and adjusted them carefully on his nose. "What is it that Reichenau wants?" he asked, frowning.

"He requires *your* written authority for Krebs to kill them both," said Kaltenbrunner.

Himmler nodded thoughtfully. "I don't see why," he said. "You can give him that."

"He has asked for your written authority, Reichsführer." It was untrue. But Kaltenbrunner had no intention of leaving his name on such a document unless Adolf Hitler's permission was first sought. Verbal orders were quite different. They could be eradicated by simply eradicating the recipient of the orders. But a written document was something else, not to be taken lightly.

"Doesn't Krebs already have a letter?" Himmler asked, trying to bring his mind to bear on the subject. "I remember signing it."

"Indeed, Reichsführer, couched in wide-ranging but general terms," said Kaltenbrunner. "According to Reichenau, Inspector Krebs is reluctant to act without your specific, personal orders."

"Why are subordinates so anxious always to cover themselves?" Himmler said testily.

Kaltenbrunner remained silent as he watched the Reichsführer-SS worrying at the problem.

"May I draft the order, Reichsführer?"

Himmler removed his spectacles. "No," he said. "Let me get some sleep now, Ernst. Tomorrow I shall fly to Berlin. I've felt all along that this matter is something for the Führer's personal consideration."

She knelt beside him on the dank floor between the rows of empty wine racks in the cellar at the Château d'Arblay, cleaning the wounds in his leg as best she could. They had hardly spoken since the heavy door at the top of the short flight of stone steps had been slammed shut and bolted.

"There, I think it looks better," Anne-Marie said.

"Thank you." Chandler smiled up at her.

They wrapped themselves separately in the blankets that had been hurled down the steps after them and lay huddled together in silence.

"Is it true?" Chandler asked at last.

"My mother was in many ways a stupid woman," Anne-Marie said slowly, staring up at the ceiling. "She believed herself to be more intelligent than she was because men flattered her. I saw it all my life in the café. She was a big woman, tall—statuesque is perhaps the word. She smiled easily and touched men. A hand on the shoulder as she served the coffee, a nudge, an arm around the waist. She manipulated men."

She sighed deeply. Chandler waited patiently for her to go on.

"As I grew up I hated her flirting and boasting. As she grew older, into her thirties, she got worse. She wasn't promiscuous, at least I don't think so. It was mostly talk about the past."

Her hair swirled about her eyes as she shook her head violently. Chandler remained silent and very still.

"Then one night, I heard her crying. I went into her bedroom. I had never seen her cry before. She had our local newspaper, the *Echo du Nord,* spread out on the bed.

There was an article on the new leader of Germany. It mentioned how he had spent the war in our area, in St-Eloi and the other villages around.''

She stopped again, breathing in deeply. ''I asked her why she was crying. She brought out a shoe box. In it was a photograph and a cheap bracelet. From him. From the new leader of Germany, Adolf Hitler. The name meant little to me then. She—she began to suggest that I was not my father's child.'' Something in her throat caught her voice.

Chandler pulled his arms out of the blanket and held her close.

''You asked me if it is true. My mother and sister were killed because of it; so were Uncle Georges and his wife, and Paul Litvinov. How can it not be true?''

By morning, the skies had cleared. The hot sun drew up clouds of mist from the rain-soaked landscape. These vanished in the warm air a few feet off the ground.

In an upstairs bedroom at the Château d'Arblay, the three men were silent. Each was drained through lack of sleep. Reichenau stood by the unshuttered, open window. Chandler and Borel sat opposite each other across a table.

''You must be wondering, Monsieur Chandler,'' Borel began, ''what I am doing here.''

Chandler shrugged, although he had never expected to see the Frenchman again.

''I'm obeying the laws of the Republic. No, the Third Republic no longer exists,'' said Borel. ''The chamber of deputies, meeting in Bordeaux, voted itself and the Republic out of existence.''

Chandler watched Borel's haggard face; the lips were turned down in what he read as contempt.

''So, I am obeying the only government in France. The government constituted in the figure of Marshal Pétain, the victor of Verdun.''

Chandler was silent. He wondered again why he was still alive.

"As I understand it," Borel continued, "in order for Colonel Reichenau and the Gestapo in Paris to make an arrest here, in unoccupied France, it is necessary to call upon the services of a French police officer. In this case, myself. That is why I am here."

"You're going to arrest me?" Chandler asked.

"Yes, for the murder of Jacqueline Claudel," Borel said flatly.

"Jesus!"

Reichenau glared from the window. "You will remain silent, Herr Chandler."

"As far as it is possible to understand these complex questions of authority," said Borel, feeling along the fringe of hair at the side of his head, "Colonel Reichenau is, I believe, my senior officer."

"Get on with it, Borel. We haven't got all day," said Reichenau.

"Time is important, Monsieur Chandler," said Borel, leaning forward in his chair. "Legality and justice come some way behind," he added pointedly.

Chandler studied Borel's face. Was he trying, in some veiled way, to tell him something, to warn him?

Borel looked over at Reichenau, but the colonel seemed absorbed in something beyond the window. From a briefcase at his feet, the French inspector took out a file and his police notebook. "I'm instructed to ask you to read a statement I have prepared from my notes, which will form the basis of the report I shall submit to the prosecutors' office in Paris."

Reichenau now watched impassively as Borel slid the file across the table to Chandler. As the American began to read, Reichenau turned back to the window.

There was no doubt in the colonel's mind: Chandler would have to be eliminated. Before Krebs's incredible outburst there had been a slim chance that this could have been avoided. Now it was necessary and inevitable. But it would still be useful to have Borel arrest Chandler. He would then be, technically at least, a prisoner of the

French government. If he were then to meet with some fatal accident, the American authorities would find it difficult to hold the German government responsible. It would go a long way to avoiding another embarrassing debacle like the Beth Kately affair.

Borel had taken a pencil from the leather spine of his notebook and was doodling idly on the flyleaf.

To Chandler, the statement was a mixture of the same circumstantial evidence Borel had questioned him about in Paris, laced with downright lies. Bilescu had made a declaration that on several occasions Jacqueline Claudel had tried to break off her relationship with Chandler and that this had resulted in violent arguments. A second forensic examination had found his fingerprints on a number of relevant items in the apartment, and the concierge, Madame Bissel, was now sure she could positively identify him as the man she saw on the evening of the murder.

Chandler threw the file back across the table. Borel warned him with a gesture not to speak.

"I must ask you," said Borel, "are you prepared to sign this statement as true in its present form?"

Chandler shook his head.

Borel checked his watch and made an entry in his notebook. "I must also ask you if you would like to make a statement of your own."

"I have nothing to say," said Chandler.

Borel noted the reply and leaned back in his chair.

"Do your duty, Inspector," Reichenau said.

Borel rubbed his chin. "In the matter of the murder of Jacqueline Claudel of Île St-Louis, Paris, I advise you, Theodore John Chandler, that you are now subject to my arrest."

"Guard," Reichenau called.

The door opened and one of the SS troopers Reichenau had brought down with him from Paris came in.

"Take the prisoner back to the cellar," said Reichenau.

The trooper took Chandler out.

Borel extracted a crumpled pack of cigarettes from his pocket.

"I plan to return to Paris today," said Reichenau. "You'll stay, of course."

"I could hardly leave a prime murder suspect I have just placed under arrest," said Borel.

Outside it was clouding over. There would be more rain.

Chapter
Eighteen

AROUND THE BIG chintz-covered armchair, every man in the dim after-dinner light fought the compulsion for his eyelids to drop, fought the waves of weariness and boredom that engulfed them all.

Slumped in the big armchair, a cream cake in one hand, which moved in pallid imitation of the dramatic gestures that accompanied his great speeches of the past, Adolf Hitler recounted the days of struggle, the moments of bitter decision, as he had dragged himself from the mud of Flanders to the leadership of the Third Reich.

Mesmerized by the waving cream cake, fifteen generals and members of the Nazi Party leadership lay back in their armchairs, praying the soft lighting would disguise the closing of their eyes. Most had heard the story a dozen times before. But the Führer was like a man with a favorite record. Night after night he would relive his past, rewriting history, obliterating truth with repetition, drugging his listeners far into the night.

There was no question of any guest leaving the small, stuffy sitting room before Hitler himself. The ladies had left hours before, when Eva Braun had yawned prettily and announced it was time for her to go to bed. Frau Fegelein, her sister, had gotten to her feet immediately. Frau Himmler had stood, more uncertainly, and Frau Jodl and Frau Keitel, the generals' wives, had glanced quickly toward their husbands for permission.

Unfailingly polite to women, though contemptuous, often crude or dismissive to men, Adolf Hitler had jumped to his feet, pulling down his rumpled jacket, brushing crumbs from the creases in his black trousers.

It was no secret to his entourage that Hitler enjoyed the company of women and that he possessed a magnetic attraction for them. Nobody now dared speak of his niece Geli Raubal, who had committed suicide for love of her strange, moody uncle. Nobody spoke of the private box at the Metropol, Berlin's only remaining girlie show. Nobody, of course, ever mentioned the existence of Eva Braun outside the magic circle.

Yet on these evenings Hitler welcomed the women's leaving. It was the signal for the small talk, the chatter, to end. Now *he* could talk about the past, which absorbed him.

When there were women present, he expected Eva Braun to lead them away within fifteen minutes of midnight. But for their husbands it was different. Whether in Berlin or the mountain retreat at Berchtesgaden or in any of his newly constructed operational headquarters, the Führer followed the same routine. Rising just before midday, he presided over lunch for fifteen or twenty staff officers and visitors. From these he would arbitrarily select half a dozen to take tea and cakes with him. Then at seven, dinner and perhaps a Hollywood movie, a western for preference. Only then, for Hitler, comfortably seated and provided with coffee and more cakes, would the day really begin, when the withdrawal of the wives left the night free to be filled by his reminiscences.

"In those days, as front-line soldiers, the very word suffering took on a new meaning," Hitler was saying.

"Fear of death or mutilation can cripple a man for a week, a month even. But it can't stay with him for a year, two years, three. Something else takes its place. We front-line soldiers in the last war learned to live on two levels of consciousness—with the certainty of death and the equal certainty of immortality."

Among the guests, only Heinrich Himmler was fully awake. Sitting upright in his armchair, he struggled to frame a question. "But Führer," he said, "even in those days, there must have been moments of quiet. Moments of relaxation?"

Hitler smiled. "Yes," he said. "I had my dog, Fuchsl, a spirited little thing. Came over from the English lines one night and attached himself to me. Two years we were together, until some swine stole him from me."

"I meant relaxation, Führer, rest periods behind the front line."

Hitler frowned. "Sometimes there was leave, even a furlough back home, but increasingly I had no wish to return to a Germany rotten with Jewish defeatism and Communist betrayal. I preferred the front line."

Keitel was fighting to disguise a yawn as a prolonged cough. Himmler sat forward on the edge of his seat. "As front-line soldiers," he said, "you took your pleasures where you were?"

Hitler grunted, uncertain what the normally prudish Himmler was getting at.

"No doubt, Führer," Himmler probed nervously, "some of your colleagues had French girl friends."

"Some," Hitler conceded indifferently.

"Some of them, no doubt, had close relations with the girls."

Hitler bit on his cream cake. "God didn't give front-line soldiers fly buttons just so they could piss in the mud," he said. Cream frothed the line of his mustache. "What was I saying—? Ah yes, Germany in those days, in those years of defeat. It was my unshakable resolve, as I lay gassed, blind, in a hospital in Berlin, that Germany hould rise again from the ashes.''

The clock above Hitler's head ticked with what seemed
o his guests a desperate slowness. By 2:30 the grating
Austrian voice had brought them to the 1933 elections.
An hour later they had barely progressed a year into the
eriod of Nazi power. And then suddenly, without
xplanation, Hitler got to his feet. The half-slumbering
roup of generals and senior Party members stood.
Himmler was already beside Hitler at the door.

"Führer," he said anxiously, "even at this late hour I
vould be grateful for a few moments in private."

Hitler yawned his displeasure in Himmler's face. "If
ou must," he said. "Come to my office."

The Führer led the way into a room across the corridor.
t was furnished with an imposing desk, behind which
vas a hard, straight-backed chair. Blank papers were
cattered across the desk top. A sunburst clock was
ermanently set at 2:20. It was a room with one purpose
nly. In it Adolf Hitler was photographed at his desk,
vorking through the night for Germany and the German
eople. About once every six weeks Dr. Goebbels would
ublish a photograph with a caption that varied very little.
"Late into the night the Führer calculates the nation's
ext step." Unknown to Goebbels's Propaganda Minis-
ry, however, the stopped clock had already been spotted
y the sharp-eyed Berliners, and in some working-class
reas of Berlin, the Führer's night activities were already
he subject of irreverent comment.

Hitler leaned against the desk while Himmler carefully
losed the door.

"What is it?"

Himmler clasped his hands behind his back. "Certain
nformation has come my way, Führer."

"Come to the point," Hitler said. "You're Chief of
Police. Of course information comes your way."

"It concerns the background of a very senior Party
fficial."

Hitler's head came up.

"Many years ago," Himmler said, "it is possible thi senior Party man had a child, an illegitimate child. Whil on active duty in France."

"Nazi Party members are lusty fellows. Especially th 'Old Fighters.'"

"Führer," Himmler said, "the woman—the mother o the child was a Jewess."

His eyes on the dark-red carpet, Hitler nodded thought fully. "A senior Party man, you say. A gauleiter?"

Himmler clasped and unclasped his hands behind hi back. "No, Führer. Much senior."

"Even so," Hitler straightened up, "I assume you're dealing with the problem. Clean the whole thing up. Th girl—I trust she has no children?"

"Not yet," Himmler said carefully.

"A fine story for the international press. A prominen member of the Party with a Jewish daughter. Who is he this man?"

Himmler stood immobile in the center of the room.

"I require to know who this man is, Himmler."

Sweat trickled down the Reichsführer's forehead an down the inside of his rimless lenses.

"Who is he?" Hitler's voice was hardly above whisper. "Not Goering or Hess?"

Himmler shook his head.

"Not you," Hitler almost smiled. "Not the grea exponent of racial purity? No, of course not. You neve served in the front line."

"No, Führer. Not me."

The smile disappeared from the leader's face. "I see," he said slowly.

"The mother was French," Himmler said. "She cam from a small village called St-Eloi."

"This daughter?" Hitler grunted. "Where is sh now?"

"I have been informed we are holding her in the south of France."

"You know what to do," said Hitler solemnly.

"Yes, Führer."

"St-Eloi you say. And the woman's name?"

"Arlette Claudel."

Hitler nodded. "She ran the café there. A fine-looking woman."

"So I believe, Führer. Her racial origins were in no way apparent, I understand."

Again Hitler nodded. "Do what you have to do and do it quickly. True or false these stories can be damaging when the jackals of the American press get hold of them." He turned and left the room.

Heinrich Himmler blinked, removed his misted spectacles and thoughtfully wiped the lenses clean with his handkerchief. At a sound he looked up.

Hitler had reappeared in the open doorway. "Arlette Claudel," he said almost to himself. "And the girl's name?"

"Anne-Marie, Führer."

"Anne-Marie, it's a good German name too. What does she look like, this daughter?"

"Like her mother, I imagine," Himmler said cautiously. "Except that her hair is dark."

"You have a photograph?"

"No, Führer."

Hitler stood in the doorway. A pale stain of cream cake on his jacket caught his attention. He scratched at it with his thumbnail. "Bring the girl to Berlin," he said suddenly. "Put her in one of your rooms with a two-way mirror; I know you have them. I am interested to see her. Just once, before you do what you have to."

He turned rapidly away, and Heinrich Himmler stood rigidly as the Führer's footsteps receded down the corridor.

At 4:20 A.M. Emil Krebs walked out into the courtyard of the Château d'Arblay. The air was sharp, and a brilliant moon threw a metallic sheen onto the surface of the puddles among which the three black cars stood ready to leave. On the telephone Kaltenbrunner had made it clear that for the Führer it was no more than a whim. What had already been done and what was about to be done was approved. Reichsführer-SS Heinrich Himmler had personally congratulated both Reichenau and himself. Of course Reichenau would claim the honors, he now realized that was the way of the world. Even the Socialist world of nationalism to which he had given his youthful enthusiasm. Even in the Gestapo, where merit, not birth, was supposed to be the rule, where all officers were supposed to rise from the ranks, where someone like Josef "Sepp" Dietrich could become a divisional commander—even in this society devoted to egalitarianism, people like Reichenau still somehow received the credit. The credit due to others.

For Emil Krebs, the Gestapo was a family. It had provided him with all the warmth and security he had ever known. It was an institution where working-class men like himself could attain positions of power and influence. But as a member of the family he had, however slowly, even painfully, come to understand that other people held the trump cards. University-trained lawyers like Reichenau.

It was only when he had arrived in Paris that Krebs had realized the sheer power of his own position. Not with prickly patriots like Borel perhaps, but with the true entrepreneurs of this world. Bilescu had dissolved before his eyes after one good beating. He had seen in the Rumanian a man who would do anything to survive. They could work together. Bilescu would organize the Jews from Paris. German refugees at first, and later, when the pressure mounted, French Jews. Jews willing to pay for a safe route to the south and over the mountains to Spain. Of course they would get no farther than d'Arblay. And what harm was done? Might and profit were National Socialist principles. Emil Krebs, a totally devoted Nazi ideologue, saw no reason why he should not profit from the power his position gave him.

Behind him Krebs could hear the sound of footsteps

escending the stair. He stood aside as his men brought
Chandler and then Anne-Marie out of the house. He
ound it difficult to suppress a smile at the girl's wild-
yed look, the flying hair and the passionate hatred in the
vay she tried to wrench herself from the grip of the
uards.

"One moment," he said.

She was dragged around to face him. She stood before
im, insolently staring. He found he could admire the
urve of her lip even when it expressed such contempt.

"Mademoiselle . . ." He reached out with one finger,
fted the hair out of her eyes.

He had killed her mother. And her sister. He smiled
gain as he looked at her, a smile of surprise at the
trength of his own feelings. Was it possible that he was
eginning to enjoy killing?

He was breathing, not heavily, but slightly faster than
sual. "Put her in the car," he said.

Chandler and Anne-Marie were handcuffed together by
he wrists and pushed into the rear seat of the second car.
he Gestapo driver and the guard in the passenger seat
vould guarantee security.

"She's very beautiful, Emil. But dangerous."

Krebs turned around to see Bilescu standing in the
oorway behind him. "You think I'm a fool?" he said.
In any case, Jewesses revolt me. With an ordinary
vhore, at least, you know where they've been."

Bilescu laughed and Krebs found himself laughing too.
He was a strange man, Bilescu. Life, death, race—did he
ke anything seriously? Except pain, of course. Krebs
emembered the stricken look, the desperate pleas.
he Rumanian took pain seriously. He reached out
nd shook Bilescu's hand. "I'll never forget your
ace," he said, "the night I persuaded you to coop-
rate."

Bilescu was no longer smiling.

"It went as white as a sheet," Krebs continued.
Blubbing a bit, weren't you. However"—he released
Bilescu's hand—"I see no reason why we can't be of

great use to each other—Peter.''

Turning away, Krebs walked toward the leading car
Climbing into the passenger seat, he nodded to the driver
The big black Citroën moved forward, breaking the
surface of the puddles in the courtyard of the château.

Chapter
Nineteen

AT SUNSET THE only bridge across the Garonne River at Bordeaux was a chaos of vehicles, some still covered with their protective mattresses; others, small pickup trucks, piled with household furniture; yet others, broken down with jets of steam pouring from their radiators. Whole families stood beside their cars arguing with other drivers, or slumped in desperate resignation. At several points, groups of men had taken it upon themselves to lift, bodily, broken-down cars and tip them over the stone balustrade into the river below. Wild-eyed drivers, struggling to protect their only means of transport to the north, fought and kicked to save their vehicles and then watched in exhausted horror from the parapet as they crashed against the granite footings of the arches and rolled into the Garonne.

The convoy of black Citroëns edged forward across the bridge. In midstream, opposite the Esplanade des Quinconces, a gutted tanker still belched smoke and flame, a victim of the final German air attack before the armistice. On either side of the tanker, ignoring the dark pall of smoke, small boats passed back and forth loaded

with vegetables from the countryside to feed the grossly
inflated population of the city. Beyond the stalled vehicles, the shouting, gesticulating men and the oily black
smoke, moored at the Quai des Chartrons, lay the long,
white United States liner *Washington* with its huge Old
Glory painted on its side.

At less than five miles an hour the Gestapo convoy
drove on through Bordeaux. Krebs bawled savagely from
the window of the leading car, but the main boulevards
were choked with abandoned vehicles and cartloads of
peasants' belongings. The side streets and alleys teemed
with people—farmers from the north, soldiers, shop-
keepers from Paris. To the refugees, the three black cars,
pushing their way forward, horns blaring, were just
another convoy of politicians or civil servants, to be
ignored at best, or shouted and screamed at as cartloads
of possessions were nudged aside or toppled onto the
sidewalk.

The airport, when they arrived, was in total confusion.
During the daylight hours, thousands of the wandering
horde had discovered it, swarming across the grass
runways, hanging rough tents from the sides of their cars,
lighting fires and bargaining for food. A Breguet transport
aircraft stood in the darkness, ignored on the far side of
the airfield, surrounded by glowing camp fires.

Krebs signaled for the Gestapo driver to stop. His
mouth compressed in anger as he turned to the agent
behind him and gestured across the field. "How long will
it take to find a police detachment to clear the runway?"

The man shrugged. "We won't find a detachment
tonight, Inspector," he said. "We'd need fifty men at
least."

Krebs got out of the car and stood glaring at the dark
figures hunched around the camp fires. Borel joined him.

"Look at this," Krebs said through his teeth.

"The Wehrmacht will be here by tomorrow," said
Borel. "Why not wait?"

"My orders are to return the prisoners to Paris tonight," Krebs said savagely. "I don't intend to let a

peasant rabble stop me. Get the prisoners. We're board-
ing the plane now.''

Borel went to the second car, opened the door and told
Chandler and Anne-Marie to get out. Awkwardly, wrists
still handcuffed together, they slid out of the backseat and
stood beside Borel. The Gestapo driver was crossing to
Krebs for instructions.

''If you've got any chance at all,'' said Borel, ''this is
it.''

Chandler felt the small handcuff key pressed into the
palm of his hand. He turned uncertainly, his eyes meeting
Borel's.

''Krebs plans to drive the refugees off the runway.
He'll never make it. The people out there are peasant
farmers. Most of them have a shotgun in their cart. The
way they're feeling, they'll use it on any aircraft, German
or French.''

They crossed the airfield, Krebs and Borel leading, the
young Gestapo men in a tight cluster around Chandler and
Anne-Marie. Under their guards' watchful eyes, there
was clearly no opportunity to escape, no opportunity even
to use the key Borel had given them.

As they pushed their way through piled carts and
stepped over sleeping children, they could see that Krebs
had reached the Breguet and was mounting the aluminum
steps. A few seconds later the cockpit lights went on.
There was no reaction from the people camped around the
aircraft. Exhausted by their journeys, confused by the
armistice declaration, they paid no more attention to the
plane than to the crated French fighters that lined the far
end of the airfield—until the engines burst into life.

With a roar that reverberated around the perimeter of
the field, the heavy engines began to turn over. The beams
of the Breguet's landing lights cut through the darkness of
the runway, touching the refugees like some electrifying
wand that dissolved apathy or exhaustion in a second.
Horses, tethered between the shafts, veered in panic from
the sudden noise and light. Women ran to drag sleeping
children from their blanket rolls, old people stumbled in

confusion to the safety of the darkness outside the white beams of light.

Infected by the alarm around them, the Gestapo men pushed Chandler and Anne-Marie through the crowd, shouting threats in German and waving their pistols. Behind her somewhere, as she clambered up the plane's aluminum steps, Anne-Marie heard a shot fired, then another. As Chandler followed her into the Breguet she registered that the third report was heavier, the blast of a shotgun.

In the body of the plane it was chaos. The last two Gestapo men to board had been hit in the legs. One rolled between the aluminum seats, blood welling through the cloth of his trousers. Krebs, in the cockpit, was shouting to the pilot above the engine's roar. As the plane jerked forward, Chandler and Anne-Marie were thrown down into the aisle, linked together by their handcuffed wrists. Over their heads, a shotgun blast tore through the aircraft's thin aluminum skin and shattered the central light. In the darkness Borel was beside them. "Undo the handcuffs," he said. "This is your last chance."

The Breguet lurched forward into the fleeing crowds of refugees. Men saw their wives spinning off its jolting undercarriage, their children screaming in panic as the great machine pursued them down the runway. Other men dragged shotguns from their farm carts and ran forward, firing blasts into the wings and body of the slowly moving plane.

From the blue-lit cockpit, Krebs could see that the runway was clearing. Hundreds of tiny figures were fleeing from the beams of the aircraft's lights. He heard his own voice screaming above the roar of the engines, urging the Breguet on. Somewhere beyond the noise and confusion, he was aware of the same excitement he had felt as he was murdering Jacqueline Claudel.

In the darkness outside, Pierre Lacave limped forward, his shotgun held tight to his chest. An air-force mechanic at the beginning of the war, he had been demobilized after an accident in which an aircraft engine had slipped from its mounting, crushing his leg. He knew the exact position of the fuel tank under the wing of the Breguet that roared toward him.

He had no idea whether the pilot was French or German, and in the rage against all authority that the refugees felt, he was in no mood to care. He had seen the arrogance of the arrival of the black cars and the murderous taxiing of the plane through the refugee encampment, and he was determined that the aircraft would never take off.

Two hundred yards before him, the aircraft was gathering speed. Ignoring the pain in his leg, he forced himself and dropped on both knees just inside the edge of the narrow runway. As the plane approached, he rose under the wing tip and fired both barrels into the joint between the engine mounting and the fuel tank.

In the rush of air as the plane passed, Lacave was thrown over. But the sharp smell of high-octane aviation fuel was already in his nostrils.

In the cockpit the pilot registered without understanding, the flashing warning light above the starboard fuel tank pressure gauge. Before him, glowing red camp fires were scattered along the runway. As the Breguet passed over them, he realized that fuel was spraying below the wing.

To the stunned refugees, it seemed that a sheet of flame leaped up rapaciously from the camp fires to the starboard wing. Among bucking horses and screaming children, they watched while the aircraft sped past, trailing curtains of flame. Then, just as it seemed the Breguet was about to leave the ground, a massive explosion tore the wing from the body and hurled it, blazing, high into the air.

Inside the aircraft, Chandler had seen the burning fuel spewing from the starboard motor. When the explosion came, he had pulled Anne-Marie down between the seats. Lost in blackness now, and shaken by the violent movement of the slewing aircraft, neither was sure whether they had retained consciousness throughout the whole ten seconds of the crash.

By the time Chandler was capable of rational thought again, the Breguet was no longer moving; smoke and bitter fumes swirled through the body of the aircraft; where the tail plane had snapped off, a vast hole opened to the night sky. He had no sense of time, no idea how long it took him to pull Anne-Marie to her feet. Around him in the smoke he could hear shouts in German and screams of a man in pain.

The single Gestapo man in the aisle lurched toward him, pulling a pistol from a holster under his jacket. The aircraft now seemed illuminated by a bright orange glow. Before the German could pull the gun clear Chandler kicked out wildly. As the man jackknifed forward, he kicked again. Scrabbling on the studded metal floor, he snatched up the pistol. The German was slumped, retching, across the seats. Chandler looked around for Anne-Marie, but the aisle behind him was empty. Then Borel's face appeared in a blazing gap in the fuselage. "Jump, for God's sake," he shouted. "She's down here."

Buffeted by gusts of heat, Chandler stood before a wall of flame beyond which he seemed to discern shadowy shapes. Behind him, a ball of black and yellow fire rolled down the aisle toward him.

He jumped and fell forward on the grass outside. He was aware of the cool air, cutting his face like an arctic wind. Then Borel dragged him by the arm, onto his feet and a few stumbling steps from the aircraft before it exploded in a black fireball that hung for a second, then ascended like a helium balloon into the night sky.

He reached out for Anne-Marie next to him, holding her tight. Refugees were pouring past them to stand in awestruck silence before the blazing remains of the aircraft. Those at the front cowered back from the rising intensity of the heat.

"Krebs," Chandler's voice issued as a croak, his throat parched by smoke and ash. "Where is he?"

Borel pointed behind them. On the edge of a ditch, Chandler could make out what looked like a bundle of black, smoking rags. It moved, slumped forward and rolled into the ditch.

"We must go." Borel took Anne-Marie's arm.

She pulled her arm free. She was staring toward the ditch. She turned toward Chandler. Her eyes blazed reflections of the burning wreckage. "Is he dead?" she said.

She saw the pistol in Chandler's hand and reached out. Instinctively, his hand tightened on the butt and drew it out of her reach. Their eyes held. He threw the gun down and, taking her by the shoulders, guided her off through the crowd.

Krebs lay on his back. His clothes were scraps of burned cloth sticking to his flesh. His eyes were open in a blackened, charred face. He was conscious, his lips moving stiffly. Then from somewhere deep inside him surged a hideous, primeval howl.

On the quayside, the last of the Americans were being processed by an exhausted consular officer at a trestle table set up at the bottom of the gangway beneath the brilliant lights of the neutral liner. Seamen from the S.S. *Washington* stood guard with pick handles behind an improvised barrier of deck chairs, but the long line, which had shuffled forward throughout the blazing afternoon, was now reduced to a last, dozen people.

At the end of the line, Chandler turned to the Frenchman. "What will you do, Borel?"

Borel shrugged in an exaggerated, Gallic way.

"I know some of the embassy people. I might be able to get you aboard," said Chandler.

Borel shook his head. "America's too far away," he said. A cigarette hung from the corner of his mouth. His hands were deep in the pockets of his crumpled trousers.

"You can't stay in France," said Anne-Marie urgently.

"No," Borel muttered reflectively, "probably not. The idea of England attracts me." He might have been discussing the relative merits of holiday brochures. "This

General de Gaulle,'' he said. ''I had never heard of him
before. But he speaks to me.''

He shook hands with Chandler, then leaned forward
and kissed Anne-Marie on both cheeks. ''Sometime,'' he
said, ''we'll have a bottle of champagne at the Lipp.''

They watched him stroll away along the quay until he
disappeared beyond the bright lights of the American
liner.

''Name?'' the consular officer said, half-eaten hot dog
in one hand, a pen poised in the other.

''Chandler. Mr. and Mrs. Theo Chandler.''

''Passports.'' The man looked at the two scarecrow
figures in front of him.

''No documents,'' Chandler said. ''No luggage. We
lost everything on the road.''

The consular officer chewed at the end of his hot dog.
Twisting in his chair, he called to one of the seamen.
''Get me some coffee, will you, sailor?'' He turned back
to Chandler and Anne-Marie. ''Okay,'' he said casually.
''Mr. and Mrs. Chandler. Cabin 16A.''

Epilogue

DURING THE SPRING of 1950, when all New England sweltered in a freak heat wave, a dark-gray Citroën with diplomatic license plates, cruised slowly down Massachusetts Avenue from the direction of Harvard Square and turned across the traffic into Linnean Street.

The young French diplomat in the rear seat lifted the leather briefcase onto her lap. Leaning forward to the driver, she pointed up the hill. "It must be one of these houses on the right," she said.

The car turned through a wooden gate, tires crackling across the gravel drive, and pulled up before a large clapboard house. A tall woman in her early thirties was descending the steps from the porch as the young diplomat opened the car door and got out.

"Mademoiselle Aries," Anne-Marie came forward and shook hands. "I'm Mrs. Chandler. My husband's expecting you."

She led the visitor across the wide hall. Sunlight streamed through long, eighteenth-century windows. Underfoot, Shiraz carpets covered the polished boards.

"Such a beautiful house," the French girl paused, admiring the sweep of the staircase leading to the upper floors.

Anne-Marie smiled. "Perhaps like me," she said, "before you came to Boston, you imagined all American houses were built in the twentieth century."

Passing through glass doors, they descended into a wide, shaded garden. Chandler rose from a paper-strewn table, his hair was now chipped with gray.

Anne-Marie introduced them. "Theo, this is Mademoiselle Aries." She smiled at the French girl and turned toward the house. "I'll leave you to talk."

Chandler offered the girl a seat, then sat down opposite.

"I hope it's not inconvenient for me to have come on such short notice," she said.

"Not at all," said Chandler. "I know quite a few people at the consulate. Why didn't one of them just pick up the phone, mademoiselle?"

She smiled evasively. "The consul asks to be remembered to you."

Chandler nodded.

The girl carefully composed her face. "I should begin by telling you of an event that occurred in the south of France last month, monsieur. Two men, both middle-aged, were dining in a restaurant in Nice when one of them suffered a collapse. His companion went to the back of the restaurant, claiming he was going to telephone for an ambulance."

"You mean he didn't?" asked Chandler.

"No. He left the restaurant and disappeared. When the ambulance was eventually called, the sick man was taken to the hospital and put into intensive care. He was well dressed and his wallet contained over fifty thousand francs. But no checkbook, no calling card, no identification of any sort."

"Who was this man?" Chandler asked, feeling strangely disturbed by the story.

"When he regained consciousness he gave his name as Georges Masson."

Chandler shook his head; the name meant nothing.

"The patient was unaware," the girl went on, "that his fingerprints had been taken while he was unconscious. Routine in this sort of case."

"And he wasn't Georges Masson," said Chandler slowly.

"No. He was quickly identified by the police as a Rumanian national named Peter Bilescu."

Chandler rocked back in his seat, staring toward the house.

The girl watched him for a moment. "I think the name means something to you, monsieur."

"Yes," said Chandler cautiously. "I knew Peter Bilescu early in the war."

"I must tell you that since the liberation Bilescu has been wanted by the War Crimes Department of the Paris Sûreté."

Chandler stretched his long legs out under the table and slowly shook his head.

"There is overwhelming evidence," the girl went on, "that Bilescu became a valued associate of the RSHA."

"It was a long war, mademoiselle," said Chandler, memories drifting back like small, dark clouds. "How does all this involve me?" he asked, after a silence.

"When the police went to Bilescu's apartment, they found it had been ransacked. The stove contained a mountain of paper ash."

"I still don't understand what it has to do with me."

"The ash was removed for examination," the girl said. "Some fragments were still legible, among them a record of payments made to you."

"Yes," said Chandler slowly, "it's true Bilescu paid me some money on several occasions. That would have been in the early part of 1940."

"What was the money for, monsieur? I must emphasize that you are under no obligation to answer."

"I've no objection," said Chandler. "It was for bringing Jewish refugees out of Germany into France. Illegal at the time, but I don't imagine anyone would condemn it today."

The girl smiled quickly. "One last question, monsieur. When did you last see Bilescu?"

"June 1940," Chandler said, then paused. "What will happen to him?"

"The French government has decided the matter is too important to delay. There is to be an official tribunal. On the basis of its findings Bilescu will stand trial or not as the case may be."

She opened her briefcase and took out an unaddressed, buff envelope. "I think you may well have guessed the contents of this letter," she said, holding it out to Chandler.

"I'm asked to be a witness."

"Yes," she said. Chandler took the letter.

The gray Citroën drove away, turning left at the wooden gate. Chandler walked slowly back into the house.

Anne-Marie sat alone in the garden. The letter from the Boston consul lay on the table in front of her. Chandler watched her for a moment through the glass doors and then went into the kitchen and mixed two large highballs.

"It had to catch up with us," Anne-Marie said, her body hunched with tension.

Chandler set down the drinks and sat at her side, putting his arm around her, feeling the warmth of her through the summer dress.

"You mustn't go," she whispered. "You mustn't go back there, Theo."

"I have to go," he said gently.

"It's a request; you can refuse." She looked at him, her eyes wide, defenseless.

"I have to go." Chandler pulled her gently toward him and kissed her on the mouth.

* * *

On the morning of May 30, 1950, the oak doors of the Château d'Arblay had been flung wide. Men with bundles of papers tied with blue tape hurried up the stone steps. Black-robed lawyers stood talking on the sunlit terrace overlooking the tumbling river. Gendarmes posted at the gate directed new arrivals. A printed notice, tacked crudely over a window, declared the château to be the site of a Special Tribunal of the Fourth Republic and there-fore, by status, a court of law during the period of the hearing. It was signed in the name of the presiding judge, Maître Roger Falcon.

In the long gallery, a dais had been constructed on which a broad table covered with dark green baize was to act as the *président's* bench. Other tables were provided for lawyers representing Peter Bilescu, the principal witness, and for Maître Henri Vezere, advocate for the French Republic. At the back of the courtroom, rows of chairs had been positioned for the press, witnesses and a limited number of spectators.

Chandler drove slowly up the dusty road. Through the trees he could glimpse the outline of the château. He felt strangely unmoved. At the crossroads before the old pack bridge, a new signpost had been installed to point out the four routes to the traveler.

Just off the road, beneath the château walls, the gendarmerie had roped off an uneven area of grass for parking. As Chandler drove in he noticed that already, an hour or more before the tribunal was to convene, there were over fifty cars hugging the wall and under the trees. He pulled to a halt under an aged oak and got out. He walked to the edge of the grass and looked down on the tiny villages huddled in the valley. Around him magpies chucked in the woods; swallows dipped through holes in long-abandoned outbuildings.

What did he really think almost exactly ten years later? It was a different world now. Nazi Germany had been more utterly crushed than any nation in history. Yet it had only been a few years since Jews wore yellow stars and were crowded into cattle cars and carried across Europe to the human abattoirs to the east. Today the whole epoch had an awful unreality, pushed aside from the minds of men. Could a tribunal in an old French château ever recreate that European twilight? The guilty should be punished, but the punishment of the guilty always involved the suffering of the innocent. Was it possible, on this occasion, that could be avoided?

He turned. A car had drawn up on the grass verge. The man who alighted was a familiar figure, heavier now, the fringe of hair around his gleaming bald head grayer too.

"Borel," exclaimed Chandler. "I suppose I should have expected to see you here." Chandler came toward him.

Borel lumbered forward and clasped the American's hand. "Ah," he snorted, "it's been a long time." He stood a pace back. "For a tall man like you, the years are kind. Kinder than to men like me." He patted the curve of his waist.

Chandler smiled. "How are you, Borel?"

Borel turned down the corners of his mouth in a familiar self-deprecating grimace. "Not bad. I have a new small daughter."

"Are you still a policeman?"

"Of course, yes. And in America, you are happy?"

"Very. I'm a teacher of Art History."

"Children?"

"Two boys."

"And your wife?" Borel cocked his head to the side.

Chandler realized the Frenchman didn't know. "I married Anne-Marie."

Borel smiled, smoothing his fringe of hair. "I'm glad for you," he said. "I'm glad for you both."

"Is it police business that brings you here?" Chandler asked.

Borel nodded. "I'm assigned to the War Crimes Department. We liaise with other forces to trace ex-Nazis responsible for war crimes committed in France. Bilescu is our biggest fish so far. He was sitting in Nice right under my nose."

They walked on in silence; then the Frenchman twitched Chandler's sleeve with his thumb. "Come and look," he said.

Leading the way among the parked cars, Borel stopped at an arched opening in the stone wall. Before them a well-kept garden sloped away toward the edge of a wood. Lines of square white posts created a short avenue between the rose beds. From where he stood, Chandler could read the inscriptions on the first few posts. They were all the same:

IN MEMORY OF AN UNKNOWN VICTIM OF THE GESTAPO.

"There were forty-three corpses found in the château's cellar," Borel said. "I was the supervising officer. To me it's a simple story. It needs no embellishment."

Chandler nodded slowly, not quite sure what Borel meant.

In the courtyard of the château, as ten o'clock approached, all was chaos. Over two hundred people from the surrounding villages surged around the blue prison van stranded in their midst. Chanting, shouting, hammering on the sides with fists and sticks, the crowd pushed aside the police escort struggling to keep them back from the van. Among the mass of villagers were members of all the close-knit family clans of the district: Bertin, the Communist mayor of neighboring Martignac, wearing his old partisan armband; Pierre Vantin from the farm on the hilltop; a group of the Lespinasse family, battering on the barred window of the prison van—Grosjeans, Saurats, Billotins.

A burst of carbine fire brought the crowd to a sudden silence. In the enclosed courtyard, bathed in sunlight, the crowd fell back a pace or two as six young gendarmes, sweat pouring from their faces, ringed the blue van. An inspector held a carbine in one hand, its barrel pointing skyward. From the side of the building, four or five more gendarmes moved through the crowd and began opening a way to the front door. Grim-faced, warily watching the crowd in front of him, the inspector nodded to one of his men. The young gendarme took a bunch of keys from his pocket and unlocked the back door of the van. As a figure filled the dark opening, press flashbulbs crackled. From the back of the crowd came a long sustained hissing. Then as the prisoner, a blanket over his head, was led into the château, the chant began and was taken up by every villager in the courtyard: "Assassin . . . Bilescu Assassin . . . Bilescu Assassin . . ."

In the long gallery of the château, at five minutes to ten o'clock, the fifty or sixty people in the room were brought to silence by an usher ringing a bell. The press, witnesses and selected local people took their seats at the back of the room; lawyers hurried in from the terrace outside; Borel and Chandler sat together in the back row of the spectators' seats.

In total silence now, everyone in the room watched a small corner door open and a gendarme enter. He stood to one side as footsteps approached and a tall figure, in his mid-fifties, tieless but dressed in a well-cut gray suit, appeared in the doorway. For a moment Peter Bilescu stood motionless, his eyes moving slowly around the room. Some newspapers would report that the smile, which undoubtedly flickered across his lips, was of contempt for the whole assembly; others believed it more rueful, a moment's wry surprise at the number of people present.

He stepped forward into a roped-off area to the side of the *président*'s bench and stood, his hands resting on the back of the straight-backed chair. A second gendarme joined the first, flanking the Rumanian. From the back of the room, an angry murmur rose and very slowly faded away.

Journalists formed sentences to describe the prisoner's face, haggard yet still somehow sleek, or sought the phrase to describe the improbable metallic quality of his well-brushed blond hair; then they abandoned their notebooks to join the rest of the court in staring at the erect figure, his eyes half-closed in arrogance or weary resignation.

Again the bell rang, and the usher asked the court to stand as Maître Roger Falcon bustled in through the same corner door. Short, stocky, in black gown and legal cap, Maître Falcon walked quickly to the green-covered table and sat.

Briskly he tapped the thick pad of white paper on the table in front of him. "The tribunal be seated." He lifted his head and surveyed the room from under heavy brows. "Messieurs," he said, "the purpose of this tribunal is simple. The purpose is to establish what part, if any, Peter Ion Bilescu played in the events that took place at the Château d'Arblay in the commune of La Maule-sur-Caveyron on a number of unspecified dates during the years between 1940 and 1944. What is known of these events will shortly be described by my colleague, Maître Vezere. I wish to emphasize that the purpose of this tribunal is one of inquiry. The purpose is not to reawaken old enmities on which, God willing, the book is closed. Yet I am not unaware of the passions rooted in the period we are about to examine. I nevertheless restate the terms of reference of this tribunal: they are that we should investigate and determine the manner in which Anne-Marie Claudel, secretary, domiciled in Paris, and forty-two other persons met their deaths in the commune of La Maule-sur-Caveyron during the years indicated."

Chandler had felt his body stiffen at the mention of Anne-Marie's name; now he spun his head to Borel in the seat beside him. But Borel had not reacted; he sat, slumped forward, his eyes fixed somewhere about the *président*'s bench.

"The tribunal will begin with a statement by the prisoner," Maître Falcon announced.

Within the roped-off area, Peter Bilescu moved forward, putting his hands flat on the table in front of him. "Monsieur le Président, messieurs. I wish first to make it clear that whatever you decide in these coming matters is of complete indifference to me. This is not a statement of disrespect for the court. From what my doctors tell me, even the harshest decision of this tribunal could not shorten my life by more than a year or two."

"The prisoner will refrain from comment upon the possible conclusions of this tribunal," Falcon intoned. "Please continue."

"I have only one final point to make," Bilescu said. "It is this: The events you are about to examine are, in time, only a few years distant. But in every other way they are events from another world. Monsieur le Président has reminded us that the book is closed on the enmities of the past. Let it remain closed. You cannot open it at one chapter only; the world will reach out over your shoulder and turn the other pages. If you decide to pursue this inquiry, you will resurrect the ghosts of the past. You will find that for some the past is not dead."

Pushing his way through the crowd emerging from the château doors at the midday adjournment, Chandler gripped Borel's arm and led him aside.

"Investigate and determine the way Anne-Marie Claudel met her death," Chandler said, his face tight with anger. "That's what the *président* said. What the hell does it mean, Borel?"

"Anne-Marie Claudel and forty-two others," Borel said coolly.

"I want an answer."

"Her name was found among fragments of paper ash, and there's other evidence," said Borel, searching for his cigarettes.

"You mean evidence that she's dead? The tribunal thinks she's dead."

"Would you have wanted the investigating team to know she is alive? Would you have wanted me to tell them?" Borel said in a fierce whisper.

Chandler was silent.

"Come on, I'll buy you lunch," said Borel.

They drove to a restaurant in the nearby village of Martignac in the hope of escaping some of the newsmen. In the event, they had only been partially successful, and the clamor for service and the continuous use of the one telephone formed a noisy background to their lunch.

"Bilescu's statement contained the hint of a threat," Borel said when the waitress brought their aperitifs. "Who was it aimed at?"

Chandler poured water into his Pernod. "Was it me? He caught my eye as he entered. He smiled."

"I don't think he was talking to you," Borel said carefully. "I think he was talking to the man or men who ransacked his room."

"Do you know who they were?"

"Someone from his old Gestapo and SS comrades," said Borel.

Chandler looked at him in astonishment.

"Don't look so incredulous," Borel said. "I have a list of over three thousand people I would like to talk to in connection with crimes committed in France alone. There you have a formidable brotherhood."

"You mean they had someone there," said Chandler slowly, "at the tribunal, listening."

"Almost certainly," said Borel.

Legal formalities had occupied most of the first morning session. Only after the lunch adjournment did the counsel for the Republic begin his opening statement. Maître Jean-Jacques Vezere was a local man, raised in the region before embarking on a successful career in Paris. Thin, aquiline and relentless in legal attack, he had served as a Free French officer in London during the war at de Gaulle's headquarters in Carlton Gardens.

"Fifteen years ago," he began, in the hushed courtroom, "I remember the commune of La Maule-sur-Caveyron. A dozen houses, not more. The Billotin family's big farmhouse. Madame Saurat, whose bread oven was fired twice a week for the whole hamlet to bake its baguettes and pies and roast lamb. Total inhabitants less than forty souls—laborers on the Billotin farm, a cartmaker, a woodcutter, their wives, grandmothers and a few children. To some the life of La Maule-sur-Caveyron would have seemed dull. Certainly uneventful. Most people raised geese or fine, waddling ducks. They made their confits and foie gras. They made their own wine from grapes grown on a half hectare of terracing among the rocks. Each year a fête was held. There would be dancing and feasting for two hot summer days, and villagers and relatives would come to La Maule from the countryside around. And, dominating the whole commune, benignly regarding its country way of life, the Château d'Arblay, the very building in which this tribunal now sits, empty since the old marquis died a few years before the war, a medieval fortress on the mountain road from France to Spain. That was the commune of La Maule-sur-Caveyron, ten years ago, in the long summer when war again exploded on Europe.''

He drew his black robe around him, his long, lined face staring down at the floor. ''In the spring of 1940,'' he continued, ''the heirs of the old marquis concluded their arrangements and put the Château d'Arblay up for sale. It was bought by an organization in Paris, the Jewish Resettlement Agency. The funds, we know, came from the private fortune of a Monsieur Paul Litvinov, himself destined to be an early victim and hero of the struggle against nazism. The object of buying the château was to provide a safe and secret haven for German Jews who had fled to France before the war and might again be in danger following a German victory in the north. A safe haven here on the border for the Jewish refugees before they continued their flight on to Spain and Portugal.''

Vezere's thin shoulders slumped suddenly, as if the energy had drained from his muscles. Then in a low voice, forcing those at the back to lean forward in their seats, he continued: ''Let us now move forward four years, from the beginning to the end of the war for this part of France.''

Maître Vezere uncoiled to his full height and stood imperiously before the judge's bench. ''Monsieur le Président, during the war the inhabitants of La Maule-sur-Caveyron came to term this ancient building, the Gestapo château. It was known, of course, that even as early as 1940 a special requisition order had been granted by the government at Vichy to a German administrative body in Paris calling itself the Commission for Jewish Questions. Throughout the war the reputation of d'Arblay changed. No longer a benign presence overlooking the valleys, it took on an air of menace. There were comings and goings in the night. Only one man from the village was employed here from the time the Gestapo took over. You will hear that he died in a road accident on or about the date the Gestapo finally vacated the château. A convenient accident, you might consider, given what he might have known of the events here during those dark wartime years.

"Monsieur le Président, I intend to bring evidence to show that Peter Bilescu was the so-called Commissioner for Jews who obtained the requisition order for this château on behalf of the Gestapo. I intend to show that he used his position in Paris, with the connivance of the Gestapo, to extract the last, hidden funds from desperate men and women by promising them a safe passage across the Pyrenees to Spain. I intend to show that from as early as 1940 onward those desperate refugees never journeyed farther than this building the tribunal sits in today.

"As a result of the rumors circulating in the villages of the district," Maître Vezere said in a low voice, "the gendarmerie carried out an examination of this château and its grounds. At first they found nothing untoward. Then a man wielding a pickax accidentally broke through to a bricked-up cellar below the watchtower. There, to his horror, he found the remains of forty-three bodies. With these were found various artifacts suggesting the deceased were all, or mostly, of Jewish origin."

In the heavy silence of the summer afternoon, Vezere ran his eyes along the front row of spectators' seats until he came to a girl in her early twenties. Dressed in a flowered Sunday frock, she sat beside her young husband, her round peasant face flushed with nervousness.

"With your permission, Monsieur le Président, I will

first call Madame Henriette Lupin, a native of the neighboring commune of Martignac.''

He gestured to the girl to come and stand before the table in front of the *président*'s bench. She came forward, visibly trembling. ''Here, monsieur?'' she asked in a voice barely above a whisper.

''Sit down if you wish,'' Vezere said.

The girl shook her head, unable to sit before this assembly of Paris dignitaries.

''Madame Lupin,'' Vezere began, his voice soft, coaxing, ''you were fourteen years old in 1940. You lived with your mother in the commune of Martignac, two or three kilometers from La Maule.''

''Yes, monsieur,'' the girl half curtseyed in acknowledgment.

''In the spring of 1940 the Château d'Arblay was bought by some people from Paris. You were employed by the new owners as a maid to assist Madame Saurat, who was acting as housekeeper. Do you remember the names of any of the people from Paris who were at the château at the time?''

''I remember I was instructed in my duties by a lady named Anne-Marie Claudel. There were several other people there at the time, but I don't remember their names.'' Having delivered herself of her first sentences, the girl looked more confident. Half turning, she smiled quickly at her husband.

''How long did you work here, Madame Lupin?''

''I was here through the spring of that year.''

''Did you see Anne-Marie Claudel often during the period you worked at d'Arblay?''

''Several times, monsieur. She came with some people who would stay a few nights. Then she would return to Paris.''

''And the people she brought with her, where did they go?''

''I don't know, monsieur.''

''Now,'' Vezere said carefully, ''you left the employ of

the new owners of the château. Why was that?"

"My mother said she needed me to work on our farm. My father was away in the army."

"But that was not the only reason your mother wished you to leave d'Arblay?" Vezere's eyebrows were raised in inquiry.

"No, monsieur." Again the girl hesitated. "My mother thought I was becoming too friendly with one of the men from La Maule, Jean-Claude Barrat."

"He was known as the boatman, is that the one? A big man, young, but very much older than you. In 1940 he would have been nearly thirty years old."

"Yes, monsieur."

"You, as a fourteen-year-old girl, found him attractive?"

Flushing wildly, the girl shrugged. "I was very young."

"Of course. And when your mother insisted on your leaving, you were upset? You wished to continue seeing Jean-Claude?"

Again she shrugged uncomfortably.

"And you did?"

"By chance, in the woods a few times. If I lost a sheep, perhaps, I would meet him cutting wood. Sometimes he helped me find the sheep," she said.

"And did he ever say anything about what was happening at the château?"

"He used to frighten me with stories about killing people and burying them in the cellar."

A silence had fallen on the courtroom. "Did he ever mention the names of anyone who was brought to the château?"

"He mentioned Mademoiselle Claudel," the girl said softly.

"Anne-Marie Claudel?"

"Yes. He said he had rowed her across the river one night when it was swollen by a terrible storm. He said she must have been one of the first."

"The first to die?"

"So he told me."

The examination of Peter Bilescu began on the second day of the tribunal.

As Maître Vezere was arranging his papers at his desk beside the *président*'s bench, Bilescu stood upright in the improvised dock, his gaze passing slowly along the lines of reporters and observers at the rear of the courtroom.

When his eye reached Chandler and Borel, sitting together near the back, Bilescu inclined his head for a brief moment, and that same enigmatic smile appeared on his lips.

After the formal establishment of Bilescu's name, age and the place of his birth in Rumania, Maître Vezere began with questions about the reason for his arrival in France shortly before the war.

"My object," Bilescu replied, "was simple. It was to live a more satisfactory life than I had achieved as a minor government official in Rumania."

"You were successful?"

"Very."

"You ran several businesses?"

"I dealt in the art market. I was a partner in 729, the most successful *maison de rendez-vous* in Paris. I was the owner of the Sappho Club, a luncheon club much favored by wealthy ladies of a certain inclination. Most financially rewarding, however, was my activity in the refugee trade."

"Will you tell the tribunal what that involved exactly?"

"Certainly. Sometime at the beginning of 1939 I met a Monsieur Paul Litvinov, a wealthy Jewish gentleman, and his assistant Anne-Marie Claudel. Between them they ran a charitable organization for the resettlement of German refugees, mostly Jewish, in Paris. Monsieur Litvinov was well known at that time for his vast fortune and his altruistic willingness to spend it in the reception of refugees. I immediately perceived an excellent business opportunity. Monsieur Litvinov was prepared to pay me a handsome sum for any refugee I brought into France. The refugees themselves were prepared to pay an adequate sum for the facilities I arranged in Germany. In Paris at that time there was no great shortage of young men willing to cross into the Third Reich and smuggle refugees back to France. Even after the war began I was able, by using American citizens, to continue my activities.''

Vezere moved across the room until he stood a few feet from Bilescu. ''Will you tell the tribunal what exactly was your moral attitude to these activities, Monsieur Bilescu?''

The *président*, Roger Falcon, leaned forward across his bench. ''The purpose of this tribunal, Maître Vezere, is to elicit facts, not opinions.''

''Monsieur le Président,'' Vezere said evenly. ''I submit that Monsieur Bilescu's attitude to his activities in 1939 will have considerable bearing on the events of later years here at d'Arblay.''

Falcon nodded. ''Continue,'' he said.

''The question is simply answered,'' Bilescu said. ''I had no moral attitudes to these activities. Why should I have had? I was doing no more than whole societies were doing. I was plundering the Jews. Throughout the war I continued to do so.''

''Are you an anti-Semite?''

''No,'' Bilescu said coolly. ''It was quite simply that, in the political conditions of the time, the Jews were vulnerable. In the Europe of our recent past I would suggest that anti-Semitism was greatly fueled by the simple desire for profit. As in my own case.''

The cross-examination was not proceeding as Vezere had hoped. He now sought to bring it back to firmer ground.

''A moment ago you used the phrase, 'throughout the war.' What did you mean by that?''

''Throughout the war,'' Bilescu said easily, ''I was in a position to extract money from Jews who wished to travel south to Spain.''

Vezere frowned, baffled at the direction Bilescu's

answers seemed to be leading. "And you admit you brought these people here to the Château d'Arblay?"

"Yes."

"Where, instead of arranging their escape to Spain, you plundered them of their valuables," the advocate paused, "and you killed them."

"They were killed, yes," Bilescu said.

The courtroom was utterly silent.

"Are you saying," Vezere continued, "these murders were done entirely for profit?"

"Entirely."

The *président* hammered with his gavel to silence the angry reaction at the back of the court.

Vezere stood, gaunt, nonplussed.

"What the hell is he trying to do?" Chandler whispered to Borel.

Borel shook his head.

"This tribunal," Vezere went on, more uncertainly now, "is specifically charged with investigating the death of Anne-Marie Claudel. She is the only named victim among those whose remains were found in the cellar. Do you admit to the murder of Anne-Marie Claudel?"

"Yes, I do."

At shortly after midday the blue police van with the barred windows drove into the courtyard and stopped before the main doors. Watched by Borel and Chandler, the gendarme driver and escort got out and entered the château.

Moments later they reappeared with Bilescu, his hands handcuffed in front of him. For a moment he stopped before the open back doors of the prison van and looked across the sunlit courtyard to where Borel and Chandler stood. That same smile, which the press had had so much difficulty in interpreting, passed across his lips. Then he took a pace forward and mounted the single metal step into the back of the van.

"They hold him overnight at the Ste-Marie prison at Limoges," Borel said as the blue van drove through the château gates. "I'm told he's been assigned one entire floor to himself. They dared not let any of the other prisoners near him."

They were walking through the arched gateway to where the gendarmerie had roped off the improvised car park.

"So," Borel said. "Tomorrow you'll give your evidence."

"If the *président* decides it's necessary after Bilescu's confession in open court."

"We shall know by tomorrow morning," Borel said. "And then, for you, home to America and Anne-Marie."

Chandler shook his head. "Anne-Marie's here in France," he said. "She checked into a hotel outside Toulouse yesterday. Most of all, she's looking forward to seeing you again."

Borel grunted his pleasure. "It will not be the celebration dinner we planned at the Lipp. But it will be good to see her again, nevertheless."

Chandler nodded, stopping beside his rented car. He was reaching for the handle of the driver's door when the crackle of shots echoed across the hillsides. For a moment both men stood trying to locate the direction of the shooting.

"It's the valley road," Chandler said, dragging open the car door. "Get in."

Accelerating across the uneven grass, Chandler turned onto the road. In the rearview mirror, he caught a glimpse of gendarmes running through the château gates as his rented car sped into the first curve, the wheels leaving the road as it crossed the hump of the stone bridge. The trees had interlaced their branches overhead, and little sunlight penetrated the thick summer woods. A hundred yards straight on, then a sharp left and the sun would bounce off the great limestone rock with a brightness made painful by sudden emergence from the deep shade.

From the angle of the passenger seat, Borel saw it a fraction of a second before Chandler. As the Frenchman shouted a warning, Chandler was already braking. The blue prison van lay on its side between the shattered stumps of the two fallen pine trees. On shrieking tires, Chandler brought the Peugeot to a skidding halt.

As Chandler and Borel ran toward the van, one of the gendarmes clambered painfully out of the front, his head streaming blood. The side of the van, Chandler saw, was riddled with bullet holes.

"They were up there on the bank," the gendarme pointed. "The shots came from up there."

Borel had a pistol in his hand. "Stay here," he said to Chandler; then he ran across the road and ducked into the undergrowth.

A second gendarme was pulling himself out of the overturned vehicle. "I couldn't stop," he muttered, then pointed to the shattered pine trees. "I just couldn't miss them."

The first man wiped blood from his forehead and pulled a bunch of keys from his pocket. Unsteadily he unlocked the back door of the van. As the door flapped to the ground, Chandler saw the crumpled body of Bilescu: a burst of fire had cut across his face, leaving his jaw to sag in a gaping, bloody smile.

Standing in the shade, Borel weighed the two spent cartridge cases in his hand. "Nine millimeter," he said. "Sten gun."

On the roadway, the police were clearing the road-block. The body of Bilescu was being loaded into the back of an ambulance.

Chandler watched Bilescu's arm hanging loosely from the stretcher. "Who did it?" he asked.

Borel rubbed his chin. "Perhaps the Resistance was not prepared to await the outcome of the trial," he said. "We know how the local people felt about Bilescu. Ten years commuted to five for ill health would never satisfy them. And the ambush technique. It's been used a hundred times in this area."

Chandler watched the ambulance doors slam behind Bilescu's head. "You may be right," he said.

"Even so, while you're here I'd like you to take this," said Borel. From a waistband holster, he drew his pistol and gave it to Chandler.

"I don't need this," said Chandler.

"Keep the gun, my friend," said Borel. "To please me. Keep it at least until I see you off at the airport tomorrow."

Chandler turned to the Frenchman. "You expected this?"

Behind them the ambulance drew away.

Borel smiled his saturnine, self-deprecating smile. "Expected, no," he said. "But I *hoped* for it."

The Hôtel de France, in the country outside the Toulouse suburb of Blagnac, was an establishment of a dozen rooms, a bar and a comfortable provincial dining room. But the pride of its owners was the garden constructed from an old terraced vineyard and now transformed into a series of walkways, covered in summer with heavily leafed vines.

Taking her drink from the bar, Anne-Marie had walked out into the garden to avoid the friendly attentions of the *patron*. She felt no guilt at the exhilaration she had experienced when Chandler had phoned to tell her of Bilescu's death. Perhaps in a sense it was not entirely unexpected. In the villages around d'Arblay there must be many who would want to avenge themselves on collaborators and who felt loathing for Bilescu's treachery. There were also Jewish organizations savagely impatient at the slow pace with which justice moved against the mass-murderers of the recent past.

But expected or not, Bilescu's death could only bring her relief. For ten years she had lived under the threat of exposure. Since the end of the war the consuming interest of the world's press in the life of Adolf Hitler had in no way abated. Her life and her husband's would never be the same if the story came out. But much more important to both of them was the knowledge that their two small sons' lives would be distorted to a grotesque degree.

More than any prince or prodigy or film star's child, their sons would grow up in the glare of insinuating worldwide publicity, the permanent victims of newsmen, perhaps even the physical targets of the deranged. Now, with Bilescu's death, it seemed likely that she and Theo could relax back into the comfortable security of their family life in America.

It was getting dark. Overhead lights shone from the canopy of shadows formed by the interlacing vines. The terracing, descending in broad steps, led down to a small willow-lined stream in the valley below the hotel. She was looking forward to seeing Borel again. Someone to relax with, someone, apart from Theo, of course, with whom to talk about the past.

Across the valley, lights from the occasional passing car flared and disappeared among the trees. They would be here soon. She turned and began to climb the broad terraces.

"Anne-Marie," a voice came from the shadows behind her. A voice with a German accent.

Entering the hotel bar with Borel, Chandler asked the *patron* if his wife was in their room.

"No, monsieur. She's taking a walk in the garden," he said.

The two men stepped out under the arched vines. Beyond the door, Borel paused to light a cigarette. From somewhere below, the scent of honeysuckle drifted up toward them. And with it a short, muffled cry.

The first blow that Krebs had struck caught her high on the side of the head. She had gone down, rolling across the terracing into the mass of thick vines on one side of the walk.

He knew he had misaimed the blow. At the Kolumbiahaus in Berlin, where he had trained, SS doctors had pointed out the precise spot below the ear where a single blow would have the effect of the hangman's knot, snapping the neck. They had even had the opportunity to practice on live victims. But the girl had moved, jerking away her head so that the front knuckles of his fist had struck too high, the blow cushioned by the thickness of her hair. Still, she would have been rendered unconscious.

He came down the terrace to where she had fallen. He could see her shoes and the paleness of her legs protruding from the shadows and was briefly reminded of the time when he had killed her mother. A better world, now so long dead.

He bent down to drag her from the undergrowth. To Anne-Marie he was a heavy, lumbering shadow, his scarred face picked out among the dancing leaves by the light positioned above his head. She felt two large hands grip her ankle and her leg just below the knee. As he braced himself to drag her onto the path, she used his weight as an anchor from which to kick down with the other leg. Her high heel split his lip and smashed through his lower teeth. He was on his knees as she kicked again, the heel gouging deep across his scarred cheek. It was his shout of pain, muffled by blood and broken teeth and the torn flesh of his lip, that Chandler and Borel heard.

Krebs pulled himself to his feet. Mounting inside him he felt the old, strange excitement. Caged by the thick vines, she had no chance of escape. Standing now, back pressed against the thick interwoven strands, her breath hissed through her teeth in some elemental feline fear.

He had only to step forward. One single blow would destroy her. But he felt the sense of prepotency rising inside him. He had searched for her too long to finish it like that. His huge hand closed on her mouth, forcing her down. His other hand groped for the coiled length of piano wire in his pocket.

When Chandler hit him, he felt it only as a dull, painless thud. He was like a boxer, anesthetized by the lust for violence. As he rolled in the pathway his hand scrabbled for the gun in his pocket. He was halfway to his feet when Chandler charged at him, hurling him backward toward the edge of the stream at the bottom of the terrace. The gun, caught in the lining of his pocket, tore free. He was pushing the safety catch when Chandler hit him again; a blow behind the jaw, by chance, at the precise point ·favored by the SS instructors of the Kolumbiahaus.

Perhaps he was dead as he rolled into the stream. Perhaps it was Borel's foot, pressing down on the back of his neck, that drowned him.

For a moment Chandler and Anne-Marie stood looking at the billowing jacket of the dead man.

"I think," Borel said, "you should leave me to pick up the pieces. Take the plane tonight."

Chandler eased his aching arm around his wife. Borel lit a crumpled cigarette. How much did the Frenchman know, Chandler wondered, how much had he guessed? Was any of this final act in the drama anticipated by this still strangely enigmatic figure with his crumpled suit and fringe of graying hair?

"No celebration drink?" said Chandler.

"Sometime," said Borel, "but not yet."

"Perhaps in another ten years," said Anne-Marie.

"Perhaps."

New York Times bestsellers— Books at their best!

___ 1-55773-044-X **THE PANIC OF '89** $4.50
          by Paul Erdman
"The pages race by," (*Wall Street Journal*), in this international high-finance thriller that's all-too-real!

___ 0-425-10924-0 **THE TIMOTHY FILES** $4.95
          by Lawrence Sanders
Shocking suspense by the author of *The Eighth Commandment*. Sanders introduces a hero for fans of his "Sins" detective, Edward X. Delaney.

___ 1-55773-113-6 **THE DAMNATION GAME** $4.95
          by Clive Barker
"I have seen the future of horror, and its name is Clive Barker."
—Stephen King "A gripping tale of hideous evil," (*New York Daily News*), by the author of *The Books of Blood*.

___ 0-425-11170-9 **MEN WHO CAN'T LOVE** $4.50
          by Steve Carter and Julia Sokol
As seen on "Donahue" and "The Oprah Winfrey Show!" How to recognize a commitment-phobic man before he breaks your heart.

___ 0-515-09226-6 **BROTHERHOOD OF WAR VII:** $4.50
          THE NEW BREED by W.E.B. Griffin
"An American epic...Griffin is a storyteller in the grand tradition."
—Tom Clancy, author of *The Corps*.

___ 1-55773-047-4 **ARE YOU LONESOME TONIGHT?** $4.50
          by Lucy de Barbin and Dary Matera
The controversial story of Elvis Presley's secret passion—and the child he never knew! "A strong, convincing story." —*Chattanooga Times*
(On sale August '88)
